JANE ANONYMOUS

ALSO BY LAURIE FARIA STOLARZ

Blue is for Nightmares
White is for Magic
Silver is for Secrets
Red is for Remembrance
Black is for Beginnings
Bleed
Project 17
Deadly Little Secret
Deadly Little Lies
Deadly Little Games
Deadly Little Voices
Deadly Little Lessons
Welcome to the Dark House
Return to the Dark House
Shutter

JANE ANONYMOUS

LAURIE FARIA STOLARZ

First published in the United States by Wednesday Books,
an imprint of St. Martin's Publishing Group

JANE ANONYMOUS. Copyright © 2019 by Laurie Faria Stolarz. All rights reserved.
Printed in the United States of America. For information, address St. Martin's
Publishing Group, 120 Broadway, New York, NY 10271.

www.wednesdaybooks.com

Designed by Anna Gorovoy

The Library of Congress Cataloging-in-Publication Data is available upon request.

ISBN 978-1-250-30370-7 (hardcover)
ISBN 978-1-250-30372-1 (ebook)

Our books may be purchased in bulk for promotional, educational, or
business use. Please contact your local bookseller or the Macmillan Corporate and
Premium Sales Department at 1-800-221-7945, extension 5442, or by
email at MacmillanSpecialMarkets@macmillan.com.

First Edition: January 2020

10 9 8 7 6 5 4 3 2 1

For those brave enough to share their honest truth
and the attentive listeners who really, truly hear it.

JANE ANONYMOUS

PROLOGUE

Dear Reader(s),

Before ten months ago, I didn't know that the coil spring from a mattress could be used as a makeshift weapon, or that the rod inside a toilet tank worked just as well as the claw of a hammer.

Before ten months ago, I never imagined that the sense of smell could be so keen—that the scent of my breath, like rotten fruit, could wake me out of a sound sleep, or that cooked rice carries a distinct aroma, like popcorn kernels heating.

Before.

Ten months.

Ago.

I'd never considered the power of light—that when one is deprived of it, illogical thoughts can gnaw like rats at the brain, keeping one up, driving one mad.

Nor had I any reason to predict how intimately I'd come to know myself: the oily stench of my own hair, the salty taste of my own blood, and the touch of my unbathed body (the scaly layer of scabbing that would form all over my skin, and the fire-ant sensation that would crawl up and down my limbs).

For the purpose of this memoir, you can call me Jane Anonymous. For the purpose of my sanity, I've chosen to do this in secret. Accordingly, all of the names in here, for both people and places, are fake. I want to tell my full story, and I can't possibly do that if I'm paranoid about being identified. And while I'm on the topic of story, until now, I've never attempted to write my own. People have asked. Film agents and publishers have tried to lure me with six-figure deals in exchange for a full account of what happened during my seven months away. I've told them all to go to hell. I need to do this my way, on my terms.

Maybe that makes me sound like a bitch.

But ask me if I care.

A year ago, at this time, I'd have sung an entirely different tune. Back then, I worried what people thought and trusted in the goodwill of others.

But now I'm a girl who sleeps in her closet with a knife tucked beneath her pillow, trusting no one but herself.

Everyone says that I should try therapy. But therapists have their own agendas, the least of which is to help me heal. They want to get inside my head, make me their prize-winning case study, sell the inside scoop to some gossip rag—to buy braces and prep schools for their kids. Did I mention that I'm paranoid too? (Yes, I think I did.) Anyway, I'm no one's paycheck. I'll get it all out here instead. And then, one day, who knows. Maybe my words will somehow help save some poor soul from making the same mistakes I did.

Yours truly,
Jane Anonymous

THEN

1

It was raining that morning, ten months ago. I remember because I'd gotten up early, hoping to go for a run. But it was already 8:15, and I was still waiting for the weather to clear. The streets were covered in puddles, and I'd recently gotten new running shoes—purple Nikes with lime-green swooshes and thick pink treads. Funny to think about them now, that I'd been so concerned about protecting my shoes, I'd let nearly a year of my life slip away.

Already dressed in my running gear, I turned from the window, knowing the clouds weren't going to suddenly part. The sun wasn't going to magically appear. The oil-stained puddles, with their spirals of blue and green, wouldn't be evaporating anytime soon.

I'd wanted to be on the road by eight o'nothing. There was a cute runner boy I'd been hoping to see. We had this thing where we nodded to one another each time we passed, usually by the water fountain and always around 8:30. What were the odds that he'd be running in the rain? *Should I just suck it up and wear old shoes?*

I went to go grab a pair when my phone quacked with a text. From Shelley: *Surprise! I'm home from Camping Hell a day early. Long story short: I rly need 2cu. Can we meet @9? Eggs & Stuff? Let's salvage my bday disaster.*

My gut reaction? Excitement. I hadn't seen Shelley, my best friend, in over a week. But not two seconds later, my brain took over and I remembered: I'd left her birthday present at work.

Can we meet a little L8R? I texted back. *I'm going for a run.*

Pleeeeeease, she typed, adding a bunch of frowny-face emoticons.

I didn't want to let her down. Her summer had sucked harder than leeches, and having to spend her seventeenth birthday on a camping trip with her show-tune-singing fam, with no cell phone reception whatsoever, was sure to have been no exception.

Ru there? she continued to type.

I looked at the clock. If I left now, I could open the store, grab the gift, and still have ample time to make it to Eggs & Stuff by 9:00. *Cu then,* I typed back.

Mom was already up, sitting at the kitchen table in her snowflake-printed bathrobe (even though it was summer). "Hey there." She peeked up from her magazine—*Knit Wit.* The cover featured a dazed-looking chicken knitting a scarf that reminded me of candy corn. "Going for a run?"

"Not anymore."

"Great, we can chat over coffee."

"Sorry, no time. You'll have to chat with Dad."

"Except Dad's still in bed—that sleepyhead." She grimaced. "Seems our days of Sunday brunch are a thing of the past."

"Time to wake him up?"

"I already tried. But he worked late last night . . . didn't get in until well past midnight."

"I'd stay," I told her. "But I promised Shelley I'd meet her for breakfast."

"She's home already?"

"Yes, so I need to get her birthday present—*stat*."

"Well, you've certainly come to the right place. I have plenty of gifts."

I didn't want to argue, but when it came to gift-giving, my mother and I were from two entirely different planets. While she resided on Planet I-got-this-on-sale-but-have-no-real-use-for-it-and-so-it-goes-into-an-already-overflowing-bin-of-tacky-random-stuff, I lived on Planet My-friends-are-my-family-and-so-each-gift-has-been-carefully-hand-selected.

Still, Mom popped up from the table and bounded across the kitchen, en route to the linen closet, where she stored her trove of "treasures." The idea of turning over some of the stuff in her stash was evidently far more enlivening than the dark-roasted coffee beans my dad had imported from New Guinea.

She came back a few moments later with a bin full of her finds and pulled out a baseball cap with melon-patterned fabric. "This would look adorable on Shelley, with her heart-shaped face."

What melons had to do with hearts, I had absolutely no idea. Mom could sense my inner snub and dove back into the bin, producing a snowball-maker (!), faux-fur glovelettes, and a turquoise watch that screamed *old lady*.

"What's wrong?" Mom asked, reading the repulsion on my face.

I bit my tongue in lieu of commenting. "I already bought a gift. I just left it at Norma's. Can I borrow the car to go pick it up?"

Mom gazed out the window, and the corners of her mouth turned downward. She has this weird hang-up about letting me drive in rain or snow (not to mention fog, slush, sleet, hail, and darkness).

"You *could* bring me yourself," I suggested, fairly confident she wouldn't take the bait. "As long as you're okay with waiting while I wrap the gift, and then driving me to Eggs & Stuff right after. I can text you to pick me up, unless of course you'd be willing to drive Shelley and me to the mall or a movie aft—"

"Take the car," she said, cutting me off. "Just drive carefully."

"Thanks," I perked, snagging the keys from the hook.

When I finally made it home, nearly seven months to the day later, my pretty purple running shoes—with the lime-green swooshes and the thick pink treads—were still fully intact, sitting in the hallway closet, spared from the wretched rain puddles.

While I, on the other hand, was far beyond repair.

Nearly broken.

In every.

Way.

NOW

2

When I wake up this morning, I find my mother staring back at me.

On the floor.

Lying by my side.

In the middle of the hallway, right outside her and Dad's room.

She reaches out to touch the scars on my hand—dark pink lines extending from my knuckles to my wrists like broken spiderwebs. Her blue eyes are illuminated by the soft glow of my flashlight. She starts to hum—one of the songs from *The Sound of Music*—just like she used to when I was little, when I'd crawl into bed between her and Dad after having a bad dream.

A puffy comforter covers me. She obviously did that. I only brought my pillow and the cold sheet from my bed.

How long has she been here, watching me sleep? I want to ask her, want to give some explanation as to how I got here too. My closet just didn't feel secure enough last night.

Once she pauses from singing, I open my mouth to explain, but I can't find the words.

"Sleep now," she whispers, tucking her arm beneath her head. No pillow or blanket for her, just skin, bones, and the thin layer of her cotton nightgown against the cold, hard wood. "Tomorrow is a new day."

Except I don't want to think about tomorrow. I want to stay in the space between days—the space where I don't have to worry about letting people down or saying the wrong thing.

The space with no expectations.

3

The streets were quiet that morning, ten months ago. Maybe because of the rain—all of those ankle-deep puddles that'd delayed me from running. The clouds kept the sky dark; I remember because the streetlamps shone brightly, painting long white stripes across the rain-soaked pavement.

I pulled into the back driveway of Norma's Closet, the clothing boutique where I worked. Norma, the owner, had given me my own set of keys two months before, having deemed me trustworthy enough to open and close the store on my own.

I entered in the rear door, able to smell the honeycomb candles she'd been trying to push—a surprisingly musty scent. Norma is really sweet, but she has all of these lame ideas for impulse buys at the register, the candles included, and so we'd been left with six bulky crates that took up valuable floor space.

I closed the door behind me and flicked on some lights. I'd been keeping Shelley's gift on a shelf behind the register for at least three weeks, telling myself to bring it home. Why I never had—despite the fact that it'd already been paid for—can only be chalked up to pure procrastination. Now it's extra ammo I use against myself.

I opened the box. Inside was a sterling silver bracelet with amethyst crystals and a dangling star charm. Amethysts were Shelley's favorite, not only for the purple color but also for their supposed ability to repel negative energy. Shelley was also into stars—gazing at them, wishing on them . . . Whenever we'd come home from a late night out, she'd look up at the sky and comment on the celestial patterns.

Her card had a star too—on the front, metallic pink against a sparkling black background that reminded me of the night sky. I'd already written my message inside:

Dear Shelley,

I'll never forget that day, thirteen years ago, when you and your mom knocked on our front door, as the new neighbors in the 'hood, looking to make friends. You asked me if I wanted to play, showed me your collection of slime balls, and my life was forever changed.

I know I've said it before, but I love you like a sister. I'll be wishing on the brightest star in the sky tonight, hoping that we'll always be this close. Happy birthday, my forever friend.

Much love,

Jane

I wrapped the box in purple tissue paper, slipped it into a bag, and tied the handles closed with curly ribbon just as a knock sounded at the door. Some guy was peeking through the glass. I pegged him to be about twenty or twenty-one, not too much older than I was.

He waved when he caught my eye. A smile burst across his lips, like we'd known each other for years. Had we? Did he recognize me from the pet shelter where I volunteered? Or maybe he'd seen me running around town?

I moved from around the counter and pointed at the sign. "We're closed," I told him.

He clasped his hands, as if to pray, and mouthed *please, please, please.* "It's my one-year anniversary with my girlfriend." His words were muffled behind the glass. "I'm picking her up in an hour, and I don't have a present. Please . . . I'm such an idiot."

He was handsome, admittedly, which definitely helped: tall, with deep brown eyes, plus a bit of facial scruff, like he'd just crawled out of bed. His faded green tee clung to his chest from the onslaught of rain soaking through to his skin. Droplets pelted against his face and drizzled down his neck.

The rain made him look defenseless somehow.

"If I screw up again, I'm done for." He drove an invisible stake through his heart and rolled his eyes upward, feigning death.

It was only then I noticed: His arms were covered in tattoos— tree limbs that grew from his wrists, tangling with the hair on his forearms and branching around his muscles.

It wasn't long before he dropped to his knees and stretched his clasped hands upward, pleading for me to open the door.

I couldn't help but laugh, couldn't help but feel a pang of jealousy too, because he was here for someone other than me.

I pulled the key ring from my pocket and unlocked the door. He smiled wide when he saw what I was doing. I smiled back. He was getting his wish. And just like that, I'd become a superhero.

He stood up and placed his fingertips on the door, and for three awkward seconds as I twisted the key in the lock, I could feel his close proximity: a flittering in my chest, a prickly heat that spread like fever across my face.

I peeked at him through the glass, noticing the shape of his lips; the top one was slightly fuller than the bottom. He swallowed hard—I watched the motion in his throat—and then gazed at my mouth.

And suddenly neither of us was smiling.

The mood had shifted.

Nothing was funny.

I opened the door and took a step back.

"Thank you," he said, closing the door behind him. "You're really saving me here." His voice had a rusty tone, as though he hadn't slept in days. He smelled like the rain, a musky, earthy scent, like something we could've bottled up and sold at the counter to impulsive shoppers. His brown eyes locked on mine for probably longer than they should have.

For someone with a girlfriend.

Celebrating his one-year anniversary.

I could tell he could sense it too—the awkwardness of the moment. He bit his bottom lip and then shifted his weight left and right on his feet. "I saw the light on in here and figured I'd take a chance."

I was really glad he had—was suddenly grateful for the rain and all of those new-running-shoe-wrecking puddles. "We obviously don't open until later, but I was here picking up a gift too."

He smiled again—bright white teeth, a dimple in his cheek. "So it was destiny, then."

I forced myself to look away, reminding myself about the girlfriend. "Do you need help picking something out?"

He looked around the store and took a few steps toward the counter. Norma's Closet prides itself on carrying the most trendsetting clothing in town, as well as a wide array of accessories, from must-have scarves to jewelry, hats, and handbags.

"What does your girlfriend like?" I asked.

"Well, she's pretty sporty," he said. "But she loves jewelry. I was thinking maybe a bracelet."

Funny that he'd pick a bracelet too. I pointed him toward the case and moved behind the counter. "Let me know if there's anything you'd like to see."

"She's pretty understated," he said. "Doesn't like to be too flashy."

"How about that one?" I pointed to a bracelet I'd been coveting since its arrival—a string of sterling silver hearts, encrusted with emeralds—but even with my discount, it was still too expensive.

"Yes." He nodded. "That looks like something she might like."

I took it out of the case and slid it across the counter toward him. He checked the price tag: $180.

"I know. It's a bit pricey, but those are real emeralds," I told him.

He ran the bracelet across his palm. The lobster clasp rested on his wrist, where the tree was rooted. "Actually, could *you* try it on? That'll give me a better idea."

I should've known then—should've guessed that someone so desperate for a gift wouldn't have been dragging his feet. But instead I did as he asked, slipping the bracelet on, fastening the clasp one-handed.

It was absolutely stunning, and I could feel it on my face—the burn of pure envy heating up my cheeks. "What do you think?"

"It's perfect," he said, meeting my eyes again. "I'll take it."

I was kind of sad to see the bracelet go. I'd tried it on a handful of times, hoping that Norma would put it on sale. But still I clipped the tag, wrapped it up in tissue paper, and turned to reach for a bag.

And that's when it happened.

His tree-branch arms wrapped around my chest.

A cloth pressed against my mouth.

I stumbled back and tried to scream. But my voice was silenced, and my legs couldn't seem to move right—*shuffle, shuffle, stomp, slide.*

I reached out. My fingers found something soft: the new silk rompers; I pictured their stripe-and-daisy pattern. I pulled—*hard*—hoping to snag a hanger, imagining using it as a weapon.

Something crashed—a clothing rack? A mannequin? The fabric slipped from between my fingers.

"Just relax," he said, holding me in place, squeezing my wrists together at my chest. "I'm not going to hurt you."

A fiery ball of light pressed behind my eyes: bright orange and yellow, erupting into flecks like straight out of a volcano.

I opened my mouth to bite, but it was filled with cloth. My tongue felt thick and heavy—too big to form words, too bulky to scream out.

There was a sticky-sweet scent.

And a bitter-fruity taste.

Plus, a flurry of thoughts and questions. *Is this really happening? This can't possibly be happening. What did I do? How did he know?*

Ms. Romer's high-pitched voice played in my mind's ear—all of her lectures on self-defense in health class.

Because Ms. Romer knew.

Because her partner was a cop.

Because she said she watched too many crime shows on TV.

"Don't let the perpetrator take you to a second location. Fight with all your might. Kick, scream, bite, scratch. Do whatever it takes."

My head felt woozy, but I refused to give up. I swung out with my arms, only to discover that they were still pinned at my chest.

I looked around for a weapon or a way out, but all that was within eyeshot were the cases full of candles: wrinkled brown boxes stacked against the wall, silver wicks peeking out at the top. I watched them darken and blur as the lights grew dim.

As my body grew heavy.

As my reality faded away.

4

Mom made an old favorite dish for dinner: homemade manicotti with Grandma Jean's plum-tomato sauce. Dad baked des-
sert: fudge brownies. The sight of the brownies flashes me back
to middle school, when Shelley bet me she could eat an entire
batch in less than three minutes. I took the bet and watched as she
stuffed her face with fistfuls of brownie. It wasn't until her cheeks
were packed like a chipmunk's that I did the chicken dance, complete with bunny teeth, rendering Shelley incapable of swallow-
ing because she was laughing so hard. A chunk of brownie shot
out of her mouth. A trickle of chocolate drooled from her nose.
We collapsed to the floor in a fit of uncontrollable laughs. And
suddenly all bets were off, because we'd both clearly won.

I miss Shelley.

A lot.

I miss Grandma Jean too. She passed away the year BIWM
(Before I Went Missing) and lives on in our food now—in the
sauces, the stews, and the hand-rolled gnocchi.

As I sit here at the dining table, going through the motions of a meal, while feeling like the ghost of my former self, I can't help wonder: *Where do* I *live on?*

Dad takes a sip of wine. The color looks extra dark, like black raspberries. Mom said he's been making his own wine for the past ten months. *"It gave him something else to focus on. Honestly, if it weren't for wine and work, I think he'd have gone completely mad."*

Her words are like acid spilling over open wounds. If it's not bad enough I screwed up my own life, I also managed to screw up his.

"How is your room working out?" Mom asks.

"My room?"

"Yes." She nods. "Do you feel like you're finally all settled in? Is there anything else you need?"

"Anything else?"

"We can go shopping if you like." Her face brightens. "Clothes, books, bed linens, school supplies . . ."

"Can I let you know?"

"Of course." She fakes a smile.

I fake one back.

"Also, I've been meaning to ask . . . Have you heard from Angie?" Mom's eyebrows dart upward as if she already knows the answer.

Angie works at the animal shelter where I used to volunteer. Apparently, she got some new dogs in, and there's one she wants me to meet.

"She called today," I say, focused on the flower arrangement in the center of the table. Water lilies. The petals look like box-cutter blades.

"Did you set up a time to see her?"

I stab my thigh, beneath the table, with my butter knife, wishing it were sharp enough to tear.

"Jane?"

"I didn't set up a time." I swallow hard, grinding the knife in deeper.

"How about Shelley?"

I gaze toward the window, picturing myself on the ledge.

"Have you heard from her?" she persists.

I want to be excused. I peek at Dad to see if he'll come to my rescue, but he's staring into his plate as if he wants to jump too.

"Shelley called," I admit. She calls all the time. Today she offered to bring me lunch—avocado, tomato, and mozzarella sandwiches, plus an Elvis Alive, made with coconut milk, pureed banana, and peanut butter. My favorites. She knows this.

But I said no anyway. "I'm really kind of busy."

"What are you really kind of busy doing?" Shelley asked.

"Maybe some other time," I told her, and I felt—in the hole-that-is-my-heart—a tunneling sensation that burrowed deep inside my chest.

"On Friday, I'm going to the movies with Mellie and Tanya," Shelley continued. "Do you want to come?"

"Since when do you hang with them?"

"Since Mellie accidentally spilled Pepto-Bismol in my lap in physics. I had to wear a lab coat for the rest of the day. Short skirt. Long story." She laughed. "Anyway, they want you to come."

"They said that?"

"Of course. We all want you to join."

Part of me assumed they just wanted the inside scoop about my seven months away. Another part figured they must feel really sorry for me. Either way, my answer was still the same: There was no fucking way.

After we hung up, I pictured the three of them in a movie theater, snarfing Sno-Caps and talking about their college plans, and suddenly I felt bitter.

Bitter.

And lonely.

And angry.

And regretful.

Because while they were enjoying life like nothing ever happened, I was stuck here living mine because of everything that had.

"Does the food taste okay?" Mom asks, pulling me off my mental ledge. "You've barely touched your plate."

She doesn't understand that tomato-based foods are no longer appetizing to me. I tried to tell her that during my first week home, when she made angel hair pasta with marinara sauce, but her face contorted into a giant question mark. She didn't understand it. She didn't want to hear it. She'd worked so hard to make the noodles and sauce from scratch, just like Grandma Jean.

"Dr. White called earlier," she says when I don't respond. "I think we should set up another appointment."

"I don't like Dr. White."

"Because she's too old?"

"Because her office smells like honeycomb candles."

Her face twists up as if my comment doesn't compute. I want to scribble the word *Listen* across both of her ears: *Listen to my words, even put them in your mouth; swallow them down like your homemade pasta noodles.* Because, the truth is, I've already tried to talk.

To her.

To Dad.

To doctors.

To the police.

They all declare a safe space and tell me I can say whatever's on my mind, but that's only really true if what I have to say is what they're prepared to hear. And so they furrow their foreheads, raise their brows, purse their lips, and shake their heads.

They look away.

They clasp their hands over their mouths.

They leave me feeling.

Even more isolated.

Than I was during those seven months, which they'll never understand.

"What do honeycomb candles have to do with anything?" Mom asks.

Meanwhile, Dad continues to drink. There are chunky bits at the bottom of his glass. He needs to refill. I need to go back to the four gray walls of my room.

"Promise me you'll go if I make an appointment," Mom says.

I hate Dr. White. "She makes me feel crazy."

"What makes you say that?"

"Because she thinks I *am* crazy."

She and Dad exchange a look, but neither or them argues for my sanity.

"I have a better idea for therapy," I offer. "What if I write about what happened?"

"Like a book?" She looks at Dad again, checking his reaction. *Why the hell doesn't anyone ever check mine?*

"You're not planning on sharing your story, are you?" she asks.

I stuff my mouth with noodles, just as Shelley did with that batch of fudge brownies, so I don't have to talk—so none of my ideas will get stomped like Dad's sour wine grapes.

5

Lying on my back, the surface beneath me rocked from side to side. I opened my eyes, unable to see. Darkness surrounded me—an overwhelming sensation that crawled like spiders beneath my skin.

I tried to get up. My head hit something hard. A car horn beeped. My heart started hammering.

I reached outward to feel all around, discovering a roof above my head. My knuckles made a knocking sound against it.

Music played—a country song, a medley of instruments: a guitar, a keyboard, a drumbeat, and a harmonica. My body jolted forward, and I smashed into another solid surface, nose-first. A trickle of wetness ran down my lip, landed on my tongue—the taste of blood.

The snap to reality.

A male voice sang, *"Don't let that lover get awayyyyy."*

Tears slid down my face. Acid crept into my throat. I reached inside my pocket, my fingers shaking, my legs quivering, relieved to find my phone. It was still there, zipped inside my running jacket. I clicked it on—two bars, three texts, and a missed call from Shelley, plus another missed call from Mom. I didn't bother to read the texts or listen to the messages. I just typed in my pass code, getting it wrong on the first try. I accidentally hit Delete on the second try.

Finally, I got it to work, and I pressed my mother's number.

"Where are you?" she answered; there was panic in her voice. Shelley must've called her when I didn't show up at the diner.

A gush of words stormed from my mouth. "*He took me. Mom . . . You have to help me, Mom. I don't know where I am. I don't know what's happening. I'm in the trunk of his car.*"

Hearing those words aloud provided a new layer of terror, because speaking them made them true, and because I'd never heard myself be that scared about anything.

"*Who* took you?" Mom asked.

"A guy. At the store."

"Norma's? John," she called to my father. "*Now.* We need to call 9-1-1."

I could hear Dad's voice in the background. What was he saying?

"She's in a car trunk," Mom told him.

A whining sound burst from my mouth when I suddenly realized: The guy who took me . . . he'd eventually stop driving. I'd be forced to get out. And what would happen then?

And what would happen then?

"*Mom,*" I whimpered.

"Listen to me carefully," she said. "Do you see a tab or latch of some sort—something that glows in the dark? Pull on it. A light should go on. The trunk will flip open."

"No!" I cried. "There's no tab, nothing glowing."

"Okay, so look around," she continued. "Is there anything in the trunk that can help you? A weapon? Something sharp?"

"A tool or umbrella?" Dad asked, now speaking directly into Mom's phone. "A screwdriver, jumper cables, cleaning agents?"

I tried to look, straining my eyes, but I couldn't see. I could only feel: a thin layer of carpeting and the interior contours of the trunk, where the sides met the roof.

"Are you able to locate where the taillights would be?" Mom asked. "There's probably a panel covering the space. Pull it out and kick at the taillight as hard as you can to break the glass. Then stick your hand through and wave so that other drivers can see you."

I felt all around, but I couldn't find anything—not a tool or a taillight. Where were the panels? Why couldn't I find them?

The music continued to play. *"Make that lover want to stayyyyyyy . . . Give her love all night and dayyyyy . . . Don't let her get awayyyyyy . . ."*

"Jane?" Mom's voice.

"I can't see," I murmured. "I don't know." *Didn't I have a flashlight app? I could've sworn I'd downloaded a flashlight app.* I looked at the screen, but I didn't see the icon: the purple flashlight.

"You need to hang up and call 9-1-1," she said.

"Mom, *no.*"

"Jane. Big breath. Daddy's on the phone with them now. He already gave them your cell number, but they want you to call them."

"No." More tears. I didn't want to let go.

"Jane." Her voice sounded stern, but I could tell she was crying too. "Let them help you. They're tracing your whereabouts. They're going to find you. We're going to find you. *Jane?*"

The car stopped.

A door slammed.

I found the panel—a piece of carpet-covered plastic—and pulled it out. My fingers found wires.

I tugged.

Something broke.

"*Jane?*"

"He's coming," I whispered. My whole body shook. I could barely hold the phone.

My mother was crying too hard for words, which only made things worse, because Mom was supposed to tell me that everything would be okay—that she'd put on her red cape and come save me, wherever this was, just as she always had.

I heard a key slide into the lock, followed by a deep *click*.

"Don't let him take you," Dad said. "Kick, bite, scratch, punch—"

"*Almost home.*" The guy's voice again. The familiar rusty tone.

Chills ripped up my skin.

"Don't take her!" Dad shouted. "I'll find you. I'll find her."

Something wet hit my face. A rag pressed against my skin. That familiar sweet scent was right over my mouth, beneath my nostrils, filling up my senses. I tried not to breathe it in, knowing it would put me out, but my head was already fuzzy and my limbs felt heavy. Inside my ears was an overwhelming itch.

Where was my phone? No longer in my grip. Had I hung up? Was Mom still connected?

A squeaking noise came from inside my mouth—the rag rubbing against my teeth, like Styrofoam on Styrofoam. I screamed out, deep from within my chest. A blood-curdling wail tore out of my throat.

At least I thought it did. But I didn't hear any sound. Had it been muffled by the rag? Or lost in the folds of fabric? My tongue felt cumbersome again—too big for my mouth. Had it muted the sound?

I tried to swipe him away, reaching through the air, swatting from side to side, only able to see the top of his head out of the corner of my eye: the spot the rag didn't cover.

Brown wavy hair.

A patch of light skin.

And a burst of black dots.

My fingers jammed into something soft. I imagined it was his chest. I wanted to get his eyes, like Ms. Romer advised in health class.

"The vulnerable five," she called them. *"The eyes, nose, throat, groin, and knees. Kick 'em where it counts. Jab 'em where it hurts. Punch 'em like you mean it."*

He continued to press the rag into my face, trying to pin me still, waiting until I passed out. In my mind, I fought back, kicking outward, flailing my legs.

I might've spun around on my back.

I'm pretty sure I managed to knee his hip.

He started to lift me out of the trunk, grabbing around my shoulders. I arched my back. The top of my spine jammed into something sharp; a biting, singeing pain radiated down my legs.

"There's no need to fight." His voice was no longer rusty. It was slow and distorted now—the vocal equivalent of molasses on ice. "It'll only make this—"

Harder?

More painful?

I could no longer decipher the words, but still he was talking. I pictured myself in an ocean with anchors tied around my feet, fighting to stay afloat by treading water with my arms. Only I kept slipping beneath the surface, making it hard to hear.

He pulled me forward—up, out of the ocean. My chin met something hard. His jaw? Or collarbone? I sank my teeth into whatever was there.

Was that a wail? Did it come from him or me? Or maybe from Mom—was she still sobbing, over the phone?

Music continued to play. Had it ever stopped? Was the ignition still running? Were we on a boat?

"*Lover, don't you want to stayyyyy? In a place where we can hide awayyyy . . . Oh, please, believe. We'll be happy and free. Oh, please, lover, please, believe.*"

THEN

6

When I woke up again, the first thing I saw was a pair of eyes—chocolate brown with upturned lashes, plus a mole by the lower lid. I wanted to reach out and poke those eyes, but my arms didn't move. I couldn't find my fingers. Everything felt thick.

And heavy.

And slow.

And warm.

The guy's lips moved, but I couldn't decipher the words. There was a buzzing in my ears and a disconnection in my brain.

I think he placed something on my face. I'm pretty sure he pulled blankets up to my chin. Maybe he sang me a song—from *The Sound of Music*. Was he wearing white ski gloves?

I blinked, but I'm not sure for how long—or if I might've nodded off—because when I opened my eyes again, he seemed closer. I felt the heat of his breath against my cheek.

He was holding something—someone's hand. It took me a beat to realize it was mine—my sterling silver ring, my clover-shaped birthmark, my week-old French manicure.

His lips drooped downward like a sad clown face. Something was wrong. His forehead scrunched up; there were deep horizontal lines etched into his skin.

He checked my pulse, holding my fingers upward. Were my veins always so blue? My skin normally so ghostly? Was I already dead? But dead girls don't smile, and a smile came to my lips—I felt it crawl up my cheeks—as I looked at those brown, brown eyes so full of concern, and as I watched the tension in his jaw and the sharp angles of his mouth as it moved to form words. It was like watching a movie where I had a front-row seat, only I wasn't sure where the seat was or how much I'd already missed.

Was I still in the trunk?

Were we past the inciting incident?

Or was this the final cut and his eyes were the last things I'd see?

7

I woke up in a bright white room with stark white walls. The furniture was white too—a table, a chair, a dresser, a mini-fridge.

I sat up. My head throbbed: a knifelike sensation that plunged through the bones of my skull. A musty smell filled the air. I recognized it right away, like rotted wood or decayed leaves. It was the scent of the honeycomb candles from Norma's store. They were burning somewhere.

I looked around, trying to locate the source, suddenly noticing that I was lying in a bed—crisp white sheets, two square pillows. What was this place? Why was I here?

Breathe.

Breathe.

"Whatever you do, try your best not to panic." Ms. Romer's voice, back inside my head. *"Be smart. Assess the situation. Figure out your best resources."*

The entire space seemed about as big as my dorm room at poetry camp, but with no windows and no doorknob on the door.

Was this a basement of a house? Was that a pocket door? The candles weren't burning here, but they were nearby for sure.

I reached into my pocket. My phone was gone. My blood turned to ice. This wasn't happening.

This couldn't.

Possibly.

Be happening.

Two bright eyeball lights shone down from the ceiling. They were caged with metal screens and secured with locks.

I stood up. My legs felt heavy. My feet tingled as they touched the floor; that was white too—painted cement. I shuffled to the door, felt all around the edges. It wasn't made of wood. Possibly steel? Or iron?

I cupped a hand over my mouth. Tears streamed down my cheeks.

"Whatever you do, try your best not to panic. Be smart. Assess the situation. Figure out your best resources."

A tall, slender cabinet stood to my right. It was attached to the wall with thick steel bolts, plus a chain. The fridge was that way too, and so were the table, chair, bed, and dresser—all secured to the walls and floor.

I moved across the room, itching at my forearms, scratching the back of my neck, then inside my ears. A side effect from the drug? Was that why my mouth felt so fuzzy? And why my skin felt so chilled?

Beyond the dresser was a doorway without a door. The space was open, about the size of a walk-in closet. I peeked inside, spotting a toilet, a sink, and a stand-up shower.

My eyes filled up again. My body began to twitch.

He was keeping me here. This was no fucking joke.

I scrambled to the door and beat my fists against it, screaming for someone to come—even if that meant him.

I kicked.

I beat.

I punched.

I smacked.

I did all of the things I was supposed to have done before he'd had the chance to take me in the first place. But it was too fucking late.

No one answered.

He never came.

There was just a nighttime silence too heavy to lift. I tried to breathe through it and felt a jabbing in my chest, cutting off my air. I sank down to the floor and tucked my head between my knees. *This wasn't happening. This couldn't possibly be happening.*

I looked at the door again, noticing a cutout at the bottom— a panel that swung open and shut, like for a pet. It was small— maybe twelve inches wide by eight inches tall.

I moved across the floor and pushed the panel open. Propped on my knees, I used the strength of my elbows to try to wriggle my way through, but the sides of the opening pinched my biceps, dug into the flesh. Barely shoulder-deep, I felt a tingling sensation radiating down my forearms, burning my fingertips. I needed to find another way.

Lying on my stomach, I stuck my head through the opening. The top of the hinge ground into my scalp. Something sharp pressed against my ear. I peered around, spotting a pile of boxes stacked in the distance, as well as another room— about three yards away—across the hall. The door crack at the bottom was filled with light, as though someone were inside there.

"Hello?" I shouted.

No one answered. Nothing happened. And so I screamed like an animal—until my throat burned raw and I could taste blood on my tongue.

Eventually, I slunk back on the bed, rolled onto my side, and stared at the bright white wall as my mind continued to race. My heart wouldn't stop palpitating. But somehow I was able to cry myself to sleep, returning to that temporary state of unconsciousness where reality doesn't exist.

8

When I woke up again, I kept my eyes pressed shut, not wanting to see what in my mind I already knew: The white wall would be there, facing me, beside the bed.

And it was.

Totally real.

I touched it to be sure, dragged the nubs of my fingers across the cool, bumpy surface; felt the hot, bubbly tears fill the rims of my eyes; winced from the sharp, wrenching pain deep inside my gut.

I was going to be sick. Acid crept up the back of my throat and filled the crevices of my mouth. I threw up beside the bed, heaved until there was nothing else left, except hot, bubbly tears and cool, bumpy surfaces.

I got up and stumbled into the bathroom. A light went on overhead, as though by motion. I stepped in front of the sink. A mirror faced me, but it wasn't made with real glass. My reflection looked distorted, my face and neck too long—like the image in a fun house. But still, the presence of a fake mirror . . . He obviously cared about vanity, and wanted me too as well, which explained the hairbrush on the hamper and the bar of soap on the plastic dish.

A bright red blob sat in the corner of my eye like spilled ketchup. A broken blood vessel; I'd gotten one before—from laughing upside down, reclining off the back of Shelley's sofa during a backbend challenge that involved Thai noodles and gummy worms.

Was this one from crying too hard?

Or screaming too loud?

Or convulsing too much?

The blob had bled over part of the green iris, turning it brown, making me look like a monster with my ashen cheeks and my swollen red lips, like *The Night of the Living Dead*.

I shut my eyes again, trying to block everything out, even for a few seconds, still able to hear my mother's sobs on the other end of the phone.

"Be smart." Ms. Romer's voice again. *"Assess the situation. Figure out your best resources."*

I peered all around, wondering if I was being watched—if the guy who took me was sitting in front of a video or computer screen.

My lips stung. I licked them to check for bleeding, but everything tasted sour like the inside of my mouth. Still, I was pretty sure I'd bitten them in my sleep, that I'd dreamed of lip piercings and salted chips.

And running in the rain.

In my purple running shoes.

A long lock of hair fell loose from its bun. I poked it back in place, secured the rubber band with an extra loop, then turned toward a tall storage cabinet. Like the furniture in the other room, it'd been chained to the wall. I opened the door. Inside I found more bars of soap: the Saint Georges brand, the same one I used at home. The shampoo and conditioner were the kind I liked as well, from Studio M, at least twenty bottles of each. Stacked on the middle and bottom shelves were towels, washcloths, boxes of tissues, packages of sanitary napkins, and toilet paper . . .

I backed away, shaking my head. A weird gurgling noise sputtered from my throat. *Just get a grip,* I reminded myself. *Assess the situation. Find my resources.*

I started to pick through the items on the shelves, but my hands wouldn't stop trembling. Bottles were toppling out. My lungs were caving in.

Was that a container of facial cream? I recognized the green-and-yellow logo. And the name on the jar: Celestial, from Lush, also my brand. I heard myself wheeze.

Think, Jane.

Don't freak out.

There's a lot here to work with.

I went to grab a bottle of shampoo—to check the ingredients list for something I could use, something to inflict harm— when I noticed a pad of paper stuck to the inside of the door. It was a checklist for things I'd need to order—for items in the cabinet I'd eventually use up and groceries in the fridge I'd yet to weed through. I also found a scorecard of some sort and a tiny wooden pencil.

EARN STARS FOR BEING GOOD

Score 1 star each for the following chores:

1. Placing dirty dishes outside the cat door after the completion of each meal.

2. Depositing trash in the bag provided and leaving it in the hall-way at least once per week.

3. Stripping bed linens weekly and leaving outside the cat door, along with any clothing items you'd like washed.

Please list your completed chores below, beside each star. After twenty stars, you can choose from the following prizes: a novel of your choice, a notebook and pen set, a deck of cards, a magazine (be specific on which type), a crossword puzzle or word-search book, or other item of your choosing.

★
★
★
★
★
★
★
★
★
★
★
★
★
★
★
★
★
★

Desired Item: _____

My head whirred. The room began to tilt. I grabbed the door for stability, but it wasn't enough. My knees gave way. And my head hit the floor.

THEN

9

Sometime later, screaming jolted me awake. My eyes snapped open, but the room remained dark.

Where was I?

Lying in bed?

The surface beneath me felt stone-cold, brick-hard. The bones in my face ached. I lifted my head just as a female voice shouted, *"It won't happen again!"*

I scrambled to a seated position, triggering the sensor light to click on. I was still in the bathroom.

The scorecard for the star points lay at my feet, along with the wooden pencil.

I crawled across the floor out of the bathroom and to the pocket door to listen. She screamed again—a tear-filled wail that radiated in my chest. I felt it in my gut. I think it shook the room.

I pushed open the swinging panel. A tray sat within reach, out in the hallway. I looked beyond it just as the girl screamed louder. My heart beat faster. I stuck my face into the opening, trying my best to see, but I only had a view of about five feet on both sides of the door.

"*Please,*" she wailed. "*I won't. I promise.*" Her voice had blades. It tore me to bits.

I wanted to call out, wanted to rip right through the wall and tell her that she wasn't the only one here.

A door slammed somewhere. Her voice got strangled. She sounded farther away now, maybe even on another floor.

Tears slid down my face as I remained curled up by the door, my mind racing, my muscles twinging.

It got.

Eerily.

Quiet.

There was only Ms. Romer's voice inside my head: "*In the unfortunate event that you do get taken to a second location, be sure to leave a trail of clues. They're like bread crumbs for investigators and go quite nicely with the main dish of DNA.*" She laughed.

But nothing was funny, because I hadn't left a thing—not a mint from my pocket or the rubber band from my hair.

Had anyone seen me go into Norma's shop?

Had Norma ever invested in surveillance cameras? She'd talked about getting them once, when the convenience store down the road had gotten robbed. But she never did go forward with the installation.

Or *had* she?

How about the toy shop across the street? Or the stationery store next door? Did they have surveillance cameras?

What did the scene look like after I passed out? Where had the guy parked his car? Behind mine, in Norma's back driveway? Did he carry me out (and leave some of his DNA en route)? Or was I able to walk?

"Hello?" I shouted after what felt like an eternity, surprised to hear my voice, that I hadn't gone deaf. That's how quiet it'd become.

What was happening? Why was the girl no longer yelling?

"Hello?" I tried again, but it came out in a cough. My throat sounded splintered. I needed water.

I peeked through the cat door again. A pitcher sat on the tray, along with a stack of drinking cups. I slid it toward me and poured water into a cup, only it lapped over the rim.

I popped the lid off the pitcher and drank from the spout, my mind reeling, my head spinning. Everything felt fast, fast, fast, and at the same time slow.

Slow.

Slow.

The liquid tasted sweet. Why was my neck wet?

Where was my phone? Would the police be able to trace it?

I looked at the tray again. There was something wrapped in foil, as well as a bag of chips, a container of applesauce, and a bruised apple. I unwrapped the foil, able to smell the item inside—the charred meat, the doughy bun. The burger felt cold to the touch. A shriveled square of orange cheese sat on top, melted into the grease, along with a thick tomato slice.

My stomach grumbled in response. My mouth started to water. I gobbled the burger down, unable to chew it quickly enough, nearly choking in the process. Then I searched the tray for a spoon to eat the applesauce. There wasn't any, so I used my fingers, lapping every last bit.

When I'd almost reached the bottom, the lights went out. I stomped my feet, hoping it would trigger a motion detector light like the one in the bathroom. But nothing happened. I remained in complete darkness.

I stood up and slid my palms over the wall, on both sides of the door—swiping left and right, then up and down—trying to locate a light switch, unable to find one. Why hadn't I noticed a switch earlier?

I continued searching, taking side steps toward the cabinet, able to feel the wooden corner at my back. Still no luck.

I moved in the opposite direction—until my calf touched the bed. Was there no switch at all? Or was it outside the door? Was he right outside my room?

My whole body trembled as I pressed my ear against the door panel. "Hello?" I called; my voice trembled too.

If he answered, I'm not sure I would've heard him. It was too loud inside my ears: the pulsating of my heart, the rushing of my blood, the storming of my adrenaline.

Was he watching me? Controlling when I slept? Playing with my mind?

I turned away from the door and ventured a step, still trying to listen for any noises—the click of a lock, the scuffle of a foot. With my arms outstretched, I moved across the room. Finally, my hands found the open doorway of the bathroom. I stepped inside, tripping the sensor. The light over the sink went on.

I let out my breath, reassuring myself; I could stay in here for as long as I wanted. But I opted for the dark instead. I snagged the hairbrush and curled up by the cat door, feeling I'd be closer to the girl that way, only slightly empowered to know I could retreat to the bathroom for light if I wanted.

Wielding the hairbrush as my weapon, I closed my eyes and envisioned using the handle to stab at his eyes.

I pictured the blood.

And imagined his wail.

I replayed the scene at least a hundred times inside my mind, my teeth clenched, my body twitching, as I waited to hear the girl's scream. I wouldn't rest until I did.

NOW

10

I'm sitting in the waiting room of Dr. White's office. It's time to go in, but I'd rather eat dirt. My mother insists—on my going in, that is.

"I'll be right here the whole time," she says as assurance, though it feels more like a warning.

I step into the office and close the door behind me. Once again, the interior smells like honeycomb candles, like hay and burning leaves. I mentioned it the first time I was here—how much it bothered me—but clearly the problem is mine.

I turn to face the door and wrap my hand around the knob, so tempted to bolt. I could say I have a stomachache. Mom would know it's a lie, but does the excuse really matter?

"Come sit," Dr. White says, a cheery tone to her voice as though we're two good friends just chatting over coffee. "It's been a few weeks. I'm really glad to see you."

I turn the knob, making sure that it works, that it didn't automatically lock when I closed the door.

"Come sit," she persists.

I picture a box of Kleenex and imagine counting up all of the tissues inside it as I pluck each one out.

"Is everything okay?"

Twenty-seven, pluck . . . twenty-eight, pluck . . .

"Come on, let's talk."

Twenty-nine, pluck . . . thirty . . .

"Jane?"

I swivel and scan the room, double-checking for windows. There's a row of four on the sidewall. I move from the door and sit across from Dr. White. Behind her is a picture of women holding hands, all of them different ages, from various countries. Supposedly, Dr. White is all about girl power and women's rights. It's why my mother chose her; Dr. White would know how to fix me.

Because I have rights. (Doesn't everyone?)

And because my situation is somehow a woman's issue (as opposed to a human one).

I reach into my pocket and hit Record on my phone in case she has anything helpful to say that I can play back later (doubtful but optimistic).

DR. WHITE: How have you been?

ME: The same as last time.

DR. WHITE: And how is that?

ME:

DR. WHITE: Did you visit the pet shelter like we talked about?

ME:

DR. WHITE: Jane? Do you need a tissue? I see you're eyeing the box.

ME: Do you mind if I just hold the box?

DR. WHITE: Of course, help yourself. We talked last time about making contact with some of your friends.

ME: I don't really feel ready for socializing yet.

DR. WHITE: Are you still having panic attacks?

ME: Yes. Once or twice a week.

DR. WHITE: When do you find that you're getting them?

ME: In the middle of the night, when I'm lying in bed, thinking too much.

DR. WHITE: Thinking about what specifically?

ME: Him.

DR. WHITE: Him? Meaning the man who abducted you? The man who locked you in his trunk and kept you captive for seven months?

ME: No, I mean Mason. That's who I've been thinking about.

DR. WHITE: I see.

ME: I miss him.

DR. WHITE: Can I get you a fidget cube?

ME: A what?

DR. WHITE: You're pulling out all of my tissues.

ME: Oh. Sorry.

DR. WHITE: Okay, so getting back to those panic attacks . . . Do any of the exercises I taught you help?

ME:

DR. WHITE: Jane? Can I get you something?

ME: No. I just need to stretch my legs. It's hard to sit for so long.

DR. WHITE: Would you like some water? There are cups on the shelf behind you.

ME: Water?

DR. WHITE: You're holding the jug. Come and sit back down. I was asking if any of the exercises I gave you helped with the panic attacks.

ME: The visualizing helps. Then, once I'm breathing better, I go into the closet. That helps too. I've set up a comfortable area.

DR. WHITE: In your closet?

ME: Is that unusual?

DR. WHITE: It's just that a lot of people who've experienced confinement often report having symptoms of claustrophobia. Does being in the closet ever bring on your panic attacks?

ME: No. I told you, the closet makes me feel safer . . . hidden.

DR. WHITE: I see.

ME: So it is unusual?

DR. WHITE: Let me get you that fidget cube.

ME: Where are they?

DR. WHITE: The fidget cubes? I have a whole basket over . . . Jane?

ME: Where are they?

DR. WHITE: Where are what? Jane, what are you looking for?

ME: Why does it smell like honeycomb candles?

DR. WHITE: Jane, please come take your seat.

ME: I knew it. I smelled it. This is a honeycomb candle, isn't it?

DR. WHITE: Jane . . .

ME: Where did you get this?

DR. WHITE: This isn't really about candles, now is it. Please, come sit down. Let's talk about what's bothering you.

ME: How about the fucking candle.

DR. WHITE: Would you like me to throw the candle away?

ME: Don't bother. I'm leaving.

DR. WHITE: But our session isn't over. Jane . . .

When I get back out to the waiting room, Mom stops knitting and drops the needles onto her lap.

"What happened?" she asks. "It's barely been twenty minutes."

"Jane?" Dr. White's voice again.

"I'm done," I tell Mom, refusing to look back.

"Don't be silly. You still have thirty more minutes." Mom resumes her knitting—her version of tough love.

"I want to go *now*," I assure her.

"No," Mom insists. Knit, knit, knit. "We planned this. You promised me. I had to move two other appointments to make today work."

"It's okay," Dr. White says, her voice as soft as shit.

"No, it isn't." Mom's fingers work faster as if a scarf will fix everything.

"How about if we give you a choice," Dr. White says. "We can try this again now, or we can reschedule for another day."

"No," Mom snaps, answering for me. "Let's be responsible adults and go to our scheduled appointments."

Poke.

Loop.

Pull.

Repeat.

Dr. White: "I'm giving you a choice here, Jane. So what do you say?"

"I'm leaving," I tell her, going for the door.

"Jane—no!" Mom shouts.

But it's already too late. Her yarn-tangled self is no match for my need to flee. I take the exit stairwell, bolt down two flights, plow through the lobby, and go outside, where the air is less stifling and doesn't smell of honeycomb.

I run for five blocks, looking all around me, jumping at the blare of a fire engine and the slamming of a car door. A girl crossing the street shouts in my direction. I freeze in place, thinking she's talking to me, but then her face lights up as a woman with blue braids waves at her.

I keep moving forward, scurrying across No Name Park and finding myself in front of Popular Chain Hotel. Here, I flag down a taxi and climb into the back, careful to close the door gently—no need for loud noises.

I lock the door behind me and try to breathe at a normal rate. Why didn't I bring my phone? Why aren't I carrying anything sharp?

"Where to?" the driver asks—an older man, at least seventy years old. He looks harmless enough, but still, I could hold my own against him if it came to that.

I check my pockets—fourteen dollars. "I have enough for an hour," I tell him.

"That's not exactly a destination."

My only destination is to escape my every thought. I don't want to answer more questions or be counted on by anyone. I just want to stare out the window at life passing by: a rush of colors, and shapes, and swirls, and obscurity.

Too blurry to make decisions.

Too distracting for future-planning.

Too far from others to disappoint.

"Could you just take 95 and then do a loop back?" I ask.

Thankfully, he doesn't say anything else. He just puts the car in drive and pulls away from the curb.

11

The monster controlled the light. There were no wall switches, only the motion sensor in the bathroom. I was reliant on him to show me the time of day. Light coincided with mealtimes, turning on just before the delivery of breakfast and clicking off shortly after dinner.

For breakfast that first morning, he left me waffles, yogurt, and a container of tomato juice (but again, with no utensils). After I was done, I squatted down by the dresser and tried to pull it toward me, as far as the chain would allow: barely three inches. I slid my hand into the open crevice and scratched at the wall, hoping to make a mark with my fingernail.

It didn't work. The nail bent. I needed something sharper.

I searched everywhere—in the food cabinet, under the bed, behind the fridge, and inside the bathroom closet—before finally discovering a jagged edge on my sweatshirt zipper, where the metal had gotten mangled. I used the edge as a pen and made my first tally mark, denoting Day One, unsure how accurate it really was.

How many days had I already missed?

And was it really, truly morning?

It could've been midnight for all I knew, but with no windows to see outside, fluorescent lights and breakfast delivery were all I had—my primitive version of telling time.

It was on the thirteenth tally mark that a male voice screamed—an angry, pleading wail that spread chills across my skin. Was it the monster's voice? Had the police finally come?

Would I finally get to find out who he was?

And what really happened?

I crouched down by the cat door just as a female shouted, *"Let me out! Please, I'll do anything!"*

Another scream followed—a hysterical one; the girl started laughing.

I pushed the panel open, able to hear more voices shouting—men and women, in different parts of the building, at varying degrees of volume:

"Hello?"

"Who's there?"

"Shut up!"

"Is he coming?"

"I don't want to die. I don't want to die. I don't want to die . . ."

"Just die already, will you?"

The police weren't here. The joke was on me. We were caged like animals, but how many of us were there? How big was this place? And what were we all waiting for?

Each of the voices seemed to be coming from at least a few floors away. At first, I assumed people were talking to one another. But then I realized no one's voice seemed to be in response to anyone else's.

We were too far apart to communicate beyond those cries. But still I cried along with them, happy to join the choir.

12

By the sixteenth tally mark, I realized I hadn't yet bathed. Or brushed my teeth. Or taken my hair out of its ponytail. I was still in my running clothes. My rain boots were still on my feet.

During those first couple of weeks, I hadn't sifted through the dresser drawers either, except to notice they were full of clothes—nothing sharp to protect myself. The fridge was stocked with drink bottles I hadn't touched (all plastic, none of them glass). The cabinets were full of snacks I had no appetite for—some of my favorites too, like the vanilla-flavored granola bars I used to bring on my runs, the peanut butter–filled pretzels Mom had to drive thirty minutes to get, and my preferred trail mix from Wild Willow Market (the kind with the dried mango bits).

But I didn't have much appetite. And I could smell my own skin, like week-old chicken left in the fridge. Meanwhile, my head wouldn't stop itching. Maybe I'd picked up lice. More likely, my scalp was caked with oil; bits of skin collected beneath my fingernails each time I scratched.

I fished inside the dresser for a fresh pair of underwear and I found several. They looked all too familiar: same green-and-yellow stripes, same floral and checked patterns.

My size.

With lace hems.

And the same soft cotton fabric.

I withdrew my hands. My stomach twisted into a knot. Were these my things? From my home?

I blinked hard as if that would change the canvas—turn the stripes into stars, make silk out of the cotton fabric . . . Then I ventured to pick up a pair, letting it dangle from my finger. The hem was pierced with a price tag, from Cha Cha La Mer, one of my favorite shops in the city, showing these things were brand-new.

Did he buy them just for me, knowing what I had in my drawers back home? How was that even possible?

It *wasn't* possible.

There had to be another explanation.

I searched the bras. They were my size as well: 32B with wireless cups (the kind I used), in seashell pink (the color I always bought because it remained invisible beneath a tee). I pulled out a pair of sweatpants and a T-shirt next—both in my size, from Run Like Wolves, a brand I loved but could rarely afford.

The scent of lavender and pine lingered in the air. It was the smell of the Cha Cha La Mer store. I'd asked about it once—what made the shop smell like that, smell so good. Was it a fragrance I could buy—something we could sell at Norma's? The saleslady told me it was the store's best-kept secret.

Was this his?

Knowing my brands?

And what I liked to eat?

Nothing made sense, except the obvious: He'd been watching me long before I was taken.

Had he seen me undress?

And pawed through my things?

Both of those possibilities rolled into a tight-fisted knot beneath my ribs, making it hard to breathe. I yanked a hoodie from the drawer and slunk down to the floor, crying into the crumpled sleeve until at last I drifted off to sleep.

THEN

13

"Well, you've certainly come to the right place. I have plenty of gifts."

"This would look adorable on Shelley, with her heart-shaped face."

My mother's voice startled me awake. I sat up, my heart pumping hard, half expecting to see her, only to discover that I was still in the room, still curled up on the floor.

My mother's voice continued to play in my head on a continuous loop. I pictured her standing at the kitchen table in her snowflake-printed bathrobe with her basketful of gifts: the melon-printed cap, the snowball-maker, the faux-fur glovelettes, and the turquoise watch . . .

And I threw up in my mouth.

"Please!" I shouted over and over again as if the monster might hear me and change his mind. I crawled to the door and listened for him to come.

But it was silent now.

There were no other voices and not a single footstep.

The only sound was the rushing of water, as though through a pipe, reminding me I still hadn't showered. The thought of taking off my clothes, after finding the underwear, was even worse than the smell of my skin, the stench of my sweat (like concentrated vinegar).

Door hinges whined from the end of the hall. I poked my face through the cat door and waited for the click of the latch and the jostling of keys. It took twenty-two steps before his legs were finally within view—faded jeans, frayed hems, brown heavy work boots.

"Please," I begged. "What do you want? What can I do?"

Why was I here?

Who were the others?

The dishes rattled as he set down a tray. I caught a glimpse of a red plaid shirt and a bright green watch. No tree-limb tattoo. Was it farther up his arm? Or maybe the monster bringing me food wasn't the same one who'd taken me.

"Who are you?" I pleaded after thirty-six tally marks. "Do you work for him? How much is he paying you? My parents will quadruple it." I stuck out my hand, trying to grab at his boots; I knew them by heart—every mark, stain, stitch, and scuff. I noticed on days when his laces were double-knotted, and when the leather was damp, when I could smell the rain-soaked hide.

On some days, I'd have given anything for him to come into my room and beat me—to throttle my neck, throw me against the wall, cut me with a knife, or set my hair on fire. At least then I would've had a fighting chance. And at least then I might've felt on the outside a fraction of what I'd been experiencing on the inside—that gnawing-singeing ache.

"Let me out!" I shouted after thirty-nine tally marks, throwing myself against the door and pounding it with my fists. I grabbed the side of the cabinet and tried to rip it from the wall. But I fell back—*hard*—hitting my head on the bed frame. A spray of flashing lights shot in front of my eyes. But still it didn't stop me.

I hurled the trays, chucked my boots, rattled the chains, kicked the table.

Shook the fridge.

Tossed the snacks.

Pulled the drawers.

And threw the clothes.

I flipped the mattress, tore up the sheets, screamed myself hoarse, and thrashed until I saw blood.

Needless to say, I was a very naughty girl, and it got me absolutely nothing, except a big mess to clean, an egg-shaped bump on my head, and a gash by my eye. The blood from the gash pooled onto the cement. I watched it for several seconds, wondering how much blood one would have to lose before passing out.

And what would happen then?

Would trays of food collect in the hall? Would the monster assume I was dead and come inside to check?

What *would* it take to die? How long would I have to bleed? My heart pounded at the flurry of questions, at this sudden surge of power.

And then I saw it.

As if by fate.

A box of Cocoa Loco brownies.

I must've whipped it across the room without having noticed the smiling square of chocolate on the cover of the box. Otherwise, I would've paused, because they were Shelley's comfort food of choice, with the layer of chopped walnuts and the drizzle of white frosting.

Had the guy assumed they were one of my favorites—maybe from spotting them in the forefront of our snack cabinet, through the window in the kitchen? Or maybe he'd seen my mom stocking up on boxes at the little red store in town.

The funny thing was we'd only kept Cocoa Loco brownies

around for Shelley's visits, and so finding them in the monster's cabinet, among all of my favorite go-to snacks, and knowing he'd misunderstood, as trivial as the detail was, gave me a smidge of satisfaction.

He didn't know everything about me.

I held the box against my chest, thinking how it'd never failed to make Shelley's face light up. When her boyfriend, Mitchell, lied about his boys' night out, or when she'd bomb a test at school, all I had to do was flash the Cocoa Loco name, and all hope would be restored.

The light in the room blinked once before going out completely and leaving me in the dark. But suddenly that was okay, because I had the box of brownies.

I navigated to the bed, pretending to be in Shelley's basement during one of our sleepovers, imagining we'd just watched a scary movie and decided to call it a night. "I miss you," I whispered into the darkness, snuggling the box closer and picturing Shelley's smiling face.

14

When I woke up again, my head ached. I lay in bed, waiting for the lights to go on, unable to shut off the memory that reeled inside my brain: One late summer night, not long before I was taken, I came home to find that the window in my bedroom had been left wide open, including the screen. I never asked my parents about it, figuring Mom must've hiked up the pane to let in fresh air.

But why would she also open the screen? And why, especially, would she do so in the nighttime, when moths and mosquitoes could fly right in? It wasn't as if it'd been left like that from earlier in the day. The pane and screen had been closed when I went out to meet Shelley at dinnertime.

Hadn't they?

I'd have noticed otherwise. Wouldn't I have?

Plus, summer equals air-conditioning, which means closed windows.

Closed windows.

Mom was always reminding me to lock mine too. Our neighbor's house had gotten broken into, after all, which was why I never asked my parents about finding the window open. Because what if I'd done it and just not remembered? Not to mention that I'd snuck in late that night, way after curfew. And who wants to stir a simmering pot?

I sat up, still waiting for the light, unable to shake the image of the monster climbing through my bedroom window, searching in my closet and going through all of my things. The image had gnawed at me for most of the night like a rat inside my brain. I don't think I slept for more than thirty minutes straight.

What time was it now?

I stood up and went to take a step, feeling a clump of clothing beneath my feet—the product of my tantrum. I scooched down to the floor and felt all around, raking my fingers over food boxes, strewn T-shirts, and a gallon jug of water. I slid the jug toward me and took a sip. Water poured down my chin and neck. The jug was almost too heavy to hold. My muscles were getting weak. I felt a tremor in my thumb.

Despite the darkness, I lifted the jug, up and down, to do biceps and triceps curls—thirty of each, with each arm, as I waited for the light. I also did fifty leg lifts and thirty squats.

Still.

No.

Light.

But the spurt of activity felt surprisingly uplifting. I used that rush to scoot down by the bed, remembering a movie I saw where the main character took a box cutter to the side of her mattress.

I pushed down on the fabric, able to feel springs. How hard would it be to pry one free and twist it into a weapon? I played the scene out in my head: The guy coming into the room; I would be sprawled out on the floor playing dead. Days' worth of food would have collected in the hallway, alerting him that something was wrong. With the spring tucked into my sleeve,

I'd wait for the guy to bend down to pick me up. That's when I'd stab him in the neck, right in the jugular vein.

Where *was* the jugular vein?

Not far from the carotid artery.

Why hadn't I listened more in bio?

After the stab, I'd kick him in the gut and run for the door. I was sure he'd have left it open. How else would he carry me out?

I ran my fingers over the mattress fabric. It felt thick like vinyl. I needed something sharp.

But I needed light more.

I navigated my way toward the bathroom, trampling over clothes and snack bars. At last, my foot met cold ceramic tile. The light burst on, which felt like a little victory. It shone into the main room, illuminating about a quarter of it—just enough to see the mess.

And just enough.

To feel.

A little less powerless.

I searched the bathroom—in the cabinet, inside the shower— but the sharpest tool I could find was the zipper of my sweatshirt: the jagged edge. Not the best pick, but it'd have to do.

I stayed in the bathroom, doing more leg lifts, trying a few pushups, using the tube of toothpaste to paint stripes on the toilet and grow flowers on the tile as I checked and rechecked the light in the main room.

But it remained dark.

Something was wrong.

The possibilities hit me like a freight train:*Whatifthatguydied andnevercamebackandthelightsnevercomeonandIendupstarvingtodeath? Howlongcanonesurvivewithoutwater?Ifthatguyisn'tdeadwillhecomein tomyroomwhileI'msleepingandwatchme/rapeme/tortureme/killme?Will Iuseupallthelightinthebathroomandendupincompletedarkness?*

I scurried back to the cat door and peeked into the hallway, but it was dark out there too.

Don't panic.

Be smart.

Assess the situation.

Figure out your best resources.

The zipper gripped firmly in my hand, I lay down on the bed and began to poke at the side of the mattress. The fabric seemed unbreakable. Only a handful of threads came undone at first. Still, I pulled and prodded each one, trying to get others to fray and loosen—until my fingers burned raw. I pictured tiny red pinpoints forming beneath my skin, and imagined sitting in the dark for days on end trying to somehow stay sane.

I really needed food, even though I didn't feel hungry. Maybe it would help me think straight.

I could smell food cooking somewhere—the scent of garlic and stewed tomatoes, like an Italian restaurant. Why hadn't breakfast come? How long had it been since he'd brought me warm food?

Not since the tantrum.

How long ago was that?

How long had I slept?

Why was I always so tired?

I waited by the cat door, chain-eating from one of the snack boxes—a package of saltine crackers—my mind racing, my insides shaking.

A knock sounded—from the wall, somewhere near the dresser. I didn't move—didn't think too much of it initially. There were lots of noises in the building from time to time: valves squeaking, pipes churning, doors slamming, toilets flushing . . .

I took a sip of water. The knocking sounded again, following a rhythmic pattern: *knock, knock-knock, tap, thud.* I crawled across the floor, feeling for the dresser. Crouched down beside it, I pressed my ear against the wall. The knocks continued—first fast, then slow, then loud and soft. I curled my hand into a fist and rapped lightly.

The knocking stopped. And so did my breath. I repositioned on my knees and placed my mouth up to the wall. "Who's there?" I rapped again.

"Mason." A male voice.

My whole body stiffened—all except for my heart; it hammered inside my chest. I felt its vibration against my bones.

"Did he take you too?" he asked.

I opened my mouth to answer, but no sound came out. Because what if this was a trick?

"There's a bunch of us," he said. "I've been sneaking through the walls, through the air vents."

A rustling came from out in the hallway. I braced myself, waiting for the room to crack open, for the monster to burst in.

"*Hello?*" Mason asked.

I held my breath and counted to five, trying once again to move the dresser farther from the wall, but the chain was too short; there wasn't enough slack. Mason was talking again—something about heating ducts and a couple of months.

"*What?*" I asked, trying to keep my voice low.

"—tell him, will you?"

It took my brain a beat to fill in the blanks of his question. But before I could answer, he told me he had to go.

"—tomorrow," he said.

"Wait. Tomorrow *what?*"

There was a clanking then, from down the hall, like a fallen pipe; it was followed by a high-pitched whistling.

"—up my plan," Mason said. "Okay?"

"Okay," I answered, not even sure what I was agreeing to.

"Wait, what's your name?" he asked.

"Jane," I told him, almost wishing that I hadn't.

"I'll see you tomorrow, Jane."

Would he? See me? I didn't know what to think. But once upon a time, I couldn't wait until tomorrow.

15

At breakfast, Mom slides into the seat across from me at the table. She's already eaten, but now she wants to watch me. "Everything taste okay?" She forces an awkward smile each time my fork hits the plate, then nods as I take a bite, as if I'm a toddler learning to feed myself.

I pick at a pancake. "It tastes great." I'm sure it does, but I haven't noticed any flavor.

She peeks at my pitiful nails. I've peeled them down to the nubs. Knowing how much I used to love changing the polish, she recently bought me ten bottles, along with a manicure kit.

"Do you like any of the nail colors I got for you?" she asks.

"I like them all." But I haven't used them yet, because I'm still waiting until I earn enough star points. There are currently six stars on my scorecard. My goal is ten, and then I'll reward myself with a manicure.

I've been giving myself one star each for the following tasks: having meals with my parents; twenty-plus-minute stints outside my room; talking to Shelley for longer than five minutes;

therapy sessions; public outings; engaging with old friends; and visits to the shelter.

"But your nails are still bare." She frowns.

I've disappointed her yet again.

"Hey, I was thinking maybe we could go to a show this weekend," she says. "Or shopping? What do you think? *Jane?*"

"Yes?"

"Why are you using your fingers? I gave you a fork for a reason."

"Oh. Right."

"I'd also be happy to arrange lunch for you and Shelley. Anyplace you want, my treat. Jack would like to see you too. I talked to his mom. She said he asks about you all the time."

I take another bite, remembering to use my fork, wishing that she would stop, wondering why my stack of pancakes won't seem to go down.

"We should also talk about your session with Dr. White."

"I'm sorry for storming off," I tell her. "For just leaving you there."

"I was worried about you. I drove around looking. You wouldn't answer my calls . . ."

"I didn't have my phone."

"Even so . . ."

I know. "I'm sorry." But words don't make it better.

"It's fine if you don't want to go back to Dr. White, but you need to continue therapy. We can find someone new if you'd like."

"I'd rather write about what happened," I say, retesting the idea on her.

"Writing can be wonderfully therapeutic." She nods. "But how can it truly help when the pages of a notebook can't talk back?"

That's actually the most appealing part.

"*Jane . . .*"

"What?"

"We'll find another therapist."

Chew.

Swallow.

Sip.

Repeat.

"Sound good?" she asks.

"What if there *is* no fixing me?" *What if I'll always be broken?*

"Every heart can heal."

"Even yours?"

Her mouth forms a tiny hole. I wonder if it matches the one inside my chest, where there used to be a heart.

"Don't worry about me," she says. "I'll heal when you heal."

As if there's not enough on my plate already. I stand from the table. "I think I'll finish this upstairs."

She rubs her temples; the conversation has given her a headache. "You spend too much time upstairs. You're free now, but still you choose to lock yourself up. You should be getting out and reconnecting with all of your friends."

I should be.

In my room.

And so that's where I go, locking the door behind me.

NOW

16

I'm not alone for long. I get through barely a chapter of writing when Mom knocks on my door, insisting we go shopping.

"What do you say we freshen up your room?" she asks. "We can give it a new look and change things up."

Before I know it, I'm inside the car.

Dad's driving us to the mall.

Music pumps from the speakers—a female vocalist, but still the instrumentals are too reminiscent, and so I ask him to shut it off.

It's weird going shopping with the two of them, riding in the back seat like a little girl. Eventually, the car stops. And that's when I notice: We've arrived. Dad's parked by the entrance. I peer out the window at the rows of cars.

"Jane?" Mom asks. "Which store would you like to go to first?"

A red-haired girl, maybe five years old, passes by our car. Some older guy is trying to hold her hand, but she keeps pulling away, scurrying out of reach.

I look closer. My nose hits the window glass. The girl sees me. Our eyes lock. I wave to let her know I'm here, watching, able to see which car the guy drives. I could call the police if I needed to.

I grab my phone and click it on, then take photos of the guy, just in case. I peg him to be around thirty years old, with a ruddy complexion and light brown hair. I zoom in on the little girl and take pictures of her as well.

"Jane?" Dad's voice.

The girl's face cringes in response to my attention. She grabs the guy's hand and clenches his forearm like a beloved doll. To her, I'm the threat. For me, that comes as a relief.

I lean back in my seat and let out a breath.

Both Mom and Dad are staring in my direction—Dad, through the rearview mirror; Mom leaning over her seat.

"Is everything okay?" she asks.

That question again. "Everything's fine."

"Which store would you like to start at?" she asks again.

I look toward the mall. "Wood & Crate," I say, reading the first sign I see.

"Perfect!" Mom beams. "We can shop for rugs, curtains, bed linens, wall art . . ."

We all go inside. But as soon as Dad spots a comfortable seat, he plants himself down, takes out his phone, and tells us he has some work emails to answer.

"Does that bother you?" I ask Mom once we get out of earshot.

"Does what bother me?"

"That he's always working? Even on weekends . . ."

She plucks a pillow from a nearby sofa. "What do you think of this?"

"Is that the reason we no longer have Sunday brunch?"

Mom's face wilts. "Would you like to do Sunday brunches

again, sweetheart? We can start tomorrow, anything you want . . . Pancakes? Omelets?"

I give a half nod. I don't want brunch.

She doesn't want reality.

So where does that leave us? Lost? Alone? On an island of pretty pillows?

Mom pats her pillow as though encouraging me to do the same. "What do you think of this fabric?"

"It's nice," I say, stroking the soft faux-fur.

"We could get some drapes to match."

I look around the store, feeling at a loss. But then I see it—in the middle of a kitchen display. My eyes zero in on a square white dining table.

I make a beeline for it, noting the wide, chunky legs. I run my palms over the smooth beveled edges. "This," I say, wanting it in my room. I squat down beneath it. The underside looks different from the table in captivity: painted instead of bare. Plus, the legs on this one are carved rather than straight, but still they're thick enough to wrap myself around.

"A breakfast table?" Mom asks.

"Yes." I nod, feeling guilty for asking, because I haven't exactly earned it.

"What do you plan to do with it?"

"I could put it in the corner, to the right of the windows. It'd be good for school projects and stuff. My desk just isn't big enough."

"You know you can always spread out downstairs, on the dining room table . . ."

I sit down in one of the chairs. "This would just be easier. I wouldn't have to worry about cleaning up after or getting in your way."

"You're never in my way. But, sure, you can have it." She smiles, just "happy" to make me "happy."

Later, in my room, while Dad puts the table together, screwing on all of the legs, Mom lingers in front of my bookcase, where I've emptied two shelves of books and replaced them with jugs of water and boxes of Cocoa Loco brownies.

"These are the brownies that Shelley likes," she says. "In case she visits?"

I shrug instead of answering.

"You know there's always plenty of food and drinks in the kitchen. You and your friends can help yourselves."

"I know, but I just like having some stuff here."

Mom looks at me, head tilted, as though I'm a puzzle she needs to solve.

"It's fine," Dad says, standing from beneath the table.

More than fine. The table is perfect.

"Thank you," I say, almost wanting to give him a hug.

Having the table here, in my room, on Pretty Pillow Island, makes me feel just a little bit more at home.

NOW

17

Sometime later, Shelley calls, offering to bring me a coffee.

"I'm a little busy," I tell her.

"Well, too bad, because I'm not taking no for an answer this time. Would you like your coffee iced or hot?"

"I'm fine—really."

"And I'm dating Prince Harry, much to the duchess's chagrin."

"Excuse me?"

"Iced it is. I'll see you in a bit."

"No, wait." I look around my room, starting with the new breakfast table. I don't feel like trying to explain it to Shelley, nor do I want to make excuses for the jugs of water or the stockpile of brownies. It's all pretty screwed up, I know, including the fact that the contents of my closet have been dumped out onto the floor—a jungle of dresses and shoes and handbags and belts—to make room for me on nights when I want to hide.

"Let's go somewhere," I say, promising to give myself two gold stars as a reward.

"For reals?" Shelley asks.

"Unless you'd prefer to do this another time."

"And I repeat: I'm not taking no for an answer. Shall I pick you up?"

"No. I want to walk. Coffee Et Cetera?"

"Great. I'll see you soon."

I hang up, feeling a pit in my gut. I picture it like a grenade, knowing my meds will do shit to disarm it. Coffee Et Cetera is a ten-minute walk from the house. I keep my hair tucked inside my sweatshirt hoodie and peer over both shoulders every twenty steps along the way.

Mr. Miller, our neighbor, is outside, watering roses. As soon as he spots me, his focus shifts. Water from the spout gushes over an open storage box. I pull my hood farther over my face just as I hear a loud *bang*.

My insides jump.

I swivel around to look, clutching the cell phone in my pocket, convinced the noise was from a car trunk slamming. I check the street, searching for anything that looks off.

"Jane?" A male voice.

Is that country music playing?

"Jane?"

It's Mr. Miller. He's still staring. His lips are moving. The water from his hose pours onto his shoe, but he doesn't seem to notice.

I turn away and bolt down the street, feeling stupid for going out. Seriously, what was I thinking?

Breathe.

Breathe.

By the time I get to Coffee Et Cetera, Shelley is already parked and waiting for me out front. The shop is on the edge of town, in the opposite direction of the high school, so not many people we know frequent the place—at least that's what

I thought. When I open the door, I see Mike Jacoby from the debate team; Sarah Snell, class playwright; the Williams triplets with their matching headbands; and the infamous Vowel Team clan (Anya, Eric, Isaiah, Owen, Uma, and EnYa).

I haven't seen any of them since BIWM.

"Do you want to leave?" Shelley asks.

Before I can answer, Jack comes out of the men's room, and my insides coil up like bedsprings.

"Why don't you get us a table," Shelley says.

I move to the back of the shop, slide into a corner booth, and snag the saltshaker, trying to focus on the tiny crystals inside and not the grenade about to go off. Ten breaths later, I peek up.

Jack is looking this way.

Sarah hooks her arm in his, staking her claim.

"Here we are," Shelley says, setting a mug of something frothy in front of me. There's a card by her wallet. It's been punched with two stars. After ten, she gets her prize, not unlike I do. She looks over her shoulder at the others. "I know. It's awkward. But try not to let any of them bother you. They're just curious."

"About me?"

"Well, um, duh." She smiles. "And you can't really blame them. They were your friends, after all."

"Since when was I friends with the Vowel Team or the Williams triplets?"

"Okay, well, maybe not *them,* but Jack."

Jack.

He and I had plans together on the night I went missing: the Gigi Garvey concert. He knew she was my favorite and surprised me with third-row tickets. Things hadn't exactly been official between us, but they'd definitely been brewing.

"He asked me for your new number, by the way," Shelley says.

"Is he seeing someone?"

"Someone like Sarah? Doesn't she wish. That girl collects boys like shoes. She'd just love him to be her next Jimmy Choo, not that I can blame her. I mean, who couldn't use an extra pair, right?"

"Excuse me?"

"Number status?"

"What do you mean?" She's speaking a whole other language.

"What's the security status on your phone number these days? Classified? Open to the general public? Only available to private lists? In other words, do you want me to give it out?"

Do I?

Plastic plates clatter in the kitchen. I picture myself huddled and waiting by the cat door.

Clamor.

Scrape.

Clank.

"Because people want to see you," Shelley insists. "They're curious."

That word again. It makes me crawl right out of my skin. I take a sip, wishing I were sitting inside a cab, headed over a bridge to someplace far away.

"I guess I'm pretty curious too," she says. "I mean, can we talk about what happened? Because I really think it would help."

"Help who?"

"Well, you, of course. I mean, how else are you supposed to get over stuff, right? Unless you're seeing a therapist, but even still . . ."

"Even still?" My head spins.

"Are you seeing someone?"

"I'm mostly just writing about my experience—as a means of therapy, that is."

"So cool," she says as if we're talking about summer plans. "I mean, I know how much you love to write. But do you want to talk about stuff too? Like . . . what that guy was like . . ."

I grab the saltshaker again, hating myself for agreeing to come.

"Was he as awful as everyone says? Did he make you *do stuff*?" She says that part under her breath, shielded by her hand, but that doesn't lessen the blow.

My eyes press shut. The breeze from an overhead fan sends shivers all over my skin.

I need.

To get.

Out.

Shelley touches my forearm. The gesture makes me flinch. My eyes snap open. My hands are covered in salt crystals.

"It's okay," Shelley continues. "I mean, I get it—why you've been so tight-lipped. It's just kind of hard for me, you know? Because we used to talk about everything."

It's true. We did. And the fact that she wants everything to zap back to the way it was BIWM is just one of the things that keeps us apart.

"I'm trying to be understanding." She sips. "But at the same time, it's, like, I don't know what to say anymore. I mean, do I talk about myself? Do you even want to know? Because you haven't really asked, so instead I end up babbling like an absolute idiot, which is probably as annoying as shit."

Her inky-black bangs form a line across her forehead, cutting it in two.

I didn't notice the bangs before; her hair has always been one length. And when did she get her ears double-pierced? Or start wearing lip gloss?

"Hello?" She waves her hand in front of my face. "Say something, will you? Tell me what you think."

"About what?"

"About what I just said, about these feelies of mine."

Feelies? Of hers?

Jack is looking this way again, flashing me back to the junior prom, when he took me out on the seaside deck and kissed me by surprise—until my lips went deliciously numb. He smelled and tasted like black licorice and confessed to having had a crush on me since the fifth grade.

So what is he doing now, hooking arms with Sarah Playwright? What are the odds that he took her to that Gigi Garvey concert?

"Ignore them," Shelley says.

But their stares are louder than words, impossible to ignore, tugging at the pin in my grenade.

"Whoa, what happened?" She points to the scars on my hand. "That looks pretty major."

"It's fine," I say, covering the scars with my sleeve.

"You're doing it again."

She's right. I am. It doesn't matter that we're sitting face-to-face. I'm icing her out, making her feel alone. The crazy thing: Somewhere deep inside me there are things I want to tell her, like that after I went missing, I still talked to her in my mind, trying to trick myself into believing that she was there with me somehow.

I want to tell her that, but I remain an ice queen instead.

"Just so you know, it's not going to work," she says.

"What isn't?"

"Your plot to sabotage our friendship." She punctuates the sentence with a clank of her spoon. "Feel free to continue ignoring my calls and texts. Don't ask me a single question—not about my day, or about my year. It sucked, by the way. Maybe you heard: My best friend went missing, because she'd gone to pick up a birthday gift for me. Because I'd gotten home from a camping trip a day earlier than planned, because I'd been such a spoiled nagging bitch to my parents, begging them to come home early."

A good friend would tell her that it wasn't her fault. But friendship is a two-way street, and I've been nothing but dead ends.

"I'm not going anywhere," she continues. "You can slam all the doors you want in my face. I'll still love you. You'll still be like a sister to me."

I couldn't hate myself more.

Every. Last. Bit.

Each.

Remaining.

Shard.

Because I don't deserve her friendship. And because it's only a matter of time before she figures that out.

18

Instead of heading straight home after Coffee Et Cetera, I go inside the library, three blocks down, because I know they have a one-person bathroom, and I know where to find the key. I grab it from the basket on the circulation desk, keeping my head low. Then I lock myself in the bathroom, so it's just me, among four white walls, under a stark-white ceiling, standing on a gray-and-white-flecked floor, with no windows to look out. And, better still, no windows to look in.

I breathe here—or at least I try to catch my breath, to will the binds in my chest to release, to slow the palpitating of my heart. But I feel so out of control—like a car skidding across ice. Relief would be a crash.

But I don't crash.

I never crash.

There's just a perpetual sense of dread, a constant bracing for the worst.

I lift the lid off the toilet tank and pluck out the rod inside—

for no good reason other than I know how to do it, and I know where it is.

The rod gripped in my palm, I scrunch down in the corner with my cheek pressed against the tile and imagine Mason's *knock, knock-knock, tap, thud,* wishing he were here, wanting to feel his hands, dying to hear his voice. I grind the end of the toilet rod into my thigh, but I don't break skin. Maybe there's nothing left to tear.

I'm not sure how long I stay, but after too many knocks that aren't Mason's, I return the toilet rod inside the tank and head back home.

Shelley's car is parked out front when I get there. Sitting on the walkway steps, she stands when she spots me.

"Is everything okay?" I ask once I get up close.

"I forgot to show you something." She hikes up her sleeve, revealing the sterling silver bracelet I bought for her birthday. The amethyst crystals glimmer on her wrist. The star charm dangles toward her thumb.

"You got it," I say, feeling my skin flash hot.

Norma must've found it on the counter at the store. Is that where I left it? Did I even have a chance to grab it from behind the register?

"I've never taken it off," she says, pinching the star between her fingers. "From the moment I unwrapped it, this bracelet was the one thing that kept me going."

She obviously expects the idea of that to bring us closer, but instead it tears me apart, because as selfish as it may sound, I never want to see that bracelet again.

I take a step back, trying to get a grip, and that's when I notice. She's holding the gift bag too—the one I'd carefully chosen, with the words *Happy Birthday* printed in big loopy letters. The sparkly purple tissue paper sticks out at the top. The ribbon still has its curl.

I clasp my hand over my mouth, remembering using the blade of a pair of scissors to make the individual tendrils.

"Here," Shelley says, handing me the gift bag; the card I picked is nestled inside it.

"You want me to have the packaging?"

She's shaking her head. Her eyes focus downward. A mascara-stained tear drizzles down her cheek. "I don't know what else to do," she mutters before turning away and heading back to her car.

I close the door behind her and try to breathe at a normal rate. My head feels woozy. I can't stop shaking.

It isn't until hours later, in the safety of my closet, with a box of tissues in my lap, that I'm able to slide the card from the envelope. The pink metallic star sparkles against the glittery black background. I open the card up. My handwriting startles me—the slanted letters, the way I like to capitalize at random. It almost looks as though I wrote the note just yesterday.

I read the words, able to feel each one in the hollow of my heart, and at last the answer becomes clear: why Shelley wants me to have this. She wants me to be reminded of how I felt about her on the day that I was taken.

The day I can never get back.

19

There was still no light, but I kept working at the mattress anyway. It gave me something to focus on: a goal, a project, a distraction from going crazy. The nubs of my fingers stung, where the skin had opened up. But at least I was able to count twenty-seven loose mattress threads now. I fluffed them out, imagining they were white, puffy, and soiled with the blood from my cuts, like Santa's mustache after a nosebleed.

I also started a mental list, trying to figure out who the monster was. Who could've been watching so closely, studying my habits, including what I wore? Someone from school? But it wasn't that big, and I knew mostly everyone. The cute runner boy from the trails at the park? But his hair was short and black, rather than sandy brown and wavy.

Maybe a customer from the animal shelter? There *had* been this one guy, a year or two before, who'd requested to work solely with me—even waited a full hour while I helped other people. I'd assumed he'd gotten a recommendation from one of my former customers, but unfortunately I never asked. Instead

I walked him around, pointing out cats and dogs and answering his every question about breed, care, and training.

He'd been around my age, hadn't he?

With curly brown hair . . .

Did he have blue or brown eyes?

There had also been that awkward guy at Shelley's house, at the end-of-the-school-year barbecue, one of her brother's friends who'd given me a weird vibe. He kept staring the whole night like he knew me from someplace. When I asked him where he went to school, he said he was an exchange student from Wales (which Shelley later told me was a lie). Apparently, the guy was a new friend of her brother's from some prep school in the city. I remembered his baseball cap had a lion logo. Shelley hadn't known him well, and I never probed further.

But why would he have taken me?

Why would *anyone* have?

What did I do? Why was I here?

A blister burst on my thumb; a sudden gush dripped. I ran my fingers over the floor to feel where the droplets landed, then used the droplets to paint a smiley face on the cement, wondering if the blister was filled with blood—if the face was red. I popped my thumb into my mouth to check if I could tell. Definitely blood—a salty, metallic taste.

I needed more paint. I squeezed the wound, just as Mason's *knock, knock-knock, tap, thud* sounded at the wall.

"Are you there?" he called.

I crawled across the floor and knocked to let him know that I was.

"You didn't tell him about me, did you?"

I pressed my ear against the wall.

"I have a plan," he said. "I'm going to get us out."

"*Now?*" My heart clenched.

"Don't I wish. I'm still working on the route, trying to

find an exit. I figure there's got to be at least five of them in a place this big. I'm bound to bump into one of them sooner or later—*bump* being the operative word. It's dark in the ducts, not to mention in this room, and all I have is a reading light, smaller than the size of my thumb. I asked for it with my points, so I could read in the dark, but it doesn't exactly project beyond the distance of a page."

"How did you even get out? Were you in a room?" Had it run out of light?

"I found a heating vent behind the bathroom cabinet in my room. You should search your room too—behind the furniture, underneath the bed . . . I sneak out at various times of the day, when he isn't doing rounds."

"How long have you been here?"

"A few months maybe. The air ducts go all through this place. I took a different path yesterday. That's how I found you."

"How many of us are there?"

"Besides us? Three or four maybe. It's too hard to tell. This place is huge. There's at least one other guy. But I've only spoken to you and one of the girls—Samantha."

"How old is she? Where is she from?"

"I'm not really sure. My age maybe . . . around eighteen? She was a couple of rooms away, so we couldn't really talk much."

I pictured the whole lot of us, scattered about the building in rooms just like this one, waiting for something to happen.

But what?

And when?

"Has he ever . . . ?" I began just as a weird sucking sound sputtered from my throat. My chest tightened, cinching my lungs. I folded at the waist and pressed my forehead to the ground.

"*Jane?*"

"Has he ever . . . ?" I tried again.

"Wait, he *who?* Ever *what?*"

"The guy who took us . . . Has he ever come into your room?"

"Negative. *Wait,* why do you ask? Has he ever come into yours? Did something happen?"

"No—at least not that I know of."

"*Shit.* You scared me for a second."

"Do you know what he wants with us?"

"That's the million-dollar question, but I'm not sticking around for an answer. Are you in?"

"*In?*"

"To escape?"

"How do I know I can trust you?"

"You don't, I guess. But what have you got to lose? Your penthouse suite? The five-star room service?"

"No room service. He stopped bringing me food, and he shut off the lights."

"Shit, *seriously?*"

"Seriously," I mumbled, holding in a sob.

I suspected that he sensed it, because he began to chatter on, so maybe I wouldn't have to talk.

"The guy likes it when you play by the rules: Set trays and plates in the hallway, empty trash once a week . . . He checks what you throw out, by the way. Like, he'll notice if you're not asking for shit, not using up all of your supplies, I mean. So use the stuff, fill out his stupid checklists, and indulge his grand plan, whatever that may be, just to buy yourself some time. And since I double as a mind reader, I bet you're wondering if I know who he is. The answer is no. I met him at a party. He seemed normal enough. We were just shootin' the shit, talking about muscle versus classic cars. He asked if I wanted to check out his ride—supposedly a '68 Camaro. I followed him outside, but there was no Camaro in sight. The next thing I knew, I was waking up in the trunk of his car."

"So he drugged you."

"An understatement, I would assume. The thing is, I don't remember him coming at me or any hint of a struggle."

"If you were at a party, others must've seen him too."

"Maybe. I mean, I guess. But I'm not really sure he knew anyone there. He seemed kind of lost, just hangin' out in the basement. The only reason I went down there to begin with was because Haley—the girl throwing the party—asked me to grab some food from the cellar. The guy said he'd made a wrong turn, looking for the bathroom, and then confessed to hating crowds. That's when we got to talking."

"Well, if he was at the party, then he must've known Haley."

"Maybe."

Maybe not. Nothing was clear.

"Now, come on, what did you do?" he asked. "To cut off your food supply and cause blackout conditions."

"You really want to know?"

"Well, that's kind of why I'm asking."

And so I told him, this stranger, this person I didn't know I could trust, so much more than he'd asked to hear—about my tantrum and about how much I missed Shelley; about the phone call I'd made to my parents from the trunk of the monster's car and how I could still hear my mother's sobbing inside my mind's ear.

"My mother is the bravest, strongest, most together woman I know," I said, "and hearing her cry like that . . ." I took a deep breath, unable to hide my tears. "I'm really sorry."

"Don't worry about it. I've been there too."

"When you first arrived?"

"When I first arrived, the day after that, and most nights thereafter. It wasn't until I found the air vent that I stopped feeling sorry for myself."

"And when did you find that vent?"

"About a week ago. But rest assured, if I got this far, I'm

going to get us out for good. So during those long stretches of time when it feels like you're going to snap, think of me in a maze of ductwork, mapping out our route."

The fact that he was including me in his plan was too much to swallow down my splintered, severed throat, and I choked up on the thought.

"I gotta go," he said. "I don't want to get caught out of my room on one of his rounds. Should I come by tomorrow?"

"Please, don't go yet."

"Okay, but just, like, five more minutes. What do you want to talk about?"

"Whatever you like." I snuggled against the wall, sucking my blood-blistered thumb, and listened while he told me about the farm where he and his dad lived, raising chickens and bees and selling eggs and honey.

I'm not sure how long he talked, because at some point I fell asleep to the soothing tone of his voice. It blanketed me like velvet and protected me from the dark.

20

As soon as I woke up, I maneuvered my way to the bathroom, having kicked a clear pathway. The sudden pop of light stung my eyes, and my lids slammed shut. I stumbled to the cabinet and peeked just behind it. No air vents.

I checked around the toilet and the sink as well. It seemed the only source of ventilation came from a baseboard unit that ran along the far wall of the main room.

Still, I continued to search, crawling beneath the bed, feeling along the walls, reminding myself that a lack of sight doesn't stop the blind. I needed to be brave. I couldn't fall apart.

I also needed my box of brownies. Where was it? I pawed through the bedcovers, knowing it had to be there, anticipating the feel of the sharp-angled corners and the long, slender box.

But it wasn't there.

Not under my pillow either.

Or behind the headboard.

In the dark, tarry recesses of my mind, losing the box of brownies felt a little like losing a friend.

I continued to search, rummaging through the clothing on the floor, untangling a webbing of sheets, and sorting through a pile of cracker and cookie boxes. I also ran my fingers inside every square inch of the dresser and cabinet.

No dice.

In a final attempt, I reached to find the handle of the fridge, and as if by magic, the obvious struck: Fridges have lights. Why hadn't I thought of this sooner?

I pulled the door open. The seal broke. A chill hit my face. But it remained absolutely dark. A working refrigerator with no light bulb.

A high-pitched growling noise erupted in the room. It took me a beat to realize it'd come from me—my frustration, my lack of control. *Just breathe,* I told myself. *The brownies are here someplace.*

In this room.

Where else can I check?

But what if they weren't? Was it possible the monster came into the room while I'd been sleeping and snagged the box away?

A knock sounded, making my insides jump. Mason was here. I scurried to the wall like a mouse for cheese.

"I brought you a piece of cake," he said.

"*Excuse me?*" My head fuzzed.

"Cake," he repeated. "With a candle for light. You do like cake, don't you?"

"Yes." I still didn't get it.

"What kind is your favorite?"

"The kind with a knife baked into the center."

"And your second favorite?"

"Vanilla with blue frosting."

"What a coincidence. That's just what I brought for you." There was a smile in his voice. "Here you go. Got it?"

"Okay." Not okay. Was he going crazy too?

"Just don't blow out the candle," he said. "Keep it lit by your bed."

"You're joking though, right? You don't *really* have cake."

"No, but if I did, I'd share it. I'd find a way to serve it somehow—even magically—through the wall."

"Well, thanks," I said, craving a thickly frosted piece.

Mason came to the wall for the next eight days. I knew it was eight days, because each time he was about to leave, he'd ask, "Should I come back tomorrow?"

As if it were even a question. I'd begun to live for his visits.

"I'd love to be able to picture who it is I'm talking to," he said on one of them.

I wanted to picture him too. But in my mind, his image had already formed. I imagined he was strong and wiry—to be able to sneak between walls—with longish hair, since he likely didn't have anything to trim it, and dark eyes.

"*Well?*" he asked.

I ran my hand over the hollow of my stomach, then slid my fingers along pelvic bones that jutted out a good four inches. I'd lost at least fifteen pounds since my arrival. The insides of my knees were purple, yellow, and black—at varying stages of bruising— from bones pressing on bones in the middle of the night.

"You first," I told him.

"I'm just over six feet," he said, "which makes slithering through heating ducts all the more interesting. I have brown hair and eyes, and a crooked nose from the time I got puck-chucked playing hockey. I normally wear contacts and wish I had them now—or at least glasses—but I had to throw them out because they got too old and dry. Your turn."

I tried to picture his crooked nose, remembering a boy in school who'd broken his twice while playing Wham-O. "I have dark hair," I said.

"Long or short?"

"Just past my shoulders." I felt it to be sure. "People say I have a porcelain complexion, but that's just code for ghostly pale. My eyes are green, and I'm short, like my mom—barely five feet two—with too many freckles, thanks to my dad."

"Freckles on your face?"

"Freckles pretty much *everywhere*," I said, wishing I could suck the words right back. Where was he picturing them? Why had I just told him that?

"Well, I happen to like freckles."

I suddenly felt each one on my face; they burned like embers, making my skin flash hot.

"So what do you like to do when you're not being held hostage by a lunatic?" he asked.

"I write a lot—poetry, mostly. I also run. And I love animals."

"You would've loved my dad's farm. The best was when he was trying to raise lambs. The babies were really cute . . . the way they'd hop around. Have you ever seen a baby lamb hop?"

I shook my head, even though he couldn't see it, almost forgetting where I was.

"I'm also big into hiking," he continued.

"In the mountains?"

"Anywhere, really—even if it takes me days or weeks. Life is short, and I want to see as many awe-inspiring sights as I can, you know?"

"Yeah," I said, even though I didn't know at all. I could only imagine what it was like to take off on a whim, on a quest for visual greatness. "Are you in school?"

"Does Life School count?"

"Sure," I muttered, my head spinning with questions. Where did he live now? Was it still with his dad? What did he do to make money?

"Are *you* in school?" he asked.

"Well, it's technically summer break."

"And Jamaica was all booked up, I take it."

I let out a laugh—my first one since being there—and I felt it in my chest, the strain of unused laugh muscles.

He left shortly after, much earlier than I'd wanted. The following day, in between working on the mattress and searching for the brownie box, I waited for him to come, pacing the floor of the room, scurrying to the wall whenever I heard the slightest clatter or rap.

I also sat on the floor, beneath the table, and wrapped myself around one of the legs. With my cheek pressed against the smooth, polished wood, I closed my eyes and pretended the leg was a person, that the wood was a cheek, and that I was embracing someone I missed—first Mom, then Dad, then Shelley, Jack. And Mason.

Additionally, in the bathroom, to help gauge the time, I plucked tissues from a Kleenex box and set sixty to the side (one for each second in a minute). I counted them over and over, finally stopping at 127 batch-counts—for two hours and seven minutes since the previous door-clank. To what that actually amounted, I had no idea, but somehow it felt like progress.

Finally, Mason's familiar knock came, and I scooted down by the dresser.

"Are you sleeping?" he asked.

"I couldn't sleep." Who knew if it was even nighttime? I still didn't have hot meal delivery. I was living off snacks, trying to cling onto pounds.

"Feel like playing a game?" he asked.

"Sure." I nestled close.

"I'm thinking of a word. You can only ask me yes-or-no questions."

"Is it a person?"

"No."

"Okay, so it's a thing? Does it have legs?"

"No again."

"Is it known for having a distinct color?"

"Yes. Well, sort of."

The word was *daisy,* and meanwhile my word was *enamored.*

I was.

Undeniably.

Enamored with his friendship, hungry for his attention.

We continued with our game, taking turns with words and guesses until it was time for him to go.

"I'll come back tomorrow," he said. "Should I bring you a brownie sundae?"

"Wait." I racked my brain, trying to think up some way to make him stay. "Where's your room?"

"At the other end of the hall, through a tunnel."

"How many doors down?"

"Why? Are you planning to pay me a visit? Shall I leave my door unlocked? You never *did* tell me if you found a vent in your room. You're not holding out on me, are you?"

I pressed my fingertips against the wall. "If only there *were* a vent in my room—or at least one I could crawl through."

"I'm not really sure how many rooms separate mine from yours since I haven't been out in the hallway. But if I were to guess . . . ten rooms, maybe twelve. Then you have to go through the tunnel. My room is on the other side."

"Wow, this place must be enormous."

"An understatement, as I'm learning, but I'm making progress. I found a pathway to the room behind Samantha's. She and I were finally able to talk."

"And so did you?" I swallowed hard.

"Just for a minute—just to confirm that she's in too."

"*In?*"

"To escape," he said as though the answer should've been obvious.

And it probably should've been, but I just couldn't help it—this wave of insecurity; it washed over me like boiling water. Would finding a pathway to Samantha mean fewer visits to "see" me?

"*Jane?*"

"Yes?"

"Did you not hear me? I said Samantha says hi."

"You told her about me?"

"Of course. Was that not okay?"

"I'm just tired," I said, which was the truth, after all—tired and hungry. Plus, I'd started my period, which is a terrible excuse, but it made me more exhausted than I ever thought possible.

"Do you want a bedtime story?"

What I wanted was not to care. But I totally *did*. And so I curled up by the wall, in a nest of strewn clothes, and listened while he told me about Huey, Dewey, and Louie, three wild turkeys that had lived on his farm, plus Libby the horse and a rabbit named Mr. Pinkney. In truth, it didn't matter what he talked about. It was his companionship that meant most—like an intoxicating drug shot up inside my veins, warming all of my cold places, lightening up my darkest thoughts.

"Do you want to hear about the time I found Conway the hen sleeping in bed with my dad?" he asked.

His voice was creamy like custard. I wanted to crawl up inside it and never let go, and so I told him yes and snuggled in closer.

21

I started my day by cleaning up the room, feeling around for snack debris and empty drink containers and depositing them into a trash bag. I also folded clothes and filed them inside drawers, and I loaded the pantry cabinet with unopened food packages, trying to guess the contents of each one by giving it a shake. *Was that the pitter-patter of salt? The shuffling of granola? The cracking of pretzel rods?*

In the fridge, I placed a half dozen water bottles to the right. The Gatorade bottles were wider, the plastic thicker. I placed those to the left and made a mental note. Additionally, I drained the shampoo from two bottles into a half-gallon jug and threw those bottles away, making it look as though I'd been washing my hair. I did the same with a few bars of soap—threw their wrappers away.

Mason was right. I needed to play by the rules, and that included calculating the contents of my trash.

It took a bit of maneuvering to push the bag through the cat door, but I managed. I was also able to pick out a strategic armload of clothing—underwear, sweats, and tees—along with the bed linens. I set those in the hallway too.

The last key ingredients were the scorecard and an order form to request more supplies (shampoo, soap, granola bars, cashews, potato chips, tissues, and water). But before I placed those in the hallway, I scavenged a cereal box and pulled out the wax-paper bag inside. In the bathroom, I tore the box open and used the back side to scribble a note to my captor:

> *Dear Person Who Took Me:*
>
> *Please, let me go. I won't tell anyone about you—not that there's much for me to tell. I don't know where I am. I don't even remember what you look like. You can drug me again, take me someplace far from here, and leave me there. I'll find my own way back. Please, I'm begging you to consider this. I miss my friends and family, and I want to go home.*
>
> *Sincerely,*
>
> *Jane*

When I woke up later, it took my brain a beat to process what my eyes had already taken in: the bright white walls, the snack cabinet, the table, the dresser and mini-fridge.

I could see.

The light was on.

I jumped from the bed and peeked out into the hallway. Everything I'd left was gone. In its place, I found a container of baked ziti, a pile of fresh bed linens, a bar of soap, two shampoo bottles, a box of tissues, and a six-pack of water. I also earned two stars—for the laundry and the trash.

I slid the ziti toward me and got to work, using my fingers, cramming the noodles into my mouth, three and four at a time.

The thick tomato sauce dripped down my chin and brought tears to my eyes—so unbelievably good, like nothing I'd ever tasted.

As I ate, I peered around the room, still searching for the box of brownies. I'd done a good job of cleaning up. The floor was mostly bare. There was nothing on the surfaces of the table, dresser, and mini-fridge.

Finally, I was able to see the fruits of my laborious project, where the mattress was frayed and splotched with blood: muted red and brown patches. At first, I didn't believe that all the blood had come from me, but the nubs of my fingers told another story. I should've asked for bandages too.

My stomach still growling, I brought a cup of green beans to my lips and poured them into my mouth, practically drinking them down like juice. I chased the beans with lemonade, then scooted closer to the bed, peeking beneath it.

What was that?

Sticking out from behind the bedpost . . .

I could barely make out the corner of a white box. I edged closer, able to see a bit of the block lettering—an *e* and an *s*—and the mitten-like hand of the smiling chocolate square.

I climbed onto the bed, my insides charged like power lines, and reached down into the space between the bed frame and the wall. I grabbed the corner of the box and pulled upward. At last, I'd found them: the Cocoa Loco brownies. I hugged the box to my chest and collapsed back onto the bed.

All of the above victories cheered me up more than they should have, distracted me from the fact that I hadn't seen Mason in what felt like days.

I curled up with the box, imagining Shelley's face, almost able to hear her voice: *Need I remind you that you're trapped like an animal? Who cares about stars for good behavior or some guy who talks to you through a wall? Why aren't you trying to find a way out?*

She was right. But what if something bad had happened to Mason? What if he'd been hurt or sick, or gotten caught outside his room?

Or worse still: What if he's spending his free time with Samantha? the Shelley voice mocked. *What if they escaped together and left you behind?*

I needed to get a grip. In the bathroom, I splashed my face with water. My skin looked sallow. Tiny red pimples sprouted from my cheeks and chin. I touched the crown of my head. My hair was an oily nest. But even more startling: My pupils looked larger than normal. A side effect of no light? Of not eating properly? Of refusing to bathe or change?

The scent of shampoo and soap bars lingered in the air—like marigolds mixed in lemon balm. I moved toward the shower, wondering what it'd feel like to stand beneath the running faucet.

I hadn't bathed since the night before I was taken, after a party; it'd been well past midnight, and I'd only spent a few precious minutes standing beneath the steady stream.

How long ago was that?

The last tally mark I'd made had denoted my thirty-ninth day. And then there was the time I'd spent in the dark . . . It'd felt like weeks, but was probably only days. How long had it been? Two months since my last shower?

I turned the faucet on and imagined warm water pelting against my back. Steam wafted up to the ceiling. I breathed it in. My eyes watered from the heat.

I gazed around the room, searching for a camera. Part of me assumed there wasn't one (since no one had stopped my mattress project). But another part knew I couldn't trust assumptions, nor could I shake the sensation of being watched.

I started with my sweatshirt, unzipping the front, tugging my arms free, and letting it drop to the floor. My skin prickled as it hit the air. I'd developed some sort of rash. Tan and brown patches stretched like rags across my forearms. I reached beneath my T-shirt, unfastened my bra, then pulled the straps out, through the sleeves, one by one.

The bra fell to my feet, but the T-shirt remained in place. I touched beneath my breasts, where the seams had made track marks, and winced from the sensation—like fire ants beneath my skin, tunneling through the nerves. I should've removed the bra a whole lot sooner and taken my socks off too. But these were my last connections to home—the last things I'd put on. Taking them off (and bathing here) felt like acceptance somehow.

I rolled my sweatpants down around my ankles, kicked them to the corner, and stepped into the shower. The water pulsated against my chest, making the track marks sting, despite the T-shirt. Still I let the water run all over my body—in my underwear, beneath my shirt, down my back, and inside my mouth—nearly drunk on its ability to make me feel somewhat human.

The bar of soap clenched in my hand, I scrubbed my arms and legs, also using my fingernails, eager for the scratch. My calves were covered in hair—two-inch-long curlicues. I hadn't shaved since BIWM.

I stroked beneath my arms. It was hairy there too—long, nappy strands like a hamster's mane, like nothing I'd ever imagine. This couldn't possibly be my body.

But it was.

And so I scoured.

Desperate to reveal my old self.

The soap burned all of my broken places where the skin had opened up: my fingers, my palms, my calves, my forearms, and behind my ears. But it was a satisfying pain, one I didn't mind a bit.

When there was nothing left to clean, I sat on the shower floor, blanketed by the stream, soothed by the sound. Being in the shower felt a little like sleep—like a temporary break from reality. And so, I never wanted to leave.

22

Mason finally came to visit me again—six hot meals, a jar of cashews, and a bag of ripple chips later. As soon as I heard his familiar knock, I darted like lightning across the room, dropping the box of brownies, crouching beside the dresser, and placing my ear against the wall.

"I'm here," I told him.

"Sorry it's been so long, but I've been sick," he said. "A stomach thing."

My eyes clamped shut. The tension in my chest released. As selfish as it was, it was relieving to know that illness had kept him away, rather than Samantha.

"Are you okay now?" I asked.

"Better, but I haven't been eating. I've been taking the meals, though, making it look like everything's normal by cleaning my plate."

"Why would you do that?"

"So I could I earn my last star."

"Forget stars. You need to stay healthy."

"My head still aches a little, but the chills are gone. And I was able to get you something."

"A sweet roll?" I asked, playing along.

"No. For *real* this time—with the stars, I mean."

Wait. "*What?*"

"I have a surprise for you. I wasn't sure what kind of poetry you like, but I remember you said you liked poems, right?"

"Yes." I still didn't get it.

"So I got you a book of poems . . . with my earned stars. I thought I could read it to you, through the wall."

My mind couldn't quite grasp it: that he'd gotten me a book of poems—that he'd waste his stars on me. I mean, he could've asked for anything: ginger ale for his stomach, a mystery novel, a deck of cards, a Rubik's Cube . . . "Mason, you didn't have to do that."

"I know I didn't *have* to. I *wanted* to."

I rested my forehead against the wall, wishing there were something I could give him back.

"I mean, I know it's not ideal," he continued. "Plus, like I said, I'm not even sure if these poems are your taste, but I thought I could read them to you. Look, if you don't thin—"

"I'd really like that," I said.

His kindness was almost too much to take in. But I ate it up like sweet rolls, hugging the leg of the table, soothed by the artful verses of poets I'd never known.

23

Using my zipper as a knife, and the box of brownies as my inspiration, I managed to make a hole in the mattress fabric. With the cuffs of my sweatshirt pulled down over my fingers to protect the open wounds, I wiggled my thumbs into the hole and pulled in both directions. The mattress split open in one satisfying tear—ten gaping inches.

I peeked inside to check out the construction. It was different from how I'd thought it would be: A network of springs, assembled as part of a metal grid, sat between two layers of foam. The foam pads appeared to be solid pieces. I sat back on my heels, unsure if I should rip the pads apart to get at the coils. Or would it be better to tear the mattress fabric around both sides to have more access to the springs? Both options were worth a try, but first I needed a break. My forearms quivered. My head wouldn't stop aching.

I took a swig of water. My stomach gurgled with hunger. The scent of popcorn kernels heating filled the air. Food would soon be coming. I grabbed my reward form in anticipation, having earned my twenty stars; it was time to order my prize.

Are you kidding? said the Shelley voice inside my head. *If you really cared about getting out of this cell-hole, you'd keep on working.*

I ignored the voice and scribbled the words *notebook* and *pen set* across the line.

Why not ask for something to help you escape? the voice continued. *Like hairpins, knitting needles, or a metal fork. I mean, seriously? A notebook? Do you plan on paper-cutting him to death? Even Mason was smart enough to ask for a reading light which doubles as his flashlight.*

I looked at the box of Cocoa Loco brownies sitting propped on my pillow. If I didn't start writing again, I was seriously going to lose it. "Writing is how I'm able to make some sense of this screwed-up world," I argued. "It's how I used to end every day."

Better to end your day on the outside, rather than in this cell-hole with a bunch of moody poems. Why is that not obvious?

I flipped my pillow over the Cocoa Loco box so I wouldn't have to "listen" anymore. If that weren't crazy enough, not five seconds later, I removed aforementioned pillow so that "Shelley" wouldn't be mad.

I know.

And I *knew*.

The voice of Shelley—my inner devil's advocate—was right. I had to keep focused. But still I pushed the scorecard through the cat door (out of arm's reach so I couldn't make any edits), and felt guilty shortly afterward.

I needed to see Mason. He would make it better, tell me that I did nothing wrong, remind me of the frivolous book of poetry he got with *his* stars points. Except the book hadn't seemed frivolous at all. It'd been the first thing since being taken that had made me feel somewhat normal.

That should've been the red flag right there. I'd been locked up in a cell, taken against my will, and treated like an animal.

Nothing was supposed to feel normal.

NOW

24

It's funny the way memory works, especially long-term memory, when the thing being remembered hits us, making the brain pop like electricity. We think it's so random—that timing of sorts. But there's nothing random about it. Our brains are smarter than we are, equipped to recall things at key times, when we're able to make the most sense of the information.

I remember something. The memory strikes me like lightning, waking me out of a sound sleep. I sit up in bed, still able to picture it—that afternoon, a few years back. Someone bumped into me downtown. It was snowing out, and the sidewalks were blanketed by at least six inches.

I fell to the ground. Snow found its way up my back, filling the inside of my sweater. The bruise I'd find on my outer thigh later looked like dead roses beneath my skin.

I didn't think much of it at the time—falling, that is. I was laughing. The guy I'd bumped was laughing.

He gave me a hand getting up. White ski gloves—the men's

version of the kind I'd been coveting at the sporting goods store in Maybelle Square.

"Are you all right?" he asked.

I dusted the snow from the back of my jeans.

"Sorry. That was definitely my fault," he continued.

"It's fine. I mean, I'm fine."

"Are you sure? Is there anything I can do?" he asked.

He nodded toward Chico's Bakery. But I didn't quite get it. Was he asking if I wanted to go there? To check out my wounds? To join him for coffee? He looked at the bakery again and then at me. An unspoken question loomed above his head like a thought bubble without words.

"Excuse me?" I asked.

He glanced at the bakery for a third time. The neon-pink sign in the front window announced hot sticky buns but provided zero clarification. "I just thought that maybe . . ." His words stopped, replaced by an awkward grin.

Meanwhile, any residual grin on my face melted like snow in fiery heat. I took a step back. Chills ripped up my skin.

But still he asked, "I just thought maybe . . . Do you want something to drink? Or are you hungry for a bite?"

He was wearing a knitted hat, an oversized parka, and a pair of blue-mirrored sunglasses. But he was tall.

Like *he* was.

And had facial scruff.

As *he* had.

And so I don't know, will never know, if he'd been watching me since then.

NOW

25

My mother calls me to come downstairs, saying she has a big surprise. I can hear the smile in her voice, and I crawl out of bed, promising to reward myself with a star for good behavior.

The surprise is sitting on the living room sofa.

Jack stands when he sees me, flashing me back to the night of the junior prom, when he sat in the very same spot, waiting for my grand descent down our mahogany staircase.

A subtle smile crosses his lips. "I hope it's okay that I stopped by."

"Of course it's okay," Mom answers for me.

He's holding a bouquet of wildflowers. Mom goes to search for a vase, leaving us alone, pretending to be busy.

Jack looks different from how I remember, up close, mere inches away. Sure, nearly a year has passed, but still, his face looks thinner. His hair is longer on top. Has he grown a couple of inches? Were his eyes always bottle green? He looks so put together in his dark-washed jeans and gray cotton sweatshirt. Meanwhile, I feel broken apart, desperate to disappear.

I sit on the edge of the sofa and run my fingers over my bed-head hair.

"So I saw you," he begins, sitting down beside me. His hand rests on the seat cushion, just a few inches from mine. "In the coffee shop the other day, and I didn't get a chance to say hello."

"Hello," I answer.

"I knew you were back, but I figured that since you were out and about, maybe you'd be open to visitors. I would've called or texted, but your number is different now. Anyway, if I'm over-stepping it by coming here, just say the word."

Instead, I draw my hand away.

"I'm really glad you're home safe," he says. "Everybody is. I guess that's pretty obvious."

Nothing's obvious to me—not anymore. "It's still nice to hear."

He angles in my direction. An invisible agenda pops above his head. "I was trying to imagine what it must be like for you . . . coming home after having been away for so long, I mean. All the changes . . ."

"It's weird," I admit.

"But change can be good," he perks. "For instance, there's a new taco place in town—Casa Buela or Buena . . . something like that. I thought of you when they were moving in and reno-vating the space."

"I love Mexican food."

"Exactly, which is why I told myself I wouldn't try the place until you got home and we could try it together."

"That's really sweet of you." I half smile. "Really sweet that you would even think of me."

"Are you kidding? I think about you all the time."

"Well, thanks," I say for lack of better words.

"When you went missing, it was, like, I don't know . . . like maybe a part of me went missing too. I mean, I know that may sound weird or cheesy or whatever, but we'd been pretty close, don't you think?"

"We had been," I agreed, though I was never quite sure just where our flirtationship stood.

"We've been a part of each other's lives since the fourth grade," he says. "Every morning before school, you were there, at my locker, with your crunchy granola bars and your daily dose of cheer. Every track meet, every cram session, every major disappointment and cause for celebration . . . you were with me, offering encouragement, advice, a shoulder, your notes . . . Whatever I needed, day or night. And then, just like that—"

"I wasn't." I nod.

"I hated that . . . every day, not knowing where you were."

A thin layer of pink creeps over his face, making blotches on his neck; they remind me of bleeding heart flowers.

"I guess I was pretty freaked out that I'd never gotten to tell you some stuff," he continues.

"Stuff like what?"

He gazes up from the floor. His eyes look bleeding too. "I mean, I know this may sound weird. Most guys don't make a habit out of talking about their feelings . . . But I care about you. I always have. And I regret not telling you that before, not making it clearer. Maybe if I had . . ."

"What?"

"I don't know." He shrugs. "Maybe you'd have been with me that morning, instead of running off to the shop. There was the Gigi Garvey concert that night. Maybe we'd have gone into the city early and made a full day of it. That's what I'd wanted, but I'd been too chickenshit to ask."

"And maybe we wouldn't have."

"I guess we'll never know, but it's something I asked myself each day that you were gone."

After I got home, it didn't surprise me to learn that my

parents harbored regrets. Mom wishes she'd brought me to Norma's herself. Dad hates that he slept in that morning.

Shelley blames herself for having made her parents cut their camping trip short.

Norma curses her decision to give me my own set of shop keys.

We've all carried our regret around like anchors, struggling not to drown. But never did I imagine that Jack carried it too. Just how many more casualties lay in the wake of my mistakes?

"I guess I just needed you to know that," he says.

I want to tell him that I knew he cared, and that I did as well, but I can't get the words to fit through the pinhole that's become my mouth. "I really wanted to go with you to that concert," I say instead: my version of middle ground.

Jack smiles—the grin I remember, that curls to one side, forming a dimple in his cheek.

He looks away, clenching the edge of the sofa. I pull my sweatshirt cuff over my scars and place my hand down beside his, about eight inches away. He probably doesn't notice. To me, the gesture is huge.

"Did you go to the concert anyway?" I ask, not sure I want the answer.

Jack meets my eyes again and shakes his head. "Once word spread that you'd gone missing, it was as if the whole world stopped. A search team got assembled. There were hundreds of people looking."

My parents said the same, but it was nice to hear again. And it was nice to sit in this space with Jack—a space without questions or expectations, beyond the four gray walls of my room.

NOW

26

After Jack leaves, Mom pops out of the kitchen before I have the chance to go back up to my room. Her face is beaming: wide, expectant eyes; round, rosy cheeks; and a smile I haven't seen on her since BIWM.

She clasps her hands together as if to pray. "So . . . How did it go?"

"Okay, I guess."

Clearly, that isn't the winning answer, because the smile fades. Her cheeks lose their puff. The glow on her face dulls. And her prayerful hands drop.

"Jack's *a really nice guy,*" she says, slowly, carefully, as if I don't quite get it. "He means well and cares about you."

"I know. He does." And so what am I supposed to do? Ignore what I'm feeling? Change myself for him?

For her?

For everyone?

But me.

"He was instrumental during your search," she continues. "So generous with his time. He made flyers, hung signs, volunteered day and night. He searched the parks, the bike paths, the alleyways, the woods behind your school . . . He turned this city upside down."

"I know." My voice cracks. "I mean, I'm grateful."

"He was instrumental," she repeats.

I bite my tongue because *instrumental* implies that it was because of his efforts that I was found. But no one found me. And I'm still searching for my missing self.

"Jack's really sweet." I nod.

"So then why don't you look more appreciative?"

"I *am* appreciative. I'm glad he stopped by."

"Really?" She combs her fingers through her hair: six inches of gray locks, from root to ear; the rest is auburn. She hasn't been to a salon since BIWM.

"I'm sorry," I utter, unsure what else to say or do.

"This is about Mason, isn't it? Why you're stuck in neutral? Why you push everyone away?"

I bolt up the stairs, back to my room. Mom follows. She stands in the doorway. Her eyes zero in on my bookcase—on my jugs of water and my stash of Cocoa Loco brownie boxes. "You could have the real Shelley at your side at a moment's notice, but instead you're stockpiling some artificial version of her. It isn't healthy. What's going on inside your head?"

I take a step back, bumping into my table.

"I love you." She sighs. "But at some point, you really need to . . ."

I love you, but . . . That's all I need to hear—all it really takes to make a fresh tear in my heart, where I thought there were only shreds.

"What happened to you was horrible and hideous and tragic

and unfair," she says. "But you're back now. You're home, thank God. And you have to go on living."

As if I don't already feel dead.

"You were gone for seven months," she says. "Don't let that vile creature take one more day."

The words *vile creature* grate like sandpaper against my skin. Because she wasn't there. So how could she even say?

"I love you," she says again, this time not altering the words with a *but*. Instead, a pregnant pause follows as does a shake of her head.

But I just can't do it: say the words *I love you* back. I haven't said those words in the months since my return. Mom's eyes fill. Her face wilts like paper in flames, and the drizzling of her tears doesn't seem to put out the pain.

"I'm sorry," I tell her again, wishing I could cry too. At least tears would show that I still have feelings, that I'm worthy of time and patience.

She leaves the room, and I pull the shades, draw the curtains, turn off the light, and lock the door behind her. Sitting in the dark, I rub my cheek against the rug until I feel a hot burn, and I grind my head against a chair, conjuring up the feeling of that time, when so determined to escape, I tried forcing my way through the cat door, nearly getting myself stuck. A layer of skin tore free from my scalp. My hair sopped the blood like a sponge, turning it bright, bright red.

But still I can't cry, even though I cried plenty then.

I crawl beneath the table and wrap myself around the leg. With my cheek pressed to the wood, I think about missed concerts. And missed days. And how much I miss Mason.

So.

Unbelievably.

Much.

An absence so deep, I can taste it on my tongue like the ashes of cremated bodies after a slow and painful death. Still, my eyes remain dry. My tears have all been shed. If it weren't for my writing, I'd have no voice either.

27

As soon as I woke up, I shot out of bed and checked the cat door. My heart leaped. Like Christmas morning, Santa had left me a present. I knew just what it was, but that didn't lessen the excitement. I pulled the bag toward me, from out in the hallway, and peeked down between the handles.

The notebook cover was marbleized, silver and blue, and bound with a shiny gold spiral. I took it out. The pages were lined with gold too, all around the edges. A pen sat at the bottom of the bag. I plucked it out, checking to see if I could use the tip as a knife, or if the cap might be sharp enough to cut. But both were plastic.

I flipped the notebook open just as I heard Mason's knock. I scurried to the wall, excited to tell him about my prize.

"I told you," he said. "All you need to do is play by the rules, and you'll get what you want."

"What I *really* want is to go home."

"Which is why I'm trying to bust us out of this shithole. I found something to help me, by the way."

"What?" I asked.

"A screwdriver. It was in one of the heating ducts. Maybe a worker left it at some point. I figure I can use it to try to pick some locks, chisel through drywall, or protect myself if I need to."

I opened my mouth to tell him about my mattress project but then fell silent. Because what would happen if Mason got caught while sneaking out? If he ever chose to save himself by telling the monster everything he knew?

"I've been meaning to ask you something," I said instead. "When you first got here, was your room stocked with all of your favorite snacks?"

"*My favorite snacks?*"

"All of the things you like to eat, that is. Was everything handpicked, as though just for you?"

"I guess, now that you mention it. But to be honest, I'm not super selective. I mostly just eat whatever's in front of me."

"Okay, so how about the clothes—the ones that were in your dresser when you got here? Was it stuff you like? Brands you'd normally shop for?"

"I'm not really a brand-name kind of guy. It was just some sweats and tees, plus one zip-up sweatshirt."

"All in your size?"

"Yeah, *why?* What are you thinking?"

"I'm thinking that he chose all of us specifically for some reason. Do you know if Samantha's room is decked out with all her favorite things?"

"No, but I can ask."

"Do you think he might've taken us for ransom?"

"Well, if that's the case, I'm screwed. I don't know anyone with money."

"So maybe he chose you for a different reason."

"Or maybe I was a spontaneous pick."

"Why would he spontaneously pick you?"

"Because of my irresistible charm?"

"I'm serious."

"I'm not?"

"My parents would pay anything to get me back," I told him.

"Were you guys really close?"

"We *are* really close."

"Sorry. That's what I meant."

"My parents have Only Child Syndrome, which basically means they're hyper-focused on every little thing I do, say, feel, or want. When I sneeze, they practically come running with tissues balled up in their hands."

"If only you were sneezing when that asshole took you, right?"

"Right," I admitted. "If only my mom had insisted we catch up over coffee. If only my dad had gotten up early instead of sleeping in."

"Why *did* he sleep in?"

"He'd been working until midnight the night before."

"But you said you were taken on a Sunday. Does your dad work Saturdays?"

"He'd started to." More and more, late into the night.

"Let me guess. Does he work in a hospital? Or at a twenty-four-hour call center?"

"He works in a bank."

"*Seriously?* A bank?"

"Yeah. Why?"

"Doesn't that strike you as a little weird . . . working until midnight at a bank? Is it a twenty-four-hour branch?"

I bit my lip, knowing it *was* weird. So why had I never questioned it? The long hours, even on the weekends . . .

"My mom took off when I was eight," Mason said. "My dad couldn't handle it and started drinking."

"I'm so sorry."

"Yeah, it sucked, especially on nights when my dad got completely wasted. He'd lock me in the basement to keep me out of his hair, then tell me it was all my fault."

"Mason, that's horrible."

"But life goes on, right?"

"I guess . . ."

"It does. I'm living proof."

"Do you know where your mom went? Or why she left in the first place?"

"Negative to both. I haven't seen her since."

For a fast and fleeting second, I wondered if his mother might've had something to do with us being taken. But that didn't make sense either. Because why would she take me? Or Samantha? Or any of the others?

"My dad passed away a couple of years ago," Mason said. "I tell myself he's probably happier wherever he is. He hated life without my mom, drank himself into a pretty bitter guy. On some nights, I think he was just waiting for the time to come— to not wake up, I mean."

"That's so sad."

"I know. But everything happens for a reason, right? My mom abandoning Dad and me, growing up with an alcoholic, having to drop out of school to pay bills . . ."

"Were there relatives that could help you?"

"If there were, I didn't know any of them. But it hasn't been all bad. I mean, I've definitely seen and learned a lot—probably more than most people my age."

"What's been your most valuable lesson?"

"Not taking on the role of victim. Even when life is at its suckiest, I try to find the bright side."

"What's the bright side of being abducted and held against your will?"

"At least I'll have a pretty impressive story to tell in the end."

"You're kidding."

"Maybe a little." He laughed. "But this isn't my first time being locked up. I got arrested once for stealing from a convenience store. Between that and a rocky family life, I've had plenty of practice at staying positive."

"Stealing food?"

"Cash."

"Oh." I swallowed hard, feeling a piece of my heart crumble.

"It wasn't anything as dramatic as what you see on TV. No one got hurt."

"Did you have a gun?"

"No, but I pretended I did. It was really, really stupid. But my father had just died—not that that's an excuse—and I was desperate and hungry. Anyway, I did my time. And I tried to stay optimistic. Because what's the alternative? Giving up? Rotting away? Passing out in the snow, like my dad, and not waking up?"

"Wow," I said, taking it all in.

"Wow, *'What a complete menace I'm talking to on the other side of this wall'*?"

"Wow, you've been through a lot."

"Do you think less of me now?"

I honestly wasn't sure what to think. Part of me felt like I'd been socked in the gut. Another part tried to imagine myself in his position, after having been abandoned by my mother, and after losing my father, after dropping out of school to find a way to make ends meet . . . But would I have robbed a store?

"Tough question?" he asked. "I can't say I blame you."

"It's not that I think less of you. There are just more layers I'm encountering."

"So now I'm an onion? I hope I never make you cry."

"Okay, that's pretty bad."

"I know, but I couldn't resist."

"If you get me out of here, I'll cry tears of joy."

"I'm working on it."

"And so am I. I've been brainstorming ideas for escape."

"What kind of ideas?" he asked.

"What if I were sick and needed a doctor?"

"You're *not* sick, though, are you?"

"*No.* But what if I *pretended* that I was? You know, like in middle school when you felt like playing hooky? Do you think that guy would open the door?"

"Maybe he'd just give you Tylenol."

"I'm serious."

"Okay, so suppose he *does* open the door. Then what?"

"Then I fight back and try my best to break free." The idea sounded laughable spoken aloud, outside the confines of my head.

"I just think he'll know if you're not *really* sick—like, he'll be able to take your temperature. Though I guess you could put a warm cloth on your forehead or gargle with hot water . . ."

"Exactly, like in middle school."

"You'd really have to play a convincing role, coughing a lot, hacking up, making yourself look groggy and weak . . . Do you have any soda water in your room? Maybe you could use it to douse your eyes and make them red. But he still might be able to tell that you're faking."

"Even if I were *really* sick?" Like if I got a headache or a stomachache and simply ramped up the drama.

"You're not planning on doing something stupid, are you?"

"Stupid like *what?*"

"Like trying to *make* yourself sick."

It was the first time the option had occurred to me—that if I'd wanted I could've downed a bottle of shampoo or eaten a bunch of soap bars; that maybe, despite the horrible circumstances and these equally horrible choices, I still retained a bit of power.

"*Jane?*"

"Yeah."

"I don't think I could handle it if you *really* got sick." His voice sounded soft and splintered. "Or if you got hurt in any way . . ."

I pressed my forehead against the wall, wondering just how affected he'd been by his mother's abandonment and his father's death.

"I mean, I know we don't even know each other well," he continued, "but believe it or not, this time we've had together . . . it's meant a lot to me."

The heat of my breath bounced off the wall, smoked against my cheeks, made my face grow even warmer.

"*Jane?*"

"I'm not going to make myself sick."

"Promise me?"

"I promise," I said, glad there was something I could give him back. And just like that, my power was gone.

28

Later that same night, I tossed and turned in bed, my mind locked on the conversation I'd had with Mason and the questions it had launched.

Why *had* my father been working until midnight on the night before I was taken . . . a Saturday night? Why had he started putting in longer days, including on weekends? The bank he worked at wasn't even a major one, just a small-town branch where he processed mortgages and car loans—nothing that'd require him to work as much as he did. Or to travel as often as he'd started to.

Was it possible that he'd been cheating on my mother? Was that the real reason he couldn't have dinner with us most nights? And why, last spring, he'd missed my poetry reading entirely. He'd said it was because of an accident on the highway, but now I had to wonder.

I wondered . . .

What was the real reason he'd started working out at the gym? He'd been shopping differently too—at the mall, rather than at megastores and discount warehouses. About a month BIWM, he'd asked me to go with him to the outdoor market-place.

"You need to show me where all the cool dads shop," he'd said.

I brought him to Cloth and Stone and helped him pick out pants, shirts, and tees, racking his bill up to over $600.

"Sorry," I told him when the salesperson said the amount.

"No worries." He smiled. "I knew what I was doing. Thank you for being my personal stylist. Now, I can look good for your mom."

Had it really been about her?

"Your dad's a good guy," Mom reminded me not long BIWM.

I'd given her a curious look, not sure why she was bringing it up. The comment had seemed so random; we'd been talking about going to see a movie, nothing even remotely relatable. Did she say it because it's what she really thought? Or did she say it because it's what she wanted to believe and needed to remind herself?

I rolled over in bed, trying my best to conjure up fonder memories, like the time I got poison sumac in kindergarten when I took a nosedive into a bush while scavenging for wild strawberries—which probably sounds weird as a "fonder mem-ory," but it was the way my dad took care of me afterward that made the memory fond. At 2:00 a.m., when I couldn't sleep because of the constant itch, he snuggled me up on the sofa in the living room and scratched my legs while we watched an all-night marathon of *Jill and Jessie*. Eventually, I fell asleep, and when I woke the following afternoon, he was still there. He'd taken the day off from work just to be with me—to make my favorite lunch (mac 'n' cheese) and play my favorite board games.

Was that same dad capable of having some secret life? *How would I know?* How could I *not* have known?

I pulled a pillow over my head as if that would stifle my thoughts. But instead the conversation I'd had with Mason played on a continuous loop inside my mind's ear:

Does your dad work Saturdays?

Let me guess. Does he work in a hospital? Or at a twenty-four-hour call center?

Seriously? A bank? Doesn't that strike you as a little weird . . . working until midnight at a bank? Is it a twenty-four-hour branch?

I tried to stop the loop with thoughts of my father again. I pictured my five-year-old self wrapped up on the living room sofa, armed with the TV clicker, as a new episode of *Jill and Jessie* appeared on the screen.

"Just scratch, Daddy, scratch," I'd told him.

Dad did as I'd said, scratching my every itch, and made me 3:00 a.m. nachos, along with a root beer float. So he wasn't a bad guy. So he'd never do anything to hurt our family. How could I ever possibly think that?

But still, I did.

29

"What if I wrote letters to the monster?"

I looked at the box of brownies sitting across from me at the table as though it could answer.

"I could write long, meaningful letters," I continued, "making sure to phrase things just right, focusing on the day I was taken."

I was still confused about the timing of it all. Had the monster staked out my house that morning, having assumed I'd go running, as I often did? Did my detour to Norma's Closet throw him for a loop? Though he'd rebounded just fine, hadn't he? With the story of his girlfriend and their one-year anniversary . . . What story would he have used if we'd met on a running trail? That he was lost and needed directions? Or that he knew me from somewhere?

I grabbed my notebook and began a draft:

Dear (I'm not sure what your name is),
  I should probably start with the basics. My name is Jane
Anonymous. I'm seventeen years old, and I live with my parents

in Suburban City, New England State. I was supposed to be entering my senior year of high school, but instead I'm here, wondering what happens next.

In my free time, I love poetry, running, and animals—in that order. Writing is pretty much my life, so thank you for the notebook and pen. I'm guessing you know a lot of this stuff already, seeing as you also know what kind of snacks I like, products I use, and clothes I wear. But I also can't assume that the person reading this letter is also the person that took me.

But if this is you, the guy at Norma's that day, I'm curious if you know me from somewhere. Have we met before? I know it may not matter in the grand scheme of things, but it definitely does to me.

I'm also curious if you have a plan. Maybe you're looking for money. Or maybe you had a plan, but now it's fallen apart and you're not sure what to do. You can talk to me, by the way—to explain the next steps or your side of things. I'm willing to listen. I'm even willing to help if it means my freedom.

Think about it and write me back. Since I have questions for you, I imagine that you have them for me as well.

Sincerely,

Jane

In truth, I doubted he had questions for me. But I wanted to make him feel as though I didn't think he was crazy, as though I believed he could've had a perfectly acceptable reason for taking me.

It took twenty-six drafts to get there.

I tore the letter from my notebook and slid it through the cat door, figuring I could leave him a new letter each day. I pictured a whole stack, collecting on a desk somewhere. *How many would I have to write until he decided we were friends? Or accidentally left a letter out for someone else to see?*

After thirty-one letters with no response, I knew I needed a craftier approach. And so, I came up with the idea of hiding a message among my words—not a letter this time, but a poem I'd write. When I was finished, I could crumple the poem up and throw it in the trash. What were the odds of some random person finding the poem and cracking the code?

Probably another long shot, said the Shelley voice, at last.

Still, I was willing to give it a shot.

<u>broken Me</u>

wrench me like a sponge
until everY drop is released
peel me opeN as a letter
And unfold my every crease
stretch ME like taffy, as far as you can,
untIl the thinneSt thread
is formed
Just keep in mind,
i cAn oNly twist,
bEnd,
spirAl,
turN,
cONtract
and Yield
so Much
befOre i crUmble,
SHatter,
and tEar.
before nothing eLse is left
except broken Pieces
and broken ME.

I copied the poem at least a dozen times, changing words, shifting phrases, and playing with the lettering to try to make the message* appear less obvious. But in the end, I flushed the poem down the toilet, along with any hope.

*MY NAME IS JANE ANONYMOUS. HELP ME.

30

With the sides of the mattress torn, I pulled up on the fabric, tucked back the top layer of foam, and exposed the network of coil springs. I wrapped my hand around one of the springs and pulled—*hard*—trying to get the coil to break, but the metal was surprisingly thick.

I continued in a back-and-forth motion, imagining my arm like a machine and the coil like a lever. With enough cranks, gold would pour out and I could stake my claim.

Finally, the metal yielded—a slight bend, right at the base—but I could no longer feel my forearm, and my skin was bubbled with blisters. Deep red lines had formed across the center of my palm. I needed to try something else.

I'd yet to check each individual tile in the bathroom, or knock on all the walls in search of hollow spots.

Now you're thinking, said the Shelley voice inside my head. *Basements aren't exactly known for their fine construction and refinishing.*

She was right. They weren't. The basement back home had a cheap drop ceiling and paper-thin walls.

I got up and went into the bathroom, triggering the motion detector light, per usual, and suddenly the question occurred to me: What would happen if any of the bulbs went out—either here or in the main room? He hadn't left any spares, not that spares would've helped with the locked metal screens. *Would he come in here and change them?* Or did he not expect me to be locked up for long? The answers to both of those questions scared me more than the thought of being in the dark.

I searched the wall tiles, trying to stay focused, looking for a crack in the grout. But it was so hard—keeping track, not losing my place. Pops of light appeared in front of my vision. I closed my eyes to keep them from playing tricks, then checked and rechecked the spaces surrounding the hopper and the storage cabinet. Nothing looked unusual.

Stepping into the shower, I jiggled the knobs to make sure they seemed fully affixed, then ran my fingers over the shower insert: a large sheet of acrylic that'd been glued to the three walls of the stall. What could I use to dissolve the glue? Nail polish remover? Rubbing alcohol? Would he give me those things if I cashed in my star points? My gut told me no.

I moved toward the sink, and the room started to wobble. The floor felt unsteady beneath my feet. Was it sloping downward? Were the walls always so slanted?

I grabbed a facecloth and ran it under the running faucet. With the dampened cloth pressed firmly against my forehead, I peeked into the mirror, and that's when I spotted it—behind me, on the wall.

One of the ceramic tiles looked chipped, right at the corner. I turned to check it out. A thin, wiry line traveled down the length of the tile square. I wedged my fingernail into the space and tried to pull the tile upward, but my nails were all broken. I needed something pointed and sharp.

I swung open the toiletry cabinet and riffled through the

supplies. Shampoo bottles tumbled onto the floor, along with tissue boxes, toothpaste tubes, hand sanitizer, and packages of cotton balls. I grabbed the hairbrush, wondering if I could yank the bristles out. But they felt too soft, like horsehair.

I sat down on the floor in the center of the room, hoping to see the space in a new way. My father used to say the same— used to pledge the importance of thinking outside the box, trying to find the unseen solution. And so I looked. Again. At the toilet flusher and the knobs in the shower. I studied the fixtures beneath the sink and the handle on the cabinet. I visually scoured every inch of the cement floor before stretching out across it and staring up at the ceiling, wondering about the cages that covered the lights. Could I pry the wire free? Or find something to pick the locks?

Finally, I got up, having to pee, my head still spinning; my mind wouldn't stop racing. I started to pull at my sweatpants when an idea hit. I lifted the cover of the toilet tank and looked downward. The scent of stagnant water wafted in my face, reminded me of dirty laundry.

Inside the tank, a thin metal rod joined a fixed pole with a floating rubber ball. I set the cover down on the seat, dipped my fingers beneath the surface of the water, and pulled the rod from the ball. Surprisingly, it came free. To my complete and utter amazement, the rod separated from the pole. In my cold, wet hand, I held a six-inch metal tube.

I brought it over to the broken tile and wedged the tip beneath the edge, where I suspected the tile had been lifted before. I pulled upward, feeling a little give. The tile fell from the wall. I caught it from hitting the floor, and I peeked into the crevice. There wasn't much space—maybe an inch at most, where the tile had been glued.

I went to go stick the tile back into place when I spotted some scribbling on the back, done in pencil:

If you're reading this, I'm probably dead.

I blinked hard before rechecking the words. What were they supposed to mean? Did I even want to know?

I stumbled back to the room and curled up on the bed. My heart wouldn't stop racing. My lungs felt full of glass. Staring at the wall, I silently counted to fifty, trying to slow the motor inside my brain. There was no sound, and yet everything seemed loud, like inside a machine shop.

Please! I shouted inside my head. If only my parents had brought me to church—if only I had a god to pray to. But I prayed nonetheless—to whatever spirit would hear me: *Please help me. Please guide me. Please show me what to do. I have no idea what to do. Please, please, please . . . I'll do anything. Just give me another chance.*

I prayed.

Until.

Every star in my mind's galaxy had turned as black as the night sky.

Until the glass in my chest had dulled, and I was able to fall asleep.

THEN

31

A scratching sound woke me up. It came from out in the hall. I clutched the box of brownies. The tile from the bathroom was still clenched in my fist.

Where was the toilet rod?

Not in my hand.

Did I return it back inside the tank?

"Jane?" Shelley's voice. *"What do you think you're doing? Get up. Get up!"*

I wanted to get up, but I couldn't move, and the scratching sound continued. It was at the door: *scratch, scratch, scratch, chisel, scrape, clink.*

"Listen to me, Jane," her voice continued. *"I'm going to get you out of here."* Was *she* outside the door?

I struggled to get up, but it was as if my legs were made of lead, as if a thousand-pound weight were pressing hard against my chest.

"Jane, honey?" Mom's voice.

My heart soared. I tried to shout—to let her know that I was here. But I had no voice. And I still couldn't move.

"*Look around,*" Mom said. "*Is there anything that can help you? A weapon? Something sharp?*"

"Jane?" Mason's voice. "Is everything okay?"

"*Janie?*" Grandma Jean? Was that her? "*Be strong now.*"

Were they all out in the hall? Were the police on the way too?

"*I'm here,*" Shelley said as though answering my thoughts. "*Can you meet me?*"

Meet her?

"*Eggs & Stuff,*" she said. "*Let's salvage my birthday disaster.*"

"Jane?" Mason again.

Knock, knock-knock, tap, thud.

Knock.

Knock-knock.

Tap.

Thud.

Finally, my leg moved. I kicked out—*thwack*. Was that the slamming of a car trunk? I shot up.

I was in the bed, at last fully conscious.

The voices of Shelley, Mom, and Grandma Jean had faded away. Only the scratching sound remained. It was coming from the wall.

I stood up.

"Jane?" Mason's voice.

I heard the familiar knock. I scooted down by the dresser, able to see a hole, like for a mouse. Mason was using his screwdriver to chip away at the drywall.

"Are you there?" he asked.

"I'm here."

"I wasn't sure. I kept knocking and calling." Without another word, he stuck his hand through the hole. His skin was dry and calloused. The creases of his knuckles looked cracked and deep.

Honey-colored hair sprouted from his wrist, where there was also a spray of freckles—orange, tan, and brown. Without a single thought, I placed my hand in his. My eyes pressed shut as our fingers clasped together. A hot, tingling sensation spread like wildfire across my skin.

How long had it been since I'd experienced human touch? Was this what it felt like for people in prison? Like a thousand exclamation points coursing through the veins? Dancing down the spine? Igniting every nerve? Did something weird happen to the body—to the vessels or the neurons—after such a long absence? Did the skin become more sensitive, sort of like when a limb falls asleep and the blood comes rushing back to the affected part of the body—that surge of electricity . . .

"Is everything okay?" he asked.

I didn't want to ruin the moment by asking him about the hole or telling him about the tile. Instead, I curled up on the floor, hoping to get a glimpse of his face. I lay with my cheek pressed flat against the cement, but the hole was way too low—only about four inches tall, barely big enough to fit his wrist, never mind allow either of us to peer through.

Still, I watched his fingers move across my palm, gliding over my cuts and blisters. His nails were short, as though from biting. His fourth finger looked slightly crooked, as though it'd once been broken.

His thumb rubbed against my wrist; somehow, I felt it in my knees. It was all I could do not to let out an aching moan.

Neither of us spoke, and I'm not sure how long we stayed

like that, just feeling each other's hands—if it was for two hours or ten. But at some point, I must've nodded off.

When I woke up again, his hand was gone.

But the hole still remained.

32

Once I'd reached enough star points to request a second prize, I thought long and hard about what that prize should be. There were things I'd wanted to ask for—items I could've used for escape (tweezers, food utensils, art tools, a nail file . . .)—but they were all too obvious to even consider.

The monster wasn't stupid.

My mind kept coming back to a book I'd read—the first in the Survivalists series. Jordan, the main character, a retired military officer, survived a plane crash and had to live on a deserted island in the middle of nowhere. The most intriguing aspect of the story was Jordan's unique talent of turning the most seemingly random items into essential pieces, and so she made a hunting spear from popsicle sticks, a telescope from a magnifying lens, and a pair of shoes from duct tape and banana leaves . . .

I needed that kind of inspiration—to get ideas, to think outside the box. What could I do with my bedsheets? How might I utilize the hinges on the cabinet? Was there some other use I could find for a coil spring?

I remembered having wanted to read the second book in the series—when Jordan supposedly gets trapped inside an underwater tank—but I'd never gotten the chance.

It was the perfect idea.

With the tiny wooden pencil, I wrote down my selection: Book 2 in the Survivalists series.

A few days later, when my prize arrived outside the cat door, I pulled it inside, feeling a pit lodge in my gut. The cover was cotton-candy pink, rather than olive-camo as I'd anticipated. The title was different too: *Forbidden,* written in pretty loopy letters, with no indication it was one of the Survivalists books. The picture on the front featured a red-haired woman, all bundled up for snow, walking toward a ski lodge.

I flipped the book over and read the description on the back. *Forbidden* told the story of a twenty-two-year-old college student who falls in love with an estranged family friend, whom she meets during winter break while recovering from a bad breakup.

Clearly, this wasn't the right book. He obviously didn't want me to read something in which the main character survived. I lowered my head to the floor and breathed through the impulse to scream.

Just hold it together, said the Shelley voice inside my head. *There's no time for self-pity. You need to keep moving forward.*

She was right. I had to figure out a next move, and it *had* to be a whole lot more cunning.

NOW

33

I sit in the living room to earn my tenth star. I know, it's stupid. I don't need stars, don't have to earn them. But despite that basic logic, they're one of the few things I have.

Five minutes tick forward on the mantel clock. Then ten.

Fifteen.

And finally, twenty . . .

Mom notices me sitting. "It's so nice to see you outside your room," she says. "Dad and I thought we could all go to brunch. How does that sound?"

"Maybe," I say. "But I have some things to do."

"Schoolwork? We won't be long." She sits down in the arm-chair across from me. "Also, I wanted to talk to you about the other day . . . when Jack came. I'm sorry for the way things ended up."

"It's fine," I say, no longer even sure what the word *fine* means.

"I should've told you he was coming. I just thought it might be a nice surprise."

"It was."

"I want you to be happy, and if Jack doesn't make you happy . . ." She twiddles her fingers as though knitting without the needles.

"It's not about Jack."

"I know." She sighs. "That came out wrong. I don't seem to know what to say anymore."

That goes for the two of us.

"I feel like I just keep apologizing," she says.

"It's fine," I say again.

"But I've been doing a lot of research," she adds. "Trying to understand things more."

"What things?"

"People who've experienced situations like yours. One girl in Montana . . . ," she begins, not even realizing she's erecting an invisible wall. "She was fifteen years old when she got taken from a highway rest stop. She was missing for more than ten years."

"Ten years."

"I know." She shakes her head and covers her mouth. "And you should see the girl's picture. So pretty. And people said she did well in school and had lots of friends . . ."

As if a less-than-pretty girl who sucked in school and had no friends would be less deserving of sympathy.

"I can't imagine the trauma that girl's parents had to endure."

"Not to mention the trauma *she* had to endure."

"Well, of course." Mom meets my eyes, maybe realizing what she's said. "But you know what? She's doing great now. She went back to school and got her GED. She's now in college, studying psychology. She hopes to one day be a family counselor."

"Because the world needs one more screwed-up shrink."

"Excuse me?" Her face furrows.

"Nothing," I say, thinking I'd be better off in my room.

"Anyway, I thought that might make you feel better—to know that there's a next page, a chapter two, a second act . . ." She smiles.

I fake one back.

"So we'll go in an hour or so."

"Go?"

"To brunch . . . I still have some laundry to fold. And Dad's finishing up some paperwork for a client."

I nod, even though I don't want brunch. I just want her to leave. Finally, at thirty minutes, I go upstairs to claim my prize. My manicure kit is already set up on the table. BIWM, nail care was one of my things—something I'd do to unwind. I'd crank the music and choose a shape and shade: gray for a gloomy day, orange and black at Halloween, French nails for sophistication, square tips for a European flair . . .

I begin by prepping my cuticles, then square off the edges. The nails are shorter than normal and not nearly as angled as I like, but they're a work in progress, just like me.

I apply a coat of Blueberry Cheesecake. The shade couldn't be prettier, with a pearly finish. I set my nails under my fan drier before adding a protective topcoat. The transformation is unmistakable. My hands look softer somehow, less damaged maybe.

But I don't yet feel unwound. On the contrary: Every inch of me feels tight, strapped, strangled, suffocated . . .

Mom's footsteps clobber up the stairs. I count the steps— eleven until she gets to the top, half the number it took the monster. I hold my breath as she passes my room and as I hear the door to her bedroom close.

My cue to leave.

I scurry downstairs, past the kitchen, where Dad's working at the island with his back to me. I whisk open the door to the hallway closet. My pretty purple running shoes are sitting on the floor, basically unworn, practically brand new, flashing me right back to that rainy morning, just BIWM.

I could throw the shoes away or donate them to Goodwill. But I refuse to let them go—refuse to let myself forget how badly I screwed up.

I slip into an older pair and pull a baseball cap over my head, careful to keep my hair tucked. The last key piece to help me feel invisible: sunglasses. I put them on, then flee out the door.

With each stride—every inch I get from home—the pressure dissipates. No one can catch me. Nothing can stop me—until I come to the highway, not quite sure how I got here.

I stand, frozen on the grass, just feet from the breakdown lane, as cars zoom by at eighty miles per hour. I track each one, searching for old sedans, circa 1980-something, picturing myself trapped in a trunk, reaching for the roof above my head, gasping for the air inside my lungs.

Breathe.

Breathe.

My skin flashes hot. A dark green sedan whizzes by. The taillights are intact; I watch them intently, anticipating a break, a waving hand.

Relax, I tell myself, forcing my eyes shut, dislodging the mental stake from inside my chest. I move to sit at the line of trees about ten feet from the road.

My phone vibrates in my pocket. I pull it out and check the screen. There's a series of texts from Mom and Dad.

Dad: *Jane? Is everything okay? Where did you go?*

Mom: *Jane??? Where are you? Why didn't you say goodbye?*

Dad: *Mom thought we were going for brunch.*

Mom: *Dad is driving around, looking for you.*

Mom: *Please call or text to let us know you're okay.*

Me: *I'm so sorry.*

Me: *I'm out running. I'll be home in a little bit.*

As if they haven't suffered enough . . . I did it again—disappeared without warning. I crawl to the edge of the highway. A car horn beeps. The driver must think I'm getting too close. If only I had the courage, but I stop here, remove my sunglasses, take off the baseball cap, and look straight up toward the sun.

The bright sting of light coupled with the sensation of the wind as the cars whip by makes my eyes run, gives me the sensation of tears. Because I *should* be crying. I wish I could.

But for now I can only pretend.

NOW

34

When I get back home, Mom is waiting at the door. The color's drained from her face. Her eyes look swollen.

"I'm sorry," I tell her again.

She still wants to take me out. Dad is home for once. "Let's enjoy some family time," she says.

I agree out of guilt, and we end up at a breakfast place not far from the plaza where Shelley and I bought coordinating black-and-white dresses for the Halloween dance, BIWM, when we dressed up as chess pieces.

We go inside, and I scan the dining area. It's surrounded by windows (twelve of them). There's an exit sign on the back wall, opposite a hallway with bathrooms. I look around at the faces of the diners to see if there might be anyone I know. But luckily, it seems safe.

We get seated in a corner booth—Mom on one side, Dad and me on the other. As the waitress hands me a menu, her eyes narrow as though there's a hint of recognition. I keep my face angled downward and order a cheese omelet.

"Are you sure?" Mom asks. "I hear the strawberry crêpes here are pretty amazing."

"A cheese omelet," I repeat.

"But you haven't even looked at the menu."

"Do I know you?" the waitress asks, launching her grenade.

I peek up, bracing for the blow.

The waitress's eyes bulge like she's one of those Panic Pete dolls. "You're the girl who went missing, right? From the news . . . With that guy—that *monster,*" she says, correcting herself, giving me a knowing grin, showing she's on my side.

Team Jane.

Girl power.

Females united.

I want to throw up. Plates behind the counter won't stop clamoring. A whiny male voice sings about lost love on the overhead speakers. I fist my spoon and jab it into my thigh, picturing the toilet rod.

Mom fakes a smile. "Our Jane is home now."

"And she can order anything she wants," the waitress says. "My treat, on the house."

"That's really sweet. Isn't it, Jane?" Mom says.

"I'll have a cheese omelet."

"That sounds good to me too." Dad collects our menus, coming to my rescue. "I'll have the same."

"So quick, you two." Mom continues to peruse her choices. "I'll need another minute. And could we get coffee all around?"

"Sure thing," the waitress chirps. "And take your time."

As she turns away, the entrance door jingles open, and Shelley, Mellie, and Tanya file in. They stand by the hostess station, waiting to be seated.

"The strawberry crêpes it is," Mom announces, setting her menu down. "Jane, did you not get a full place setting?"

"A what?"

"You didn't get a spoon or fork?"

"I did. It's just . . ." I set them on my plate, wanting to crawl beneath the table. "I need to go to the restroom." Keeping an eye on Shelley and the others, I slide out from the booth. They haven't spotted me yet.

The restroom door swings open. Unfortunately, it isn't the kind that locks. Inside, I find six stalls, including a handicapped one, plus a large sink area and three windows. I go into the handicapped stall, lock it behind me, and sit on the toilet with my feet tucked beneath me.

I breathe here, flashing back to the last time I saw Shelley: at my door, with the year-old birthday present. We haven't called or texted one another since. How long ago was that? And what will I say now? That things are going great?

And, yes, we should get together soon.

I know; I'm loving this weather too.

I tell myself the exchange will be quick and painless. There's no need to pluck the rod. But then the bathroom door whooshes open. And the voices of Shelley, Mellie, and Tanya pour in.

MELLIE: Wait, those are her parents, right?

SHELLEY: Yes, and so now I'll need to go say hello. Her mom will ask why I haven't stopped by.

TANYA: And you can't exactly say it's because her daughter's being a brat.

MELLIE: But who can blame a bratty attitude? I heard that guy raped her.

TANYA: No, he *didn't* rape her.

MELLIE: How do you know?

TANYA: My dad told me. He knows someone who worked on the case.

MELLIE: So then was she tortured in some way?

TANYA: Who knows? People are saying she's totally messed up—that she doesn't really get what happened to her.

MELLIE: I saw a picture of that guy on the news, and I hate to say it, but he looked like someone I might've gone out with. Do you think that made it any easier?

TANYA: Made what easier? Isn't that the key question?

MELLIE: I just mean that, whatever did happen . . . at least it didn't involve some three-hundred-pound ogre with pockmarked skin and really bad teeth. Right?

TANYA: I'll try to forget you just said that.

SHELLEY: I really want to be there for her. But it's, like, she's not even trying.

MELLIE: She's probably not capable of trying.

SHELLEY: Okay, shall we? I need to get this over with. Plus, our table is probably ready.

TANYA: Strawberry crêpes, here I come.

I count to fifty before climbing off the toilet, opening up the tank, and plucking the rod out. I keep it concealed with my sleeve and return to the dining area.

"Shelley's here," Mom bursts out as if that will make me happy.

"I don't feel well. I'm going to walk home."

"What happened to your nails? That was such a pretty color."

I look down to see. My Blueberry Cheesecake nail polish is all scraped off. Did I do that? Sitting on the toilet? "I don't feel well. I'm going to walk home."

"What? No." Mom's face scrunches like a prune. "Look at you, you're shaking. Here. Take a sip of my juice. You just need something to eat."

"I just *need* to go back home."

"No. Sit," she insists. "We've already ordered."

I shake my head. "You don't understand." My insides are burning up.

Clamor.

Clank.

Smack.

The smell of garlic fills the air, reminds me of the monster's stewed tomatoes with the bits of oregano.

Dad fishes the keys from his pocket. "I'll drive you home."

"No," Mom says for a third time. "I thought this was what you wanted."

I'm ruining breakfast. This was supposed to go smoothly. Dad slides out from the booth.

"This is crazy," Mom insists. "We should be able to go out for a simple brunch."

Still, Dad ushers me out—through the dining room, past Shelley and her friends.

"There's my girl," the waitress says, fist-pumping the air.

Dad drives me home, not uttering a single sound. Instead, he offers me his sweater, even though it's eighty degrees. I happily accept it, poking the rod deep into my thigh, still able to hear the voices of Shelley and her friends.

In my room, I close the door behind me, crawl beneath the table, and wrap myself around a table leg. But it isn't enough. And so I crawl into the closet. But it's too quiet.

I can't breathe.

I need air.

What will it take to drown my thoughts?

Still holding the toilet rod, I go down the hall into the bathroom and lock myself inside. I turn on the shower faucet and let the water run. The steam hits my face. The warmth slows my pulse.

I step inside, in my shorts and tee, and sit on the bathtub floor. My thigh is red from the rod. I jab at the spot—over and over—as water rushes over my head, as I try to get a grip, and as I remind myself that home is better than being locked up in captivity.

That home is better than being locked up in captivity.

That home.

Is better.

Than being locked up.

In captivity.

THEN

35

In the monster room, with the toilet tank rod gripped firmly in my hand, I squatted down by the bed to work on the mattress spring. The rod was surprisingly strong for its size and shape—about six inches long with the circumference of a pen.

I braced the rod behind the spring and yanked forward and back, again and again, pushing and prodding from side to side.

It wasn't until my shoulder stiffened that I noticed a definite impact. The coil warped, like a mangled *S*. I kept on working, motivated by the progress. The metal seemed more malleable now—weaker maybe, thinner hopefully.

When I could no longer focus on the added step of positioning the rod, I used my hands, wriggling the coil every which way, trying to get it to loosen. I repeated this motion at least a thousand times—until at last it happened. The top end of the coil broke free from the grid.

Using the cuffs of my sweatshirt to protect my blistered palms, I wrapped my hands around the spring and pulled hard. No go.

The mattress slid toward me a few inches, but the spring remained attached.

I tried again, holding the mattress in place with my feet. My forearms twitching, I counted to three and yanked—*hard*.

I fell back against the floor. My head smacked the cement with a deep *clunk*. Staring at the ceiling, I suddenly realized the coil was still in my grip, but no longer attached to the mattress grid.

I'd done it—broken a spring, earned my prize.

I lay in the middle of the floor with the coil pressed against my lips, nearly punch-drunk on the victory. I wanted to tell Mason—so unbelievably much; it just didn't feel as monumental inside the confines of my head. But I was still so scared, because what if he were questioned?

What if I were, as well? Would I rat Mason out just to save myself?

I looked over at the box of brownies and waved my prize in the air, and though I imagined Shelley's voice cheering me on for a job well done, it wasn't the same. I needed to see Mason—even if it meant not sharing this news, but simply sharing the moment.

"I found something," I said when at last he came to the wall. I told him about the bathroom tile and the message scribbled across the back.

"What were you doing behind bathroom tile? And how is that even possible?"

"You're missing the point."

"You're not holding out on me, are you? Is there some secret passageway you're not telling me about?"

"Mason—*no*."

"Okay, so what did the message say?"

"It said, 'If you're reading this, I'm probably dead.'"

"Wait, *what?*"

"Do you think it's true? That the person in this room before me is now dead?"

"Well, I didn't want to say anything . . ."

"*What?*" I asked. Blood rushed from my face.

"Samantha's gone now too."

"What do you mean *gone?*"

"I mean, she's no longer in her room—or at least she's not answering when I call out to her."

I pressed the end of the coil into my leg, wondering if it was Samantha I'd heard screaming that day, begging for forgiveness. Had she been too defiant or tried to break free?

"I found something too," Mason said. "A window. I just need to figure out how I'm going to bust the glass without getting caught. It's on the third floor, where I'm pretty sure he sleeps, so I need to time things just right."

"Wait, are you *kidding?*"

"I don't joke about windows. My only fear is that the glass might be tied to an alarm. I've heard high-pitched beeping at various times in the building, like someone typing a pass code. It's usually followed by a door slam. Have you heard it too?"

I wasn't sure, but I'd definitely heard whistling, as though from water pipes, but maybe it was a beep. "Isn't an alarm a good thing?"

"Well, yeah, if an outsider hears it, but not if he does. Plus, there's the added complication of the bars on the window."

"Bars, like in a prison, meaning we can't get out?"

"Trust me; finding a window is major progress. When I know for sure he isn't around, I'll break the glass. If an alarm goes off, I'll take the heat, whatever it is. *Deal?*"

I dug the coil in deeper—through the fabric of my sweats, into the flesh of my thigh.

"*Jane?*"

"Yes," I muttered, breaking through skin.

"Are you okay?"

Not okay. I winced from the pain, picturing my mother's face. What was she doing? Were people still looking? Or had everyone assumed I was already dead?

"I just really want to go home." My voice wobbled over the words.

"I know, and you will, but you have to hang in there, okay?"

"I wish I knew how my parents were doing."

"What if they're doing better than you think? What if your disappearance has made them stronger or brought them closer?"

"They already *were* close."

"I'm just trying to be optimistic. I have to believe there's a reason for us being here—that we'll learn something or grow in some way, including your parents. Because what's the point, if not? We may as well be dead."

I bore down on the cut, using the cotton fabric of my sweats to clot the blood.

"So what do you say? Are you with me?" he asked.

"*With you?*"

"On the I-refuse-to-be-a-victim train? Trust me; it's the best ticket in town."

"Your optimism is nauseating."

"But you know you love me for it."

"*Love* is a pretty strong word."

"And so is *coffee*."

"*Excuse me?*"

"A six-letter word for something strong, bold, and addictive. Want to play?"

"I'd rather we knocked down this Great Wall of Separation."

"*Now* you're talking."

"So then, you agree? We should make the hole bigger? Then we could actually see each other when we talked. Plus, I could help you navigate through the walls and ducts."

"I thought about that too, but are you really okay with it looking as if you tried to chisel your way out?"

"What do you think would happen?"

"*Nothing*—unless that guy comes in here and sees. Are you willing to take that chance? Because I could definitely make the hole bigger if you really want me to. It wouldn't be so hard."

I really, really did. But maybe he was right.

When I didn't say anything more, Mason poked his hand through the hole. I pulled my sleeve down over my cuts, then placed my palm on his.

"Think about it, okay?" he asked. "Maybe the benefits would outweigh the risks. Or maybe I could find something to conceal the hole. The problem would be traveling with that something through the air ducts."

"Is there anything in the room you could use?"

"Not that I've been able to see with this useless reading light. *Unless* . . . Hold on . . ." He pulled his hand away.

I could hear him moving on the other side of the wall—the sound of his knuckles cracking and his shoes scuffing. "Mason?"

"I could try one of the ceiling tiles. They're not very big, though. Maybe fourteen by fourteen . . ."

"Let's sleep on it."

"Are you sure? Because I'll bet we could make it work. I could try to fuse a couple together."

"Let's talk about it tomorrow. I really need to rest."

"How about we rest together?" He sat back down.

"What about getting caught?"

"I don't care about getting caught."

"Yes, you do." I wanted to be wrong.

"I know. You're right." He poked his hand back through the hole and slipped his fingers beneath the cuff of my sleeve so we were touching skin to skin. "Good night," he said, leaving me wanting more.

After he left, I lay with my face pressed against the hole. The absence in my heart was like nothing I'd ever experienced: a wrenching-burning pain.

This isn't real, said the Shelley voice inside my head. *Your emotions are heightened because you're starving for companionship. Don't let it cloud your smarts.*

"I'm not," I said, sitting back up.

I searched my sweats for the hole I'd made. I was in control, my smarts fully intact. I dug the coil back in.

36

"I have a surprise for you," Mason said one day at the wall.

"Sweet rolls?" I asked, happy to play along.

"Better." He poked a chocolate bar through the hole. "I got it with my star points."

"So then why haven't you eaten it?"

"Because I wanted to share with you." He took the bar back, tore off the wrapper, then passed it through the hole again.

I bit into the smooth, dark block. It tasted bittersweet—the kind of chocolate my dad liked to eat, with a velvety texture and a high percentage of cocoa. I passed the bar back.

"Good, right?" Mason's voice was thick with chocolate.

"More like great." I took the bar again, unable to help notice the bite mark he'd left—a half-moon impression in the top corner. I placed my mouth in the very same spot and pressed my eyes shut.

"I should've asked for marshmallows too," Mason said, continuing to chatter on—something about camping trips and graham cracker dust.

I took another bite. The block melted against my tongue and slid like syrup down my throat. We went back and forth until the very last bite, which he insisted I eat. But I wasn't ready to be done. Instead, I brought the bite to my lips, imagining his kiss, wondering what it'd feel like.

"I wish I had something to share with you," I told him.

"How about a secret?"

"What kind of secret?"

"I don't know. Something nobody else knows."

"*Hmm . . .*" I pondered.

"Or how about something you did that you're not exactly proud of? Sort of like my convenience store mistake . . ."

Stretched out on the floor, I rested my cheek against his palm and brought his fingertips to my lips. They tasted like the chocolate.

"*Well?*" he asked.

I could tell he was lying down too—that his mouth was a mere whisper away, on the other side of the hole.

"I didn't have coffee with my mom on the morning that I was taken," I told him. "Instead I answered a text, and now I'm here."

"Okay, but do you really think that compares to my convenience store robbery and stint in the slammer?"

"Why not? That's some therapy-worthy regret right there, don't you think?"

"Try to go deeper."

"How deep?"

"To that tiny place inside you that holds a secret regret—something you don't like to think about."

"Do you double as a therapist?"

"I just read a lot of soul-searching stuff."

"Because . . ."

"Let's just say that my life, thus far, has given me ample motivation."

"And apparently your life just keeps on giving," I said, referring to his current captive status.

"A regretful moment, please," he insisted.

"What I regret is too embarrassing to talk about."

"Well, now you *have* to tell me."

My face burned just thinking about the incident. Could he feel it too, in the center of his palm?

"It happened in third grade," I told him. "We had a pet hamster in our classroom."

"*Seriously?*" I could hear his smirk.

"The teacher used to let us take turns feeding the hamster and changing the water. I'd wanted my own pet for years, but my parents didn't think I was old enough to take care of one. And so, I'd see the hamster at school and ache to bring him home."

"Cute."

Not cute. "One day, I was the first person in the classroom. My teacher was running late, caught in city traffic, and the other kids were still in the hallway, putting away their coats and bags. My heart practically exploded as soon as the idea hit: What if I brought the hamster home and kept him in my room? I had a ten-second window to decide what to do, and in that window, I unhooked the latch on the cage door, scooped up the hamster, and brought him to my lunchbox. But then I decided against it. I mean, it was way too risky. I'd either get caught by the teacher or by my parents. Still, I did it anyway—shoved him inside the box, closed the metal cover, and sat down at my desk like nothing happened. Only *everything* happened: My stomach started hurting. My skin broke out in a rash. Everybody in class asked if I was feeling okay. It wasn't until lunchtime that people noticed the class pet was missing. By that time, there was no turning back. I told everyone I still had a stomachache so I wouldn't have to open my lunchbox. When Mr. Turner noticed the open cage door, he blamed himself, saying he must've forgotten to latch it properly and so the hamster got away. By the time I made it home from school, the hamster had suffocated."

"Yikes."

"I know." I was still able to picture the disappointment on Mr. Turner's face. He kept shaking his head and looking away as though unable to face us. Watching him confess to something he hadn't done was almost as horrible as finding our dead class pet inside my lunchbox. "I still have nightmares about it."

"I'm sorry."

"No—*I'm* the one who's sorry."

"No wonder you work at an animal shelter now."

"You *do* double as a therapist."

"And as your therapist, I say it's high time you forgave yourself. You were a kid, don't forget. You saw something you wanted and acted in the moment."

"How did we even get talking about this?"

"I asked you to share a secret."

"Oh, right, *that*—trying to get inside my mind to see all of my flaws."

"Correction: trying to get *to know* you better. But since you mention the mind . . ."

"*What?*"

"I've been curious about what goes on inside the head of the guy who took us . . . like, what are *his* secrets? What makes him tick? What leads someone to take a bunch of seemingly random people?"

I'd been trying to understand the monster too, at least on some level, as I was writing the letters. "Do you think he regrets taking us?"

"I don't know. But it's sort of easier to think of him as someone who made a mistake—someone who still has the power to correct it. I mean, think about it. We're not dead hamsters inside a box. He can still let us out."

"Do you think that's how people back home see us . . . as dead hamsters?"

"Who are you talking about, specifically?"

"My parents, my friends, Shelley . . ."

"Shelley's your closest friend, right?"

"Right," I say. "Does *she* feel regret?"

"Regret *for* . . ."

"Cutting her camping trip short, sending me a text on the morning I was taken. I'd been on my way out for a run, but she really wanted to meet. She *begged* me."

"Why did she cut her trip short?"

"It was her birthday, and she didn't feel like spending it in a tent with her family."

"Wow."

"I know." The excuse sounded stupid. If Shelley had been sick, or if there'd been an accident, or if something monumental had caused her to come home early . . . But it was none of that. And meanwhile I was here.

"And so now you're stuck asking yourself *what if*. What if she hadn't sabotaged the trip? What if she'd never texted you that morning?"

"Unfortunately, yes. I ask myself *what if* all the time."

"What if you never joined me on this adventure in captivity? We never would've met."

"Do you always look for a silver lining?"

"I always try. And how about a boyfriend?"

"What do you mean?"

"I mean, how come there was no guy looking out for you that morning?"

I bit my lip, unsure how to answer, but knowing I didn't want to talk about Jack.

Mason wriggled his fingers beneath my cheek to get my attention. "Is that a tough question?"

"Do *you* have a girlfriend?"

"Not exactly, but pre-abduction, there was someone I'd *wanted* to be my girlfriend. Does that count?"

"Did she know how you felt?"

"Negative. She didn't even know I existed. Though you may find this hard to believe, outside the bounds of captivity, I'm not the charming, confident, and charismatic soul you've grown to know and love."

"So then what *are* you?"

"Shy, awkward, often tongue-tied in front of pretty girls."

"Where did you and the girl first meet?"

"More like *where did I first see and fall hopelessly in like with her?*"

"Okay, that."

"It was at the beach, maybe four or five years ago. She was with some friends. I overheard them talking about getting dinner and going for a swim . . . Anyway, I couldn't exactly intrude."

"Wait, you saw this girl *four* or *five* years ago and she *still* doesn't know you exist?"

"Hey, don't judge. I tried to talk to her a couple of times— once at a party and another time while running errands in town—but both proved mortifying."

"Why? What happened?"

"Spontaneous mutism at the party; I totally clammed up. I promised myself that if I ever got another chance, I'd at least get her number. That second chance came: I saw her on the street. In my mind, I asked her to lunch. In reality, I made weird guttural sounds."

"I'm sure it wasn't that bad."

"Tell my shrink that."

"Ha."

"Exactly. My romantic game's pretty laughable. But back to

your love life . . . If you were my girlfriend, I wouldn't let you out of my sight. I'd always be looking out for you."

I pressed his fingers against my face, wishing that Jack had felt the same—that he'd have been the one to call or text me that morning.

"I should probably go," Mason said.

"Not yet." I held his hand captive.

"I don't want to get caught." He tugged.

I tugged back. "And I don't want you to go."

"Even after we get out?"

"Especially not then."

"You mean it?"

"I mean it."

"Okay. I won't go."

I snuggled against his palm and then closed my eyes for sleep.

37

I paced the floor of my room for at least twenty miles. And filled sixty-four pages in my journal to help pass the time.

I also changed my bed linens twice, washed my dishes in the sink, set out three bags of trash, doodled an animal farm, picked and batch-counted eighty-nine tissues (forty-three times), worked out with water jugs, read the novel *Forbidden* (admittedly unable to put it down), and earned enough stars to ask for something new.

If all of that wasn't enough, I took a (clothed) shower, carved soap animals using the edge of a toothpaste tube, and plotted an escape that involved shimmying through a heating duct, sneaking up on the guy who took me, and stabbing him in his sleep—through his back. I pictured the metal coil poking out his chest.

Additionally, I made friends with a spider: Tiger, I called him, because of his orange-and-brown stripes. I watched his spinnerets as he wove a web that reminded me of stretched cotton and that joined the dresser to the wall. How had I never noticed this miracle of spiders—this innate ability to construct a network of silken ladders?

Last, I crafted yet another calculated letter to my captor:

Dear Person Who Took Me,

I'm wondering if that day at Norma's, you saw a brief window of opportunity and acted in the moment, not really giving it much thought. And so now, here I am. And meanwhile, there you are, on the opposite side of the door, not really knowing how to fix things.

Am I right?

Even a little?

If so, please know that I'm willing to help. Believe me, I've done things I've regretted before too.

Please write back.

Yours,

Jane

I did all of these things as I waited for Mason. I hadn't seen him in twelve meal deliveries, and I had no idea why. Had I said something to offend him? Did he get caught out of his room? Was he stuck somewhere, in an air vent or heating duct? Each time I thought I'd heard a familiar knock or clamor, I flew to the wall, only to be disappointed.

Where?

Was?

He?

Didheescapewithoutme?DidhelieaboutSamantha?Maybeitwasherhe caredabout.Maybetheyescapedtogether.Maybeheneverhadanyintentionof savingmetoo.

After the fifteenth meal since his last visit, I didn't feel well. There was a twisting in my stomach. I lay down on the bed, curled onto my side, trying to remember what Mr. Yeager had said in bio class . . . when he talked about which position to sleep in for best food digestion. I tried my left and then my right. But nothing felt better, and I wanted to throw up.

I dangled my head over the side of the mattress. Strands of spit trickled from my mouth, eventually dripping onto the floor. Was this an allergic reaction to something I'd eaten? But everything had tasted fine: the manicotti with marinara sauce, the baked ziti, the slices of pizza . . . I'd practically licked them all off the plate. So maybe it was the broccoli spears in my last meal? I could still taste them somehow—with each sour belch.

The knife in my stomach turned. I let out a moan, flashing back to a girl in French class who used to make herself puke. I stuck my fingers into my mouth and pressed down on my tongue, wondering if I could do the same, but I gagged in the process, letting out a loud, retching wail.

The door at the end of the hallway whined open. Was it mealtime again already? I listened for the click of the latch, the jangling of keys, and the twenty-two footsteps as he got to my door.

"Please!" I shouted at the clack of a tray. "I need help!" I pleaded at the rustling of a trash bag and the clamoring of dishes.

The knife twisted again. Bile shot into my mouth. The contents of my stomach lurched onto the floor, splattering over the side of the mattress: a mound of red tomato mush mixed in mangled green bits. "Please," I repeated. Tears filled my eyes, and my throat burned with acid.

I tried to get up—to grab some napkins and clean up the mess—but the knifelike sensation had transferred to my head, straight through the crown, slicing my skull in two.

Scrunched up by the dresser, I poked my hand through the wall, still waiting for Mason to come, even four additional trays of food later. At one point, I got up and grabbed my score sheet.

On the line for my prize, I scribbled the words *stomach medicine*. On the back, I wrote another note:

Dear Person Who Took Me:
   I don't feel well. I threw up a couple of times. My head aches, and I have the chills. I'm not sure what kind of medicine would help, but maybe an antacid. Or could you bring me to a doctor?
   Also, I've run out of paper and would like to keep writing, so if you wouldn't mind getting me a new notebook and pen. Thank you for considering.
   Jane

When at last my prize came, it was on a tray with unbuttered toast, a bottle of ginger ale, a journal and pen, but no antacids. My gut reaction: It was all my fault; I never should've asked for more than one thing.

I tried a bite of the toast. It went down easily at first, but the pain quickly returned. I writhed on the floor, letting out a long and labored moan, my eyes watering, my body burning from the inside. I threw up once again, but this time I didn't have the strength to clean myself up. It was all I could do to grab a blanket and drape it over me in an effort to stifle the chill. Then I lay by the hole, praying to the god of death to take me in my sleep.

THEN

38

"It's time, Jane."

Time? For what?

Someone squeezed my hand? *"Jane? You're freezing."*

It was Mason's voice.

My body twitched.

My eyes fluttered open.

I lay on the floor, by the hole. Mason cradled my hand in his grip.

"It's time," he said again. "I found a way out."

Wait, *what?*

"I would've come sooner," he said, "but that guy came into my room with a baseball bat while I was in the shower."

"*What?*" I moaned. It was too much to process.

"I tried to fight back, but I was totally unprepared."

"Mason . . ." I curled my fingers inside his.

"The first blow was the worst—right to my ribs. I heard a loud pop, thought I was going to die right there, that he was going to beat me to death. I kept wincing and gasping, huddled on the floor, unable to fight back."

Mason went silent for seconds—at least I think he did, but maybe I'd fallen asleep between words.

"What's wrong?" he asked.

My stomach wrenched; if there had been anything left inside, it would've erupted once again.

"*Jane?*"

My legs felt wet. Had he asked me another question? Did I have an accident in my pants? He continued to talk—something about the window, but I only caught a piece of it, the part about a broken bar. My heart palpitated, and my teeth began to chatter.

"*Jane?* Shit, your hand is like ice."

I could feel the tears in my eyes, like hot dripping wax.

"Can you walk? Do you think you'd be able to sneak through walls? How about if I get you something—some medicine? A pain reliever? I still have some stuff from the time *I* got sick—antacid stuff I got with my star points."

I closed my eyes. The room started to spin.

"I'll be back," he said.

I'm not quite sure if he said anything else, because my world faded to black, and I drifted off to sleep.

39

When I woke up again, Mason was there. His fingers clasped mine. I didn't have the strength to clasp his back. At first, I assumed I'd only nodded off for a few moments and that he hadn't yet left.

But then he said, "I'm sorry it took me so long to get back here. I barely slept last night. That guy's been lingering outside my room. It's got me completely paranoid."

I was paranoid too. What if that guy came into my room? What if Mason didn't visit me again for days? I also worried about my temperature. How high was it? At what point did the brain start to fry?

He let go of my hand and slid a plastic container through the hole. Inside were some pale pink disks, the size of half-dollars, and a handful of white pills. "That's the pain reliever from the migraine I had during my second week here, and some antacids from that stomach bug I got. I took a couple of the pain pills. They didn't kill the migraine, but they definitely helped. I didn't touch the antacid because it smelled like mint and I have an allergy. Next time I get abducted and sick, I'll remember to specify: non-mint antacids. Live and learn, right? Do you have some water?"

I reached for the bottle and popped a pain pill into my mouth. I drank it down, desperate for relief.

"I think you're supposed to let the antacid dissolve in water."

"What if I puke up the water?"

"Silly rabbit. That's the whole point of an antacid—so you *don't* puke. I need you to get better."

"And what if I don't?"

"Don't think like that. You *will* get well, and as soon as that happens, we're out of here. I've found us a way out, but you'll need your strength for climbing, jumping, scaling . . ."

"I'm scared," I admitted, able to hear the fear in my voice: a deep and scratchy wobble.

"I'll stay until I know you're okay."

"I don't want you to get caught."

"I care more about you than I do about getting caught. Hopefully, between the antacids and the pain pills, you'll get some relief. If not, I'll demand you get help. I'll bust down the wall, even if it means sacrificing myself."

I tried to break the antacid with my fingers, but I didn't have the strength. My muscles quivered. My joints ached. I popped the disk into my mouth and crumbled it with my teeth, then spit the pieces into the water and watched them dissolve—like a snowstorm, only pink. I drank the liquid. It smelled like peppermint but tasted like liquefied chalk.

Mason placed his hand, palm open, through the hole. "I'm going to stay here while you sleep. Just in case."

"In *case* . . . ?"

"Don't worry. Just focus on getting well."

"*No.* Tell me."

"Nothing. It's just, like I said, I had the pain med, but I never tried the antacids. I'm sure they're fine, just like the capsules were fine. But I like to be extra cautious, okay?"

Not okay. My heart filled with panic.

"Look, if he'd wanted to drug or poison either one of us, he could've done so a hundred times over by now. I mean, think about it—the guy prepares all of our meals."

I was too tired to talk. And so, I curled up on the floor, with my hand pressed in his palm, closed my eyes, and waited for the effects.

40

That night, a tiger-striped spider wove a web shaped like a heart. I fell into the heart like falling down a well—only this well was bursting with pastel-pink snow. At the bottom, I found a stationery store, with aisles upon aisles of paper and pens.

I started collecting notebooks in my arms, unable to find a carriage. The covers smelled sweet, like peppermint candy. I put them in my mouth because they kept slipping out of my hands. The paper melted against my tongue and tasted like sticky buns— like the kind at Chico's Bakery.

I brought the notebooks to bed and snuggled the pages like a blanket. The spiral wires pulled the ends of my hair. Spines pressed against my back. Crumpled pages nestled my neck like a pillow. And, meanwhile, a snow squall of pink loomed above my head, helping me sleep, easing my pain.

"I love you," said the spider.

My heart swelled. "I love-love-love you right back."

NOW

41

Unable to sleep, I wander down the hallway to peek into my parents' room. The soft glow of the night table lamp shines over the vacant bed, as well as the spill on the floor: cards and letters, strewn on Mom's side of the room like a paper carpet. After I went missing, people sent my parents notes of sympathy and encouragement. Mom keeps these notes in a pillowcase and reads them over and over, as though still looking for consolation for the daughter that remains at large.

I cross the room, seeking consolation too. Sitting on the edge of the bed, I fish a letter from the heap.

Dear John and Mary,

I can't begin to tell you how sorry I am about the news of your daughter. I know what you're going through because my son went missing two years ago.

He was taken from a restaurant, during a mommy-and-son lunch that was supposed to have been a treat. He went to the restroom and never returned. He was nine years old at the time—

maybe too young to be allowed to go off on his own. Not a day goes by that I don't blame myself for allowing him.

Some nights, just as I'm nodding off to sleep, my brain reminds my heart that Nathanial's still missing and I wake up with a viselike tightness in my chest—my body's way of telling me that I don't deserve to rest.

People tell me it wasn't my fault, but that doesn't help to fill the hollowness inside me. I won't ever be whole without my Nathanial.

For now, I go through the motions of life, often surprised to find that people are still living theirs—that the world didn't just stop on the day that Nathanial disappeared.

I don't say any of this to make you feel worse. I say it so you know that you're not alone in your pain. I hope that's helpful, at least on some level.

Please know you are in my prayers.

Liza Stone,

Small Town, Michigan

I run my fingers over the words, able to relate (at least, somewhat). But still there's a part she doesn't get: If Nathanial ever were to come back, he'd only be back in body. Dead or alive, his spirt is long gone.

I return the letter to the pile and go downstairs. Mom's sitting in the living room with her back toward me.

The TV isn't on.

Music doesn't play.

The house is completely silent except for the cracking of the chair as she rocks back and forth. A glass of something golden sits on the table beside her. The graphic on her nightgown—the big balloon heart—peeks through the slats of the chair. She's got the nightgown on backward.

"You're still up," I say, standing just behind her, making my presence known. "Is Dad home?"

"He's working."

"It's after eleven."

"He's always working. You should know that by now. It's his drug of choice." She swivels to face me. A doll sits in her lap— Pammy, my childhood doll.

Mom strokes the doll's hair like the mane of a cat. Pammy's eyes are as green as ever, despite being closed up in a box. A patch of freckles bridges her nose and cheeks. When I was little, Mom used to say that Pammy looked just like me—that we were like two inseparable sisters.

"Look familiar?" Mom asks.

"Why do you have her?"

"After you went missing, the detective asked your dad and me to gather as much information about you that we could find. Your bedroom had been well-scavenged territory, but no one had looked in the basement, so I made that my mission and went through countless bins and boxes. I found Halloween costumes from when you were little: Wonder Woman, Amelia Earhart . . . I also found your old cook set with the plastic food, and your collection of Polly Pocket dolls . . . Pieces of you that I could never let go of, including Pammy here."

I picture my mother sitting on the floor in the basement, trying to assemble all of the pieces—to make sense of my disappearance.

"I'd sit here, with Pammy in my lap, at the end of most nights," she continues. "And I'd tell myself that you'd be home soon."

I move closer, able to recognize Pammy's smile. There's just a peek of teeth. A chip of paint is missing from her bottom lip from when she fell out of my bike basket. "Did you really believe I would be?"

Mom hums instead of answering, snuggling Pammy close— the tune from *The Sound of Music*. The tags of her nightgown stick out the front, right at her neck, jabbing into her skin.

"Mom?"

She nods to the table by the entryway. "You got some mail—something from Jack—maybe an invitation."

But she isn't beaming this time.

Her face shows no expression.

It's as if she has zero expectation, which somehow makes things worse.

She turns her back to face the wall again, takes a sip from the golden glass, and then continues to rock and hum.

I grab the envelope, go up to my room, and close the door behind me. With my back pressed firmly against the door panel, I breathe in and out, but it doesn't help. The air doesn't seem to be coming quickly enough.

I crawl beneath the table and wrap myself around a leg. A box of Kleenex sits at my feet. I pluck out all ninety-six tissues and count them four times before remembering Jack's card. I tear it open.

Dear Jane,

It was really good to see you the other day. I'd been wanting to visit since the moment I heard you were back. So many times, I'd drive by your house, tempted to stop by, but I wanted to give you time.

I remember needing time after Becky died. Once word had spread that she was gone, so many people came around to offer their support, but I couldn't even tell you who they were now. I was too busy processing what her death meant for me at that time—no more blanket tunnels connecting our rooms. No more food fights at the dinner table. No more listening to her nag me for the last piece of cake. I would never have to compete for the TV clicker again. But I would never get to hear her say my name again either.

None of this is to say that our experiences are the same. The

*death of a sibling is completely different from what you've been
through. But I'm hoping you can still relate, at least a little,
because loss is loss, and you lost seven months.*

*Another reason I bring up Becky is because after she died,
nothing was the same. My parents were physically present, but
emotionally they'd been washed out to sea. Meanwhile, everyone wanted to fix me—to take me to parks, to toy stores, or out
for ice cream—basically, to help fill the hole. But whole was with
Becky, and there was no shiny thing that could ever take her
place.*

*Anyway, the fact is, I don't know what you're going through,
and maybe I'm wrong to compare anything. But I'm here if you
want to talk. I'm also here if you don't. We can just get together
and breathe. Or you can call me and breathe too. I promise not to
hang up. Feel free to send me breathing texts while you're at it.*

*Lastly, if you've made it this far (without pitching this letter
in the garbage), I want you to have my number (in case you don't
have it stored somewhere). I hope to breathe with you soon.*

Love,

Jack

His number is scribbled at the bottom. I store it in my phone
and open a text box.

Me: *Hey, it's Jane.*

Me: *I got your letter.*

Jack: *Glad to hear.*

Me: *Thank u.*

Jack: *No problem.*

Me: *Some of the things u said . . .*

Jack: *What?*

Me: *I don't know.*

Me: *Maybe we can breathe together sometime.*

Jack: *Anytime. U name it.*
Me: *OK, so you have my # now.*
Jack: *Yes. Saving.*
Me: *Good night.*
Jack: *Night, Jane.*

NOW

42

The following morning, I head out for a run. But instead of speeding by the animal shelter, I stop and go inside.

"It's so great to see you," Angie exclaims.

I clench my teeth, waiting for her to ask me about my seven months away, but instead she hands me a bag of catnip and tells me to come see the renovated cat lounge.

I follow behind her, thinking how the word *renovated* applies to pretty much everything since I've been back. My favorite movie theater burned down five months ago. Two new restaurants opened up in Maybelle Square. Jay and Lexie are back together on *Proctorville,* my favorite show. And Ms. Lacey, my fifth-grade teacher, the woman who taught me all about free verse and sonnets, passed away while I was gone. I never got to say goodbye. Even Angie's hair: it's gotten so long, way past her shoulders. I remember the day she cut it short, right over the trash barrel by her desk, using everyday scissors and the mirror app on her phone.

"Well?" Angie asks, standing in the doorway of the cat lounge.

I peek inside. A network of climbing shelves, made to look like branches, forms a maze all over the walls. Patches of cheetah-print pop from the floor and cat beds.

"It looks great," I say, spotting Lemon, the resident shelter cat, perched high up on a shelf against a nest of painted leaves.

Lemon lifts her head when she sees me and climbs down three levels of branches, stopping just inches from my feet. I pick her up. She's bigger than I remember; her back paws dangle past my hips. But her purrs are the same—deep and palpable; I can feel them against my chest. Lemon rests her head on my shoulder, just like old times, as if I've never been away. Somehow, I'm still the same old Jane to her.

"Come on," Angie says. "There's someone special I want you to meet."

I reluctantly put Lemon down and follow Angie into the dog wing. She leads me to the cage at the very end. Inside is a medium-sized dog with patches of brown, white, and black. Its snout is pointed like a Doberman's, but it has the blue eyes of a collie, the fluffy tail of a Siberian husky, and the wrinkles of a shar-pei.

"What did I tell you?" Angie asks as though reading my mind. "She's a total mutt. But I have a feeling you two will be close."

As if on cue, the dog starts to bark: thick, hungry yaps.

"What's its name?" I ask.

"*Her* name," Angie corrects me. "And I thought I'd leave that up to you, Dog Whisperer."

"What if I'm not ready to come back?"

"Better get ready, then, because this dog needs you, and I know you wouldn't want to let her down."

I know what Angie's doing. It's so obnoxiously transparent— as if taming this dog will somehow give me a sense of purpose, a reason not to fade into the four gray walls of my room.

I squat down to meet the mutt's eyes. Its tail sticks straight out, and it continues to bark, as though it wants to rip me to shreds. But little does it know, I'm already in tiny bits.

"She arrived approximately twenty pounds underweight," Angie says. "With a burned hind leg and an infection in her eye."

I can see the burn. The hair above the knee has been shaved away. "Where did she come from?"

"Not the happiest of situations, but nothing we have to get into right now."

Translation: The dog has been abused. We've seen it countless times before: animals coming from the Land of Deplorable Situations, left outside in frigid temps, tied up in basement cellars, and caged without food or water. The one difference now: I'm from the Land of Deplorable Situations too.

I move a little closer to show it that I can. The barking intensifies like rapid gunfire, but it doesn't bother me one bit, because part of me wants to bark too.

"So what do you say?" Angie asks. "Think we can work out a schedule?"

"Okay," I agree, but I'm not doing it for Angie, nor am I doing it for the dog. Coming here allows me to slip into my old me costume, even for a few moments, and as an added bonus, I can hear those barks again.

43

When I woke up again, I was lying in bed. My stomach grumbled with hunger for the first time in days. The scent of cooked food wafted from behind the door—baked chicken and boiled rice; I was almost sure.

A female voice cried from somewhere in the building: a pleading wail. Maybe she'd only just arrived. Maybe I'd become too desensitized to care.

I rolled out of bed, wearing a T-shirt and underwear. Where were my sweatpants? Had I tossed them through the cat door? In a fit of chills and fever? I peeked through the door flap. The food tray sat within reach. I pulled it toward me and removed the domelike cover, really wishing whoever was crying would give it a rest.

A bowl of chicken-and-rice soup sat beside a package of crackers and a container of applesauce. I took the bowl over to the hole and drank the broth, waiting for Mason to come.

But he didn't come—not even two showers and seven additional meals later. *Did he get caught out of his room? On his way back from bringing me medicine? Had he stayed with me too long?*

I lay down beside the hole, trying to be optimistic like he was. Maybe he was taking advantage of every free moment by working on the escape route. I vaguely remembered him saying something about a broken bar over the window he'd found. Could he be working it as diligently as I did the mattress spring, not having time for anything else?

Still, after the delivery of three more meals, any hint of optimism evaporated like snow in water. I stuck my hand through the hole and closed my eyes, needing some trace of him—some tangible piece—to prove that he was real.

Because what if I'd only imagined him—if my mind had conjured up his existence as a means of coping with the horror of being taken? I'd asked the monster for the meds; maybe he'd been the one to bring them, rather than Mason. Was that true? Could that possibly have been true?

I reached deeper into the hole, desperate to find proof, imagining—for no logical reason—that he'd left his sweatshirt on the other side of the wall. But the narrowness of the hole stopped me at the wrist. I pushed harder, telling myself that the sweatshirt prize would be worth the tearing of skin.

At first, it was just a scrape; the raw edge of the drywall ripped the top layer of my hand. I clenched my teeth and pushed through the pain—until the scrape morphed into a gash. Blood spurted out, painting the wall red. My skin flapped open, and I let out a whimper, but still I kept reaching. *Just a few more inches.*

A piece of the drywall broke free, fell into the other room. I went to pull my hand out, wanting to get up, wincing from the burning-wrenching-throbbing sensation as my skin twisted away from the flesh.

I stumbled into the bathroom. Despite a woozy head, I removed the lid of the toilet tank and stuck my good hand inside. I pulled the rod out. Blood dribbled over the floor: the smell of raw meat; the feeling of combustion, as though my insides would explode—from my gut, straight up my esophagus, and shoot out my mouth.

I moved back to the dresser, opened a drawer, and fished out a T-shirt. I bit the fabric like a dog, securing it between my teeth. Then I wrapped the cut one-handed, creating a makeshift tourniquet.

The rod gripped firmly in my uninjured hand, I crouched down by the hole and did my best to chisel my way through. The drywall continued to chip, but not enough. I needed more power. My left hand wasn't nearly as strong as my right.

I stepped into my rain boots and sat back. Propped on my elbows, I kicked outward—again and again—grinding my heels into the hole, not even stopping to question if the monster would hear me, if he'd come into my room, if he'd beat me with a baseball bat the way he did Mason.

The drywall cracked, making a zigzag line. But I needed to chisel more. I got up on my knees. Blood seeped through the cloth. Still I used that hand, reliant on its strength, and gripped the toilet rod like a carving knife. I stabbed at the wall—over and over—as I worked my way upward from floor to eye level, picturing the monster's face, imagining slicing through his jugular.

I assumed he must've gone out for a bit or that he was on the top floor of the building, far from all of my noise. Part of me wanted to scream out: *I'm breaking down walls, and you can't stop me! I'll find Mason and the others, and we'll bust out of here.*

I hammered away, my forearm singeing, my fingers throbbing. Finally, I was able to see inside the other room. It was completely dark—no windows. I kept on working, making the hole bigger. A giant chunk of the drywall crumbled to the floor, revealing a couple of plywood boards, running vertically, from floor to ceiling, set about ten inches apart.

Light from my room shone through the planks, enabling me

to see about two feet inward. The room looked mostly vacant, as Mason had said. It wasn't another cell. There was no bed.

I got up on my feet and squeezed through the planks. The air smelled musty from lack of circulation. I moved toward the wall that I assumed would have a door and searched it with my hand, trying to feel for a light switch. I found one and flicked it on—a pale yellow glow shone from a bulb by the door; none of the other bulbs were working.

The size of the room was similar to mine—about eight by ten feet, with cement walls, drop ceiling tiles (as Mason had also mentioned), and eyeball lights (but without cages). A mound of insulation had collected on the floor by a desk that sat against the far wall. The desk wasn't real; it'd been put together with cement blocks and plywood.

Unlike the pocket door in my room, the door in this room had a regular knob, but the keyhole was on this side of the wall. I wrapped my bleeding hand around the knob and tried to turn it, but it didn't budge.

I searched the room, looking for a heating vent. Aside from one that ran along the baseboard, similar to the one in my room, I couldn't find any traces of ductwork—not along the walls or on the floor. I gazed up at the ceiling, right above the pile of insulation, confident a duct was hidden beneath the tiles, that the insulation had fallen during Mason's frequent visits.

I climbed up on the desk, imagining Mason having done the same. The plywood surface wobbled beneath my feet. I bent forward to keep from hitting my head and then pushed upward on one of the tiles. It lifted about eight inches. In that space, I saw more insulation—fistfuls of it, like cotton candy.

I reached my hand inside, feeling for a steel opening or grate. A cool draft filtered over my fingers. I strained my arm to reach a little farther, just as the end of the plank shot up, plunging me forward. By quick reflexes, I managed to step back, anchoring the plank down, avoiding the fall.

My heart pounding, I continued to look into the space, beyond the insulation, but it was too dark. I'd need to remove all of the tiles if I wanted to find the vent.

I jumped back down, thinking I could use the loose board from the desk to strip the ceiling or even break one of the lights. How could broken glass help me? Aside from providing another weapon . . . Did I really need more than my coil spring?

Where even *was* my spring? Why didn't I have it? I slipped back into my room to retrieve it, reminding myself of the ticking clock. The guy who took me would be returning soon. My last meal had been hours before.

I racked my brain. What could I use to pick the lock? I tried the tip of the spring, but it was far too big. My sweatshirt zipper was too mangled and wide. I needed something thinner, longer . . .

Imagining myself as the main character in the Survivalist series, I picked through the bathroom cabinet, checking out packaging construction. Could I take something apart? I tried pulling at the door, getting the hinges to break free, but each hinge had been secured with eight brass screws.

I looked upward. The eyeball lights glared down at me, producing tiny black dots that danced in front of my eyes. The lights in the other room—without the cages—were sure to have wires. Could I use those wires to construct a key?

I hurried back through the wall and lifted the plank from the desk, revealing the cement blocks underneath. And that's when the idea hit: a solution far better than stripping the ceiling tiles or constructing a wire key.

I retied the T-shirt around my cut, using my teeth once again to secure the fabric. Then I picked up a block, grateful for all of my strength training. It had to have been at least twenty-five pounds.

Using both hands, I carried the block over to the door. The muscles in my forearms quivered as I hoisted it to my chest. In one quick motion, I brought the block down on the knob. It barely hit the edge of the metal before falling to the floor with a loud, hard crack.

I jumped back to avoid getting hit, then held my breath and listened for footsteps, the sound of him coming, the vibration of my world ending. But luckily, it remained absolutely quiet.

I picked up the block again, visually calculating the number of steps I'd need to take—three long strides—to gain enough momentum to smash the block down on the knob.

I inhaled a full breath and lifted the block high above my head. My biceps quivered. The wound on my arm continued to pulsate. But I was able to hit the knob at just the right angle.

There was a deep *clank*. The knob clamored to the floor.

And the door creaked open.

NOW

44

I startle awake. And click on my flashlight. I'm in my closet, not lying in a bed with a torn-up mattress, not clutching a coil spring.

Not surrounded by four white walls.

It was just a nightmare, but still I can feel it: the sensation of stiff, cold sheets against my bare legs, plus warm, soft skin sliding over my knee.

I can still picture it too: honeycomb candles burning in the shape of a heart, under a ceiling of pink snow, while a tiger-striped spider wove a web of silk all around the bed like a princess canopy.

I also saw drooping bedroom eyelids.

And tasted hot sticky-bun kisses.

And felt someone's fingers on my back, kneading down my spine, encircling my waist, as hot, tingly kisses grazed my neck. Was that a finger on my chest, drawing pinwheels on my skin?

Sitting in my closet, not lying in a bed with a torn-up mattress, I remind myself this was just a dream. Don't take it too seriously. There is absolutely no reason for this sudden rush of panic, especially because there were other images in my dream too—of Jack's hand, sliding out through the hole in the wall, with his palm facing upward. He was wearing his braided leather bracelet. I recognized his olive jacket and his long, wiry fingers. In my dream, I placed my hand in his, and he held me tight—all through the kisses.

And the kneading.

And the encircling of my waist.

And the stiff cold sheets against my bare legs.

"It'll all be over soon," he promised.

But I'm still waiting, trying to breathe at a normal rate and convince myself I'm free. *It was just a dream,* I remind myself. *Don't take it too seriously.*

There is absolutely.

No reason.

For this sudden.

Rush.

Of panic.

NOW

45

I get up and change into fresh clothes. Downstairs, I pull on a coat, unable to stifle this chill.

Mom looks up from her mug when she sees me. Her eyes stop at the coat: a black puffer jacket. "It's going to be a hot one today."

"I'm going to the shelter," I say as though that explains the Thermo-Fill in summer.

"Would you like me to drive you?"

"Thanks, but I'd rather walk. I need some fresh air." More important, I need to get away.

"How about breakfast? I bought blueberry muffins."

"Angie usually gets doughnuts." A lie.

"Okay, well, maybe we can go to lunch when you get back." She reaches for a plate. It clanks against the granite—like fingernails on chalk. Like dishes in a hallway, stacked up behind a cat door.

I think I say goodbye. Maybe I shut the door behind me. I

count twenty-two steps twenty-two times, purposely ending at the shelter to keep good on my word.

Angie beams when she sees me. "I knew you couldn't resist the challenge of a damsel dog in distress. Isn't that right, my resident dog whisperer?"

I want to see Lemon. I head for the cat lounge. Lemon sits in the center of the room, facing the door, as though she's been waiting for me all morning.

I scoop her up, wondering how long she waited while I was away. How many days, weeks, or months did she sit in the same spot until it no longer made sense? I take her in the rocker and cradle her like Mom did with my Pammy doll.

Lemon purrs in the crook of my neck. The warm weight of her body against my chest makes me feel a little less broken. I stay here, in this moment, the same way I stay in the shower, craving the space between days.

But soon, Angie makes herself known, passing by the doorway a handful of times. I have to get up.

Her dog project barks as soon as she sees me. I reach into my pocket for a handful of treats and toss them inside the cage. While the dog sniffs around, gobbling them up, I brush myself against the bars, spreading my scent the way Mason spread his. On so many nights, I'd sit by the hole, sniffing my hands, breathing in the lingering scent of his skin, like lavender soap.

After the dog finishes her last treat, she looks at me for more. I sit in front of her cage and pull a toy from my pocket—a rope that's been tied into a loop, with a hard rubber ball on one end, about the size of a tennis ball. I feed it through the bars. The dog gloms onto the ball, sinks her teeth right in, growling, seething, and foaming at the mouth.

I tug on the rope, using both hands, getting the dog to slide toward me, across the floor. It pulls right back, yanking my arm forward. I release my grip to let the dog win. She spits the toy out and backs away, still wanting to play, still eager to fight back.

I snatch the toy and continue our tug-of-war game, finally deciding on a name. I'm going to call the dog Brave, and each time I say it will be a reminder to myself for how I aspire to be.

46

The hallway was nothing like I imagined—not nearly as long or wide. A smoke detector on the ceiling blinked bright neon green. There were also two tiny night-lights plugged into the wall—Mickey Mouse and Daffy Duck—as though for a child's room.

I kept the door open, taking advantage of the added light, then moved down the hallway, spotting crayon marks on the wall—faded blue and green words, done in a child's hand:

I AM SORRY.
PLEEZ FORGIVE ME!!!!
I WILL BE A GOOD BOY.
PLEEZ LET ME OUT!!!

Crayon stick figures played across the wall: soccer, Frisbee, card games, and basketball.

Were children being kept here as well? Was it a child who wrote on the tile in my bathroom? Had he or she escaped the room? And, if so, where were they now? Did I even want to know?

I moved down the hallway, trying my best to keep quiet, even though just moments before, I'd been feeling so brave, making as much noise as I'd wanted.

I passed by a couple of rooms; the doors were closed. I imagined house equipment inside them—a furnace, a water tank, a breaker panel. I counted ten steps until I reached the door—*ten* steps, nowhere near twenty-two. Had he paced the hall each time he'd brought me food? Did he want me to believe the hallway was longer than it actually was?

I wrapped my hand around the knob and tried to give it a turn, knowing what would happen. Still, my stomach sank when the knob didn't budge. I pressed my forehead against the door, able to hear the jostling of keys, the click of a lock, the clobbering of footsteps, and the clanking of food trays: ghostly sounds, haunting me, echoing inside my brain, playing with my mind.

I moved back to the room to grab the cement block, dropping the coil spring in the process; it rolled across the floor. I scurried to pick it up, poking it into the hem of my sweatpants. The block secured in my hands, I hurried down the hall, charging at the door, my teeth clenched, my forearms trembling.

I rammed the knob with the block, anticipating the break. A loud clank sounded as stone met metal. The block came crashing to the floor, landing on my foot—the toe of my boot. I let out a catlike whine.

My foot seared. The toe throbbed.

The knob was still in place.

I picked up the block again, held it at my chest, and took a couple of steps back; a burning sensation radiated up to my ankle. Lifting the block high above my head, I came down on the knob with the force of a wrecking ball. The knob gave way but stayed in its socket, angled downward. I repeated the motion two more times.

Finally, it worked.

The knob clamored to the floor.

But still the door remained closed.

Why wasn't it opening?

There was just a hole where the knob should be, with a metal bar running across the space inside the wood. I needed to break it open.

My arms quivering, I slammed the block against the hole. No go. I tried again.

A cracking sound.

The door busted open.

I hobbled through it, searching for Mason. Where was the tunnel he'd spoken about? His room would be a few doors down, on the other side of it.

A set of stairs faced me. Was the door hidden in the wall, to the side of the steps? I raked my hand all over the wall panels, searching for a seam or crack. "Mason?" I called, trying to keep my voice low.

I took the stairs, hoping to find some other way to him. Another door faced me at the top. I went to twist the knob, suspecting it wouldn't turn, but it did, and I scurried through, shutting the door behind me.

It was different up here on the second floor—blond wood floors, off-white walls. I took another step. A kitchen stood to my left. A living room was at the right. I peeked behind me. Doors lined the hallway on both sides.

"Mason," I whispered, completely confused. This wasn't an abandoned warehouse. It was someone's home. The only sound was my breath.

I searched around, looking for a phone. A TV hung on the wall. Curtains covered the windows. Dirty dishes collected on a table.

My head spun. My body twitched. *Should I look outside to try to see where I am?*

Or check the doors.

Or search for a tunnel.

Or continue to look for a phone.

I moved down the hallway and opened the door on the right. A small bathroom. I recognized the storage cabinet; it was just like the one in my room. I tried the knob of the next room down, but it was locked, as was the next door I tried.

"Hello?" I knocked.

No one answered.

Where was Mason?

And what about the others?

I took a deep breath and tried a door on the left—a bedroom, much like mine. I flicked on the light. A single bed sat in the center of the room, surrounded by a dresser and a wooden desk. Was this Samantha's room? Was her absence the reason it'd been left unlocked?

The next room down was another bedroom. There were bright white walls and white bed linens, plus an adjoining bathroom, and a table with a chair. It looked almost like an exact replica of my room, except for one major difference: a window on the far wall. Were those steel bars, peeking through the window blinds?

Was this the window that Mason had been talking about? Except this wasn't the third floor.

Or *was* it?

Maybe all the windows had bars?

I wanted to check it out, but I couldn't bring myself to step into the room for fear the door would close, that I'd get locked up again. The thought of someone watching made my insides writhe.

"Hello?" I called, louder this time. I continued down the hall, beating on locked doors, yanking on knobs. I could always go back downstairs, retrieve the concrete block, and use it to crack these rooms right open.

"*Mason?*"

Where was he? Trapped in the vents? I slapped my palms against the wall—to check for hollow spaces or hidden doors, suddenly realizing my bandaging was gone; my cut was totally exposed, bleeding down my fingers.

My bandage lay crumpled on the floor. I scurried to pick it up, looking into the kitchen, unable to help noticing the window above the sink.

No bars.

A shade hung down, slicing the glass in half.

I took a few steps closer. My heart pounded at the sight of it all: the exposed branches, without leaves; the thin layer of snow that blanketed the ground; and at least a cord of wood stacked up in a corner. I touched the glass. The chill rippled through my body.

I wanted to get out.

I needed to breathe fresh air.

The sky glowed a rich melon color. It painted the snow pink. I wanted to jump through the glass.

A door off the kitchen appeared to lead onto a back deck, but I couldn't leave yet—not without Mason.

Where could he be?

What should I do?

I moved back toward the hallway, noticing the handle of the fridge. It'd been colored blue, as though by markers. A photo stuck to the surface, held in place with a strawberry magnet.

A picture of me.

Wearing a blue crewneck sweater.

I remembered the day the photo was taken because it'd been the one and only day I'd worn that sweater; it'd itched me all through school, and so I gave it to Goodwill.

The photo shows me crossing the street, by the post office. It was mid-autumn; all the leaves had turned orange and red.

Beside my photo was a poem I'd written a couple of years before: "Love for Sale." It'd been published in the school's literary magazine that following spring.

What did it mean now—here, on this fridge? Had I known my abductor from school? Was this a random poem he'd picked? Or had it been chosen for the theme of unrequited love?

My insides shaking, I continued to search the house—the living room, two closets, the entryway, and a pantry—finally uncovering the missing piece. A pocket door at the end of the hallway.

It was barely visible; the metal had been painted over—white, just like the walls. The handle was no more than a sliver in the wood, barely able to fit a couple of fingers. I tugged the handle. It didn't budge. I pounded my fist against the panel. "Mason!" I shouted, convinced he was on the other side. I needed something sharp to try to pick the lock open.

I stumbled back to the kitchen and started yanking open drawers. At last, I found the utensils and fished out a knife—one with a pointed tip.

Back in front of the door, I jammed the tip into the lock. To my complete and utter shock, it went in. I tried to turn it. The lock moved at least a millimeter, but it didn't click. I pulled the knife out and flipped it over, pointing the tip the other way.

At the same moment, I heard a *click*.

But it wasn't from the pocket door.

It was someplace else, inside the house—like a key in a lock, like some kind of release. The sound penetrated my ears, sawed through the bones of my skull.

I took a step back. My whole body shook.

This was really happening.

I wasn't just dreaming.

Was that the creaking of wood? Were those footsteps I just heard? Where was the main entrance? Had I even seen it? *Was that the whining of door hinges?*

I turned to look. The hallway appeared clear. I took tiny steps toward the kitchen. A ball of tension formed inside my chest, knocked on all my ribs, pounded against my spine.

My legs felt hollow, as though with one wrong step they could snap in two. Still, I continued forward, noticing a set of stairs to my left. It led to an entryway. *Was that the one he used? Did he go downstairs? Or maybe there was something I wasn't seeing.*

Another hidden door?

One that would bring me to a tunnel?

A banging noise sounded—like planks of wood. A door squealed open. It was followed by shuffling, like someone digging through boxes, sifting through bins.

I took another step, my foot singeing. My hands wouldn't stop trembling. The knife slipped from my grip and clamored to the floor.

The shuffling noise stopped.

My breath formed a dagger and jammed inside my chest, stabbing through my lungs. I covered my mouth, trying to hold in a wheeze, and scurried through the kitchen, taking giant strides to avoid the impact of extra steps.

I reached the sliding glass door and gripped the handle. Fresh blood from my hand dripped onto the glass. I tried to open the door.

No go.

I turned the latch.

Still nothing.

The dagger in my chest plunged deeper. A gasping-sucking

sound erupted from my throat. I whipped my head to look over my shoulder. The sudden motion tilted the room, shot a spray of white lights in front of my eyes.

A kitchen stool sat within reach, tucked beneath the counter. I went to grab it, desperate to bust through the glass door. But at the same moment, I spotted it; a butter knife was wedged into the space, on the door track, between the floor and the bottom of the door, like a makeshift doorstop, keeping it closed. I plucked the knife out and slid the door open.

A screen separated me. I placed my fingers into the slot for the handle, expecting another barrier.

But the door opened.

I stepped outside.

The chill in the air seeped into my pores, crawled beneath my skin, made me tremble all over. I hobbled toward a gate, still trying to catch my breath, spotting a ceramic frog planter and an old hibachi grill.

A stick broke somewhere—a splitting-cracking sound that cut through my core. But I kept moving forward, never stopping to look back.

THEN

47

I ran as best I could through the gate, up a short set of stairs, and down a long dirt driveway. *Where was this place?*

I headed for the street, struggling for breath. The woods bordered it on both sides. There were no other houses or buildings in sight, not one other person I could call on for help.

Gravel shifted behind me. A high-pitched humming noise blared inside my ear. I focused on a cluster of trees, just as my ankle wrenched. A loud popping sound. My knees buckled forward, and I collapsed to the ground. I turned to look, anticipating the monster.

But he wasn't there.

I shot back up.

Limping now, I kept aiming for the trees, still several yards away. I entered through a couple of tall, barren trees. The sun sank low. Rays of orangey gold melted down tree trunks, shining onto the icy ground. Night would be here soon. It was already freezing.

I scurried among limbs, hating the swish of my body as it

brushed with branches and the trampling of my feet over twigs and fallen snow. Most of the trees were barren, but there were evergreen and pine trees too—clusters of them, towering over me, creating a maze of sorts.

I paused a moment to catch my breath. Was I being followed? Had I truly gotten away? I continued to stagger forward, swiping branches and brush from in front of my face. Where was the street? Why couldn't I find it now? The sound of my panting cut through the sudden stillness. Could he hear it too? Was he hunting me like an animal?

I squatted down, imagining myself like a squirrel—an animal that had the ability to blend into its surroundings—and waited to hear his next move. But instead I heard another sound: the swoosh of a car as it sped by on the street. I looked up, catching a glimpse of red taillights. How much time had passed?

My hand throbbed. I tightened the bandage once more. On my knees, I crawled in the direction of the taillights, grappling over gravel-laden snow. *What month was it? When had winter come?* The gravel burrowed into my palm. *Just twenty more yards,* I told myself. *Just fifteen more, just over that log . . .*

My palm met something sharp; a wincing pain radiated to my shoulder. I turned my hand to look. A chunk of glass stuck out from my skin—a sideways slit, right through the flesh. Blood trailed down my wrist.

I grabbed a corner of the glass and tried to pluck it out with my bandaged hand, but the wrenching motion made my insides coil. I needed to pull harder; the chunk was in too deep, cutting off nerves. My fingertips started to tingle. Maybe it was best to leave the glass in place. Maybe pulling it out would cause too much damage.

I began forward again, clenching my teeth to the pain, supporting my weight with my fingertips, cautious not to bear down on the glass chunk.

Just five more yards.

Just two feet away.

At last, I reached asphalt. I lay with my cheek pressed against the pavement and rested my hands on a patch of snow, like an ice pack of sorts; my body shivered from the cold. Was my hand turning blue? Had an animal gotten hurt here? Or were my wounds the cause of the bloodstained snow?

I looked up at the stars. Were they really, truly spinning? Was the street slightly tilted? Would I roll down the hill?

I closed my eyes and tried to control my breath—until I heard it: the hum of an oncoming car. I opened my eyes. Headlights shone in the distance: bright white beams, reflecting off the road, lighting up the asphalt.

What do you think you're doing? Shelley's voice was back inside my head. *Get up. Get up. This may very well be your last chance.*

I did as she said, struggling to my feet, stumbling onto the pavement. The stars remained spinning. The bones inside my ears ached.

I stood, facing the headlights, waiting for the car to stop. It was still a good distance away. But it wasn't slowing down. My clothes were too dark, too camouflaged by the night. I tried to flag down the driver, but a lightning-rod sensation jolted my muscles, stopped me from extending my arms above my shoulders.

Meanwhile, the car was getting too close. Had it actually sped up? I jumped back, toppling down, landing on my side.

The car came to a screeching halt. A blue pickup truck. The driver—a guy with shaggy brown hair, a matching goatee, and almond-shaped eyes—rolled down his window. His mouth was moving; he was saying something.

I got up. My head continued to spin, but I was determined to stay focused. The car I was taken in . . . was that a pickup too? No, it'd had a trunk. It'd been a sedan. But maybe he'd traded that car in, sometime after he took me. Maybe he'd bought a pickup truck like this one—blue with a dented fender . . .

"Well?" the guy asked.

Well?

"Do you speak English? I asked if everything was okay."

I looked toward his arms—to see if they were covered in tree-limb tattoos—but he was wearing a heavy coat, plus a wrinkled leather watch.

"Do you want a ride or don't you?" he asked.

"Don't I?" I asked, trying to process his words and assess the situation.

"I can take you to the nearest bus station. You really shouldn't be . . ." He stopped talking. His gaze met my arm—the make-shift bandage, the blood soaked into the cotton fabric.

Was that a shovel in the back of his truck?

Were those rubber gloves on the passenger seat?

And the scratch marks on his neck . . . Were they from jagged fingernails—from victims trying to break free?

"Hey, did you have an accident?" He was looking toward my other hand now—the piece of glass, sticking up from my skin. "You should really get that tended to."

I studied his face. His mouth was still moving; his pale, thin lips sloped downward.

A loud, piercing wail tore through the silence. It sounded like a wildcat, which is what I'd thought it was. It took me a beat to realize that the cry had come from me—a primal instinct, a visceral reaction.

Something inside me had crossed over. And so, I darted back into the woods: the huntress, not the prey.

THEN

48

I cut through the woods, dodging trees, boulders, and brush as though I'd been living a lifetime in the wild. The faint glow of the waxing gibbous moon cast a light over my path, enabling me to see just enough to maneuver forward.

My breath left my lips in puffy white bursts. What was the temperature? No more than thirty degrees at most; I imagined a snow squall inside my bones, pushing against my ears.

At one point, I thought I heard the hum of an approaching vehicle. I stopped to search for headlights or taillights, listening for the inevitable swish as a car passed.

But nothing happened. I didn't see anyone.

Maybe the sound was in my head, just like Shelley's voice: *You need to get some water,* she told me—as if I didn't already know. My throat stung with thirst.

I squatted down and raked my fingertips over a mound of snow, then fed the snow into my mouth as best I could. It melted against my tongue. Gravel collected in my teeth. I spat it all out and continued to rake. The ground was frozen solid. Still, I dug my fingernails in, using my bandaged hand, managing to scrape a layer of soil. I smeared my face with the dirt. I also tucked my hair into my sweatshirt and pulled up on my hood, hoping for insulation from the chill. I moved forward again—into a darker patch of forest, cautious of each step.

Finally, when I felt as though I'd gotten far enough away, I began toward the street, crossed it, and entered the woods on the other side. Here, I found a clearing lined with silvery-white birch trees that stretched up toward the sky. The moon shone down over the space, allowing me to see: a dirt-paved pathway that tunneled through the woods, beyond the clearing.

I followed the path, imagining people using it to walk their dogs or take a shortcut. Where would it lead? It was too dark to tell; the nighttime had swallowed me whole. Still, I kept a steady pace, no longer even able to see my breath. Time was ticking. Mason was still missing.

The path stopped. My foot hit something hard. I reached down to feel what it was. A stone wall, about three feet high. *Should I turn back around? Or try to climb over?*

I sat on the wall and let me feet dangle over the side, then turned slowly, supported by my elbows. I lowered myself down, reaching out with my foot, searching for stable ground. But it wasn't there. Meanwhile, my muscles quivered, and both of my hands throbbed.

Please, I screamed inside my head. My teeth clenched, I could feel myself slipping, could hear myself whimpering. *Just hold on for a couple of more inches, just a few more seconds.*

But my arms gave out. My feet hit the ground, and I folded forward, landing on my face, unable to protect myself with my arms. A twig dug in just below my eye, stabbed the skin like a needle. I plucked it out. My eye teared up. Blood came away on my fingertips.

I rose from the ground, and my knee gave way. Luckily, I

was able to catch myself from falling once again. I meandered forward, still unable to see. It didn't seem there were any trees or brush around me. Had I reached another clearing?

I proceeded in a forward direction, able to hear something behind me again—branches breaking, twigs snapping. I quickened my pace. At the same moment, a light turned on, and I was able to see.

A farmhouse.

With an attached barn.

I was standing in someone's front yard. Spotlights gleamed over a wraparound porch and a side driveway. Had I tripped a motion detector light? Or maybe the lights were on a timer?

I headed for the porch and climbed the front steps, two at a time, nearly tripping en route. My ankle still ached. The top of my foot throbbed.

Standing in front of the door, I could still hear a humming in my ears. I lifted my foot to kick the door, but stopped just shy of hitting the wood.

Because what if the monster lived here? What if this was his main house, if where I was being held captive was his best-kept secret?

A crackling sound made me jump. I turned toward the woods, squinting to see. What if I was walking right into a trap?

I waited a moment for something to happen or for someone to reveal himself. When neither did, I turned to peek into the window that ran alongside the door. It was dark inside the house, despite the outside lights. Was no one home?

Except a Jeep sat in the driveway.

What were the odds . . . ?

I approached it slowly, thinking how the Jeep reminded me of Jack's—an old '70s model, with a giant eagle decal splayed across the hood. I went around to the driver's side and tried the door. It opened, but the courtesy light remained off. I sat behind the wheel, remembering how Jack had once stuck a screwdriver in his ignition to start it up when he couldn't find the key.

What could I use? I started to search, leaning over to open the glove box, accidentally bumping the glass piece stuck in my hand. A singeing sensation shot across my wrist, brought more tears to my eyes. I riffled through the contents, careful to use only my fingers. I pulled out an owner's manual, a stack of napkins, some plastic utensils, and a golf ball.

Finally, I found something half-worth a try: a bottle opener. I ran my finger over the pointed end, noticing more tingling in my fingers. Was I starting to lose sensation?

Keep focused, insisted the Shelley voice.

Would the tip of the bottle opener fit into the ignition? I went to try it, and my heart instantly clenched. A key was already in the ignition.

I turned it.

The engine choked.

I tried again.

There was a solid rumble.

I peeked into the rearview mirror just as another light flicked on somewhere behind me, illuminating a corral.

I put the Jeep in gear, stepped on the gas, and peeled out of the drive, almost unable to believe that this was really, truly happening. I flew down the street, unsure where I was going. The roads were dark. I clicked on the high beams. The gas gauge on the dashboard read just above empty.

It seemed I was on a hill. The road spiraled downward. My ears clogged from the altitude. I clenched the wheel tighter and slowed down, trying to focus on the dotted lines of the street to avoid going over the edge.

Finally, when it seemed I'd reached the bottom, I sped up again, spotting a car at the end of the road. I followed it, desperate to find a town. The license plate said *New England State*. I was still relatively close to home.

The car pulled over. I sped right by it, turning left, then right. A sign was up ahead. I pressed on the gas pedal to see what it was. At the same moment, I noticed the car I'd passed following me—a red sedan. Its high beams glared against my side mirror; they flicked on and off as though to get my attention.

I sped faster and wrenched the wheel, making a sharp turn down a narrow road. The Jeep tilted onto its side. I braced myself for a crash, but the Jeep smacked down on all four tires, and I came to a halt.

Loose items—a soda can, a handful of coins—tossed inside the car, rattled against the windows. Something hard pelted the side of my head.

I took a deep breath, trying to get my bearings. The car was gone now. I heard its screech from down the street. I stepped on the gas pedal, eager to keep moving.

At last I'd found it.

A tiny town.

I blinked hard, but still the town remained. This wasn't just a dream or mirage. Two streetlamps shone over a mini-mart, a post office, and a police station. If it weren't for the illuminated *P* of the police sign, I'd have sworn it was a ghost town.

I pulled up beneath the *P,* flung open the Jeep door, and headed inside.

NOW

49

After a couple of weeks of visiting Brave, I take her on a walk around the shelter building, inside the gate. I could just as easily let her off the leash and give her free rein inside the yard, since no other dogs are out right now, but she needs to learn to walk with others. This is part of the process, not so much unlike mine.

She has to learn to trust people too. Up until now, she probably hasn't had much reason to trust, but I've been trying to change that with routine visits, where I bring her treats and listen to her barking.

She's listens to me too. I've been starting most of my sessions by sitting outside her cage and telling her about Mason—about his visits to the wall and how much I relied on them. "Sometimes I imagine I can still hear his voice," I tell her. "Inside my head, when I'm deep in sleep, I can hear him telling me it'll all be okay, that I'm stronger than I think, and that he cares about me too."

I let Brave lead me around the shelter property, wondering what would happen if I didn't show up for days. Would she eventually get sick, just as I did? Would she lie awake, anticipating the clank of the dog wing door, the way I did Mason's knock? And wait to hear my footsteps approaching her cage, only to be disappointed when it wasn't me? The possibility of that dependency is just one of the things that keeps me coming back.

Brave and I do several laps before I bring her back inside. The dog lounge is empty—the perfect time to go in. She isn't ready for socialization yet, but she still can get used to the space by smelling the scents of the other dogs.

I unhook her leash and let her roam free just as my phone vibrates with a text from Jack.

Jack: *Any chance you're free today?*

Me: *I'm at the shelter.*

Jack: *Until when? It'll just take a bit.*

Me: *What will?*

Jack: *Can I meet you somewhere after your shift? I have something I want to give you.*

I watch Brave lick the corner of a pull toy—slowly, cautiously, and from different angles—as though testing to see if it might spontaneously combust. When she's sure it won't, she takes the toy into her mouth and carries it to a corner of the room, where she gnaws on the rubberized handle.

A series of question marks appear on the chat screen. Jack is waiting for my reply. I know he means well, but, like Brave, I don't feel ready for socialization either.

Me: *Maybe some other time.*

Jack: *Please. I promise, it won't take long.*

Me: *OK.*

Me: *How about 4?*

Jack: *Perfect. Anyplace you want.*

Me: *Hilltop Park?*

Jack: *Perfect again. I'll see you then.*

The park is just a block from the shelter and is usually bustling with power walkers, track team runners, baby strollers, coffee drinkers . . . We can sit on one of the benches, apart from the action, but still be surrounded by people.

With my phone gripped firmly in my hand, I count the steps all the way there (eighty-four). Jack is already sitting and waiting on the bench by the swings. He waves when he sees me. I wave back, wanting to feel excitement, but overwhelmed with trepidation.

"Hey," he says, standing as I approach. His gaze goes to my shoulders, and he inclines slightly forward as though he wants to hug me (because we used to hug all the time). But then he backs away, knowing better, wanting to make me comfortable.

I take a seat. He does too, leaving about eighteen inches between us.

"Thanks for coming to meet me," he says. "How are you doing?"

I open my mouth to give him my stock answer: *fine, not bad.*

But then: "I'm sorry," he says. "That's an obnoxious question, isn't it? A better one would be: How was your lunch?"

"My lunch?"

"Yeah, isn't that a much more interesting question? What did you have?"

"A bagel with avocado."

"And was it good?"

"Delicious." I smile—a genuine one.

"See that?"

"Maybe *you* should be my therapist. Between good questions and amazing letters . . ."

"Do you *need* a therapist?"

"My mother insists, but personally, I think they all suck."

"It's true. I'll bet that if you lined up ten shrinks, only one or two of them would be any good. I speak from experience; I went through six before finally finding my lucky number seven. You should've met number four. The guy actually fell asleep, mid-session."

"You're lying."

"No joke. The guy snored so loud; it sounded like a vacuum."

"That's horrible."

"For him or me? But then, three shrinks later, I met Dr. Jim, who really helped me figure stuff out. Plus, he never fell asleep and didn't constantly scratch his groin like therapist number two."

"You're kidding."

"Who'd kid about that? I didn't know where to look."

"Lately, I've been using writing as my main therapy source."

"Writing *what?*"

"My story, what happened—the during, the after . . ."

"The after?"

I nod. "It's not all ice cream and roses. It's scary and confusing, and sometimes even more isolating . . . Anyway, writing it all down—chronicling 'the then' and 'the now' . . . It's just my way of trying to process everything and make sense of it somehow."

"And how's it going?"

"Depends on the day—like everything else, I guess."

"Do you plan to ever share your writing?"

"Maybe one day."

"Well, I'll be first in line if and when you do." His gaze falls to my hand resting in my lap.

I look down at it too, noticing how pronounced my scars look in the sunlight. I pull my sleeve down over them.

"So I have something for you," he segues, reaching into his backpack. He hands me a brown paper lunch bag.

"You brought me food," I say, peeking inside. I pull out a square wrapped package, but it isn't food. It's a music CD: Gigi Garvey.

"From her concert tour," Jack says.

"The concert tour I missed."

"The one we both missed. But no big deal; we'll just catch the next one. And in the meantime, you have this." He flips the CD over. Gigi Garvey's signature is scribbled across the front, along with the words *Stay brave, Sweet Jane. Love, Gigi.*

I clasp my hand over my mouth.

"Do you have a CD player?" he asks. "I wasn't sure, but I couldn't pass it up, even if you didn't. I figured you'd be able to play it somehow."

"I'm sure my parents have one somewhere."

"Well, then, good." He smiles. "Because you're seriously going to love it."

I run my fingers over the inscription, wondering if Jack told her what to write, or if she heard about my story. "How did you even do this?" I ask him.

"I have my ways."

"This is so unbelievably . . ." I shake my head, too over-whelmed to even process what this feels like: glee, regret, self-pity, gratitude . . .

"You're welcome," he says. "And it wasn't unbelievably any-thing. It was just necessary. Those are some classic tunes on there. You *need* them. It's not a choice."

Words of thanks swim inside my mind but never make it to my mouth. Instead, a surge of blood rushes from my head, and I clench the edge of the bench.

"Jane? Are you okay?"

Not okay. I take a moment to breathe. It's all too much. And I have no idea why. My face flashes hot, but my insides are shiv-ering.

"I'm sorry," I tell him, feeling like a complete and utter flake.

"Do you want some water?" He fishes for his wallet. "There's a vendor by the basketball court."

"No. I should be fine." I rise from the bench. The ground feels slightly tilted. "Thank you for the CD, but I have to go."

"I'll walk you." He stands up too.

"I'll be okay," I tell him, turning away, exiting the park, hating myself every single step, especially when I realize that I didn't take the CD. I left it on the bench as though I don't even want it, when, in reality, there's nothing I want more.

NOW

50

Hours later, cuddled up in bed, I send Jack a text. Luckily, he responds right away.

Me: *I'm really sorry about earlier.*

Jack: *No need to apologize.*

Me: *Yes, there is. I freaked out, and I'm not even sure why.*

Jack: *Trust me. It's OK.*

Me: *And on top of acting freakish, I left the CD, like a complete idiot!*

Jack: *It's fine. No worries.*

Me: *You're way too nice.*

Jack: *I can drop the CD off in your mailbox sometime soon, OK?*

Me: *Thank you so much again.*

Me: *Seriously . . .*

Jack: *No problem.*

Jack: *Good night, Jane.*

Me: *Night.* ☺

51

The walls of the police station were lined with flyers—for no smoking, town meetings, voter registration, and rules for dog licensing . . .

I hobbled toward the front desk. To my complete and utter shock, Ms. Romer, my health teacher, was seated behind it. She didn't see me at first—too busy typing away on a laptop. I approached her slowly, as though she were an apparition and going too fast might scare her away.

Her head snapped up. I noticed the red glasses first, then the wrinkled skin and the sunken cheeks. It wasn't Ms. Romer. I took a step back.

"Can I help you?" she asked.

Help me? A mental block formed inside my brain. It wasn't a trick question. "I need to talk to someone . . ." My voice sounded hoarse. "A police officer. A friend is in trouble."

The woman's gaze landed on my bandage job—the blood-splotched T-shirt. My fingers were bloody too—dried drips, encrusted nails. I flashed her the chunk of glass lodged into my palm.

The woman stood up and signaled to an officer in the cubicle behind her—an older, wiry guy who reminded me of Mr. Yeager, my old bio teacher. Why did everyone look familiar?

Even me.

My old face.

Tacked up on the wall.

I took a few steps closer to the flyer. The photo had been taken at the track banquet last spring, when I'd flat-ironed my hair. The words MISSING PERSON cut across my neck, stealing my breath.

"I'm going to have you speak with Officer Jones," the woman said, buzzing me through a locked door behind the front desk.

Officer Jones introduced himself. His eyes searched my wounds—my face, my hands, my shoulders. And suddenly I wanted to hide. I followed him down a hallway into a tiny room.

"You can take a seat," he said.

"My friend needs help," I insisted, picturing Mason trapped somewhere—stuck inside an air duct or locked in a secret room.

"It looks like you could use some help yourself," he said, nodding to my hands. The one with the glass absolutely throbbed. "We've already called a medic," he continued.

"But there isn't time."

"This is just standard procedure. Have yourself a seat, and I'll be right back."

I stood with one leg out the door. A fake wood table and four metal folding chairs sat in the center of the room. A mirror was built into the wall; it was the two-way kind. I caught a glimpse of my reflection—of the dirt on my face, the cut below my eye, and the heap of hair on my head. When had I gotten the slash across my cheek? A six-inch red mark.

"*Hello?*" the officer asked. He was sitting at the table now. When had he come back? "The medic will be here shortly. Now, can you tell me your name?"

I sat down across from him. The tip of his pen angled against a notebook page, ready to write. He gazed back up when I didn't answer right away.

"Jane Anonymous."

His eyes locked on mine, and his upper lip twitched. "Can you please repeat that?"

"My name? It's Jane Anonymous."

He got up and darted from the room, returning a few moments later with a female cop. She looked too young to be an officer; maybe she'd just graduated from the police academy.

"My name is Sergeant Mercer," she said. "And you are?"

"Jane Anonymous," I repeated; hadn't the Jones guy told her? "My friend Mason is in trouble."

"Jane Anonymous from Suburban Town, New England State?"

"Yes."

She slid out the chair beside mine. I didn't want her to sit next to me, but she did it anyway, proceeding with questions that wasted my time and kept Mason in danger. "What are your parents' names?"

"*Didn't you hear me?*"

"What are your parents' names, Jane?"

I took a deep breath, hating this game, desperate to leave. *Tick tock, tick tock.* The feet of her chair scraped the floor, making a grating sound that sent shivers down my spine.

"*Jane?* Your parents' names?"

"John and Mary."

"And you're a student at—"

"No Name High—at least that's where I used to go."

"What year are you in school?"

I peered down at the glass in my hand. My fingertips looked gray. Where was that medic? "I should be a senior. What month is it?"

"You don't know the month?"

Why else would I ask? "Where am I, even?"

"It's March," she said. "And you're in Berkshire Town, New England State."

Three hours from home.

Seven months gone.

What time was it again?

"Where have you been for the past several months?" she asked.

"In a building, locked up in a room."

"If it's okay, I'd like to take you into one of our interview rooms."

"It's not okay. My friend needs help." Why did I come here?

"Okay, let's go to the interview room and get all of the details so that we can help your friend. In the meantime, would you like anything? Water, soda, something to eat? I know we've got someone coming to check out your wounds."

"You aren't hearing me."

"I am," she said, sticking her face in mine, overly confident I wouldn't bite.

"Mason needs help," I snapped. "He's back there. I left without him."

"Wait, who's back there?" Jones asked.

"*Mason!*" I shouted. Why weren't they listening? "He's back at the building. I couldn't find his room."

"Which building? Where is it?"

"Let's take a deep breath." Sergeant Mercer breathed for me— in an out, a new form of torture.

I wanted to strangle her.

"There's no need to rush," she said.

The hell there wasn't. "Mason's still back there. You have to find him."

"We *want* to find him, but you have to help us too. Is there anything you can tell us about the place you were being kept? Anything notable—cars, building, or house color? Distinguishable architecture or landscape?"

"It was up in the mountains." I spiraled down like a funnel. "There were woods all around, and a pickup truck, plus a horse ranch."

"A building on a mountain?" Mercer's forehead furrowed.

"Maybe it was a house." Hadn't I remembered thinking that? When I'd gotten up to the second floor and seen the kitchen and the living room—that it'd looked like a normal residence. There was a back porch. "Wasn't there?"

"Wasn't there *what?*" Mercer asked.

"A back porch."

She jotted down the detail and added a bubbly question mark, which annoyed me just as much as her perfectly manicured nails.

"How did you get *here?*"

"I drove. Someone saw me. The lights went on." My mind raced; my words couldn't keep up. *Where was my coil spring? No longer in the waist of my pants.* "Did anyone report a stolen Jeep?"

Bingo.

The right answer.

Someone ran to check; I heard the clobber of footsteps.

"So let me get this straight," Jones began, "you were being held captive at the residence of a Jeep owner. Is that where you believe your friend still is?"

"I need to go."

"Please answer the question."

"No!" I shouted. "The horse ranch was somewhere nearby. At least, I think it was a horse ranch. There was a corral maybe and a paved street. A pathway in the woods took me to the house; it was behind a stone wall."

"The house with the corral was behind the wall," Jones said to clarify.

I think I nodded. I know I got up and went for the door. The knob turned.

A third officer stopped me. His chest was like a wall. Still, I pushed against him, my wrists aching, my fingers tingling, imagining he was the monster—with his wavy hair and olive-toned skin. He grabbed my forearms and restrained me from behind, pinning me in place, flashing me back.

"Just relax," the officer said. "I'm not going to hurt you."

The monster had said the same. *"I'm not going to hurt you."*

Shelley's voice came next: *He's not going to hurt you.*

Mom always told me: *"No one intentionally wants to hurt you."*

Ms. Romer constantly reminded us: *"If you're smart, you won't get hurt."*

I opened my mouth to bite, wanting to sink my teeth deep into the monster's flesh. But my mouth filled with the cloth from my bandage. There was a sweet, metallic taste. And a lavender scent: the smell of the detergent the monster liked to use when he washed my laundry, when I snuggled up in fresh sheets.

I squeezed my eyes shut, imagining the bright white wall and my bright white bed, and Mason's *knock, knock-knock, tap, thud.*

Knock.

Knock-knock.

Tap.

Thud.

When I opened my eyes again, I was still in the hallway, but crouched on the floor. The officer's arms were still restraining me. Had much time passed? *Did I somehow fall asleep?*

"You're safe now," a male voice said.

The words churned inside my belly, because *safe* wasn't here. These people weren't helping. No one was listening.

"Jane? I'm here to help you." Another voice. A female one; it had a soft, melodic tone.

I saw her tan suede boots—the shearling kind. My gaze traveled as far as her knee. Blue jeans, the fringe of a purple scarf. Not a police uniform. She'd been called in. Just for me.

The T-shirt still balled up inside my mouth, I crammed it in deeper—way down my throat—creating a gag reflex.

Fingers poked at my lips, pulled at the cloth. Voices continued, talking as though I weren't there, were no longer conscious:

"She's hyperventilating."

"She's going to pass out."

"She needs a little something."

She.

She.

She.

Because even they knew: I was no longer me.

THEN

52

When I opened my eyes again, a white wall faced me. My sheets were white too, and so was my pillow. I rolled over in bed and stared up at the bright white ceiling, wondering if it'd all been a dream—busting through the wall, escaping from the room, grappling through the woods, and finding the Jeep.

I rolled over in bed. The motion stirred the covers. Something hit the floor with a clatter. The coil spring? The toilet rod?

"Jane?" Mom's voice. She rose from a chair. Her hand clasped over her mouth.

I sat up. I was in a hospital. A TV hung from the wall. A table was at my side; on it was a box of tissues and a potted plant. The leaves were red, yellow, and pointed; they reminded me of poison ivy.

Mom's mouth moved to form words, but only cries came out—soft, pleading whimpers, like a wounded bird, like she'd broken her wings.

"Jane?" she repeated, shaking her head as tears streaked down her face.

Was she happy or sad? I couldn't tell. I could only feel a sense of confusion. What had happened? Where was Mason?

Mom continued to cry.

An overwhelming urge to make things better cauterized my every emotion. "It's okay," I insisted. "I'm in one piece." *Just broken into bits.*

Mom looked broken too—smaller than I remembered, fragile like a finch—with rounded shoulders and lines that cracked her face. When had she gotten so many wrinkles?

"How did I get here?" I tried to grab at the ache in my head, discovering my hands had been bandaged. The glass had been removed. "Do I have stitches?" I tried to remember the sequence of events—looking into the two-way mirror, breaking down at the police station, seeing the pair of shearling boots . . . Had I passed out? Or did someone give me an injection?

Mom dropped her keys; her hands wouldn't stop shaking. I recognized her dress: navy blue with a belted waist and a scoop neck, the same one she'd reserved for jury duty or parent meetings.

She sat at the foot of my bed, as though any closer might've caused me pain. I wanted to ask if she knew anything about Mason, but before I could, she folded forward on the bed. Her tiny shoulders jittered. Thick, hungry sobs spouted from her mouth as though someone had died. Maybe that someone was me.

"Where's Dad?" I asked.

"He'll be here," she uttered, rubbing my leg beside my knee like a genie's lamp, as though the old me might magically emerge.

"*Mom?*" I asked.

The rubbing got harder. A gurgling noise sputtered from her lips like she was choking on her own spit. She sat up. Her mouth stretched wide, and she began to wheeze—a gasping-sucking sound. Her hands pressed against her chest, over her heart.

I looked toward the door. It was closed. My face flashed hot. A call switch sat on the table. I punched it with my bandaged hand—again and again. Mom's eyes locked on mine; the pupils appeared dilated. Her tongue inched out, between her teeth.

"Please!" I shouted, tearing out of bed, going for the door.

A nurse intercepted and went for backup.

A wheelchair was rolled in.

My mother was rolled out.

And just like that, I was alone again, in a stark white room.

THEN

53

I wasn't alone for long. A woman came into the room—midthirties, sleek black hair. She was dressed in a steel-gray suit. Her skin was the color of mocha. Behind her was an older guy—gray hair, dark suit, at least fiftysomething.

"Good morning," the woman said, extending her hand for a shake. "I'm Special Agent Ann Thomas, and this is Special Agent Nathan Brody."

"How are you doing?" he asked.

I looked toward the windows, but the shades were drawn closed. "What time is it?"

The woman peeked at her watch. "It's 8:30 a.m. I'd like to ask you some questions, if that's okay."

"How is my mother?"

"She'll be fine. They've got her in a room."

"And my dad?"

"Last I heard, he'd boarded a plane and should be here later this morning." She pulled a chair from the corner—the one my mother had used—and sat down beside me, leaving the guy to stand. "He was away on business when he got the call that you were found."

"I escaped," I said, correcting her.

"Right." She mustered a smile.

The guy pulled a second chair from the hall and sat by the door, taking a notebook and pen from his jacket.

"Is Mason still there?" I asked. "Did you find him . . . or any of the others?"

"The good news is that we managed to find the location of the place where you were being kept."

"And Mason?"

She shook her head. "Who *is* Mason? Could you tell me about him? How you met? What he looked like?"

"He was taken, just like me. But I never saw him. He'd been sneaking around, inside air ducts, traveling all over the building, trying to find a way out. We used to talk through the wall. Sometimes we held hands."

"I see." She nodded. "So there was a hole in the wall?"

"Didn't you find it? It was tiny, though, like for a mouse, so maybe you didn't see it."

"We found a wall that'd been pretty smashed up. Know anything about that?"

Oh, right. "I did that." I gazed at my bandaged hands, both of them well padded in hospital gauze. Only the tips of my fingers were visible.

"Pretty impressive."

"Did you also find the air ducts? They were up in the ceiling tiles."

"We're working on it, still investigating the space."

How much time had passed?

More than twelve hours.

"Didn't you find the other rooms where people were being kept?" I asked. "Were any clues left behind?"

"Do you know Mason's last name?"

"Um, no." I took a deep breath. Were those blades inside my chest?

"How about where he was from?"

"He said he grew up on a farm, that his father used to raise chickens and bees and sell eggs and honey."

"Locally?"

"I'm not really sure. I mean, I think so."

"Do you know how old he was?"

"Nineteen, but he wasn't in school . . . unless Life School counts—traveling and sightseeing . . ."

"Do you know how he got there—how he was taken, I mean?"

"He was taken from a party."

"Whose party? What happened?"

I told her the full story—about the girl named Haley and how the monster had duped Mason by goading him outside to check out a Camaro that didn't exist.

After a slew of questions about said party, Agent Thomas asked, "Is there anything else you can share about Mason that you think would help us?"

I gazed toward her watch. *Tick tock, tick tock.* How much more time had passed?

"*Jane?* Is there anything else you can share?"

"Just that if it weren't for him, I probably wouldn't even be here right now."

Her eyebrow raised. "What makes you say that?"

"Haven't you been listening? He risked his life to be with me, to offer me hope, to get me things I needed."

"He was a faithful companion."

"You make him sound like a dog."

"That wasn't my intention."

"Your intention should be to find him."

"As I said, we're working on it. We have a team of investigators going over every square inch of the place. If he's there, we'll find him. You can trust me on that. Now, if it's okay with you, I'd like to switch gears."

It wasn't okay. I wanted them to leave. The guy sitting behind her—Special Agent Something—was feverishly taking notes, recording my every word.

"Could you tell me what happened on the morning of Sunday, August 11?" she asked.

What day was that? My face scrunched in confusion, but then the answer finally clicked: Sunday, August 11, was the day that I was taken.

I methodically went over the details—from the rain that day to the boxes of honeycomb candles. I told her about the car trunk and waking up in a daze, able to see the guy's face—his brown eyes, the mole on his lower lid . . . I also talked about my days in the room, with little interaction aside from talking to Mason.

By the time she was finished, there'd been two hours' worth of questions.

No, the monster didn't come into the room.

No, I didn't know who he was or why he took me.

Yes, he may've looked slightly familiar that day at Norma's, but I'm not really sure.

No, he didn't touch me in any weird way, as far as I knew. There was only the obvious contact made during the abduction.

No, I didn't see him after that first night and have no idea what his intentions were.

Yes, there were others. I heard their screaming. I found a note scribbled on a bathroom tile. Mason had also spoken to a girl named Samantha.

Finally, when it seemed she was somewhat satisfied, she stood up. "I'm going to have an artist come in to do a sketch of the suspect. Someone will also be coming to give you a thorough physical exam."

"And you'll let me know when you have news about Mason."

"You bet." She smiled.

I curled up on my side. My stomach grumbled for food. It took me a bit to notice the tray on my table and the white plastic dishes, just like in the room. I lifted the dome-like lid, uncovering a biscuit and sausage patty, both drizzled with gravy the consistency of sludge. It made me want to heave. I needed something bland, craving the toast I'd had in captivity, with the crusty ends.

Some guy knocked on my door. He was holding a pad of paper. "Jane Anonymous?"

He sat beside me without waiting for a response.

With my descriptions, he sketched the face of the guy who took me. He also drew the tree tattoo. "Someone will be back to have you look at photos. We're also getting a computer composite done."

"Was that guy caught on surveillance camera?" I asked. "Have you heard anything about Mason?"

No.

And *no.*

My head wouldn't stop aching. My bandaged hands itched.

Not long after he left, Special Agents Thomas and Brody came back. They had me detail, once again, every single speck of Sunday, August 11, that I could recall, right down to the fabric of the romper I pulled off the hanger in my struggle to escape (silk, for the record).

After that, a nurse came in for my physical exam. Without uttering a single sound, she poked and prodded, inspecting every inch of my skin, my back, my teeth, my scalp.

My every.

Single.

Open and exposed space.

And when she was done, I rolled over in bed, facing away from the window. My insides shook. I couldn't stop trembling. I imagined ice water inside my veins, that that's what the nurse got when she took my blood: a vial of coldness, like from inside a corpse.

I closed my eyes, trying to forget where I was. Eventually, I fell asleep and dreamed about Mason—about holding his hand through the hole in the wall.

When I woke up, hours later, I could still feel the heat in the center of my palm, as though he were really, truly there. I snuggled up in the sheets, keeping my eyes closed, wishing the sensation were real. Was it so far-fetched to believe the investigators found him and brought him to my bedside?

I opened my eyes to check, startled to find Dad there, sitting at my side.

"Hey, sunshine," he said. My old nickname. It no longer fit. He squeezed my hand. There were tears in his eyes. "Thank God you're back." He scooted closer and wrapped his arms around me.

Since when did he talk to God? Why had he never introduced me?

He stroked my matted hair. I still hadn't showered. He smelled like ground coffee beans—like the kind he used to buy, kept secure in the silver tin.

"I got here as soon as I could," he said.

Memories played on a projector screen inside my head:

Dad scratching my back, on the living room sofa, when I was five years old and couldn't sleep because of a bad case of poison sumac.

Me, learning to tie, using red string licorice, making knots on my father's wrists while he read me fairy tales.

And me, sitting by the hole, while Mason asked me questions

about why my father had stayed in bed on the morning that I went missing:

"*He'd been working until midnight the night before,*" *I'd explained.*

"*But you said you were taken on a Sunday. Does your dad work Saturdays?*"

"*He'd started to.*"

"*Let me guess. Does he work in a hospital? Or at a twenty-four-hour call center?*"

"*He works in a bank.*"

"Seriously? *A bank?*"

"*Yeah. Why?*"

"*Doesn't that strike you as a little weird . . . working until midnight at a bank? Is it a twenty-four-hour branch?*"

An awkward pause had followed.

"Jane?" Dad asked.

I pulled away, breaking the embrace. A nurse stood at the door, her eyes wide and expectant, as though something magical were about to happen. She was hoping for a show. I could see it in the parting of her lips and the clasping of her hands. To her, this was like something you'd see on TV: a father reuniting with his long-lost daughter. For me, the memories wove a quilt that suffocated any possibility of goodness.

"I don't mean to interrupt," the nurse said. "Jane, could I get you a snack or something to drink?"

"Have you heard anything?" I asked her.

"*Heard anything?*" she repeated. Her smile faded.

"About Mason," I said.

"*Mason?*" Dad's face was a giant puzzle. He was two steps behind.

I didn't have time to catch him up. "*Has anyone heard from Mason?*" I snapped.

She turned away and left the room without a word. What did that mean?

"*What does that mean?*" I shouted, getting up from the bed.

Dad got up too, as though to stop me, but I was already in the doorway. The nurse stood at the desk.

"Do you know something?" I asked her. "Why won't you tell me?"

Dad reached out to touch my bandaged arm, but I snatched it away. "Bring the detectives back!" I shouted.

"It's going to be okay," Dad said. "You just need to get some rest."

"I've been gone for seven months. How would you know what I need?"

Dad took a step back like I'd just slapped him in the face. I went out into the hall, searching for one of the agents.

Another nurse trailed me. "You need to go back to your room."

I needed to get out.

I pushed open an exit door. A buzzer sounded. Someone grabbed me from behind, wrapped his hand around my bicep.

Fingers pressed into my wrist.

Was that an elbow at my spine? A needle in my skin?

"*If only you were sneezing when that asshole took you, right?*" Mason's voice.

"So much for happy reunions." An unfamiliar voice.

"*Scratch, Daddy, scratch.*"

"I'm sorry," I said. At least I said it inside my head. I'm not sure if the words actually hit the air. I was sorry for feeling suffocated, for not thanking God too, and for breaking the embrace after licorice-lace fairy tales and poison sumac dreams.

54

I sit up in bed, unable to sleep. I keep tossing and turning. My legs won't stop itching. I pull up on the length of my pajama bottoms. The hair on the front of my legs is a few inches long now. I run my palms over the skin, creating a sensation of déjà vu.

When have I felt this before? The tugging of calf hair as I stroke toward my knees? The tingling of nerves as I continue over my thighs? A mix of pain and pleasure that feels eerily familiar.

It takes a few moments before I notice what I've done: scratched bright red track marks across my skin. They're littered with bloodred pinpoints. No razors necessary. When one is this broken, the blood just comes. The memories seep in.

I go down the hall, step into the bathroom, and grab my razor on a mission to forget. I run the faucet and moisten every millimeter of skin, from ankle to knee, because this hair has to go.

My foot propped on the toilet seat, I shave it away in rows, imagining a tractor in a field, on a farm with chickens and baby lambs. The hair collects in the bowl, floats at the surface. I flush three times, eliminating the evidence.

There's no proof now.

Nothing to be remembered.

But still when I close my eyes, I picture a hand on my leg, stroking my calf. I see fingers making spirals over the kneecap. I feel a swell of heat spread across my thighs.

I look in the mirror and see the image of a victim. But a victim of what, exactly? Do I even want to know?

I grab a pair of scissors from inside the medicine cabinet and start to cut—first just a strand of hair, by my ear, then a solid chunk, enough to make a ponytail.

But it isn't enough. I still look the same.

I grab a fistful at the crown of my head and go to cut just as I hear the floorboards crack.

"Jane?" Mom's voice. She's standing in the doorway. Her gaze falls to the floor—to the clumps of hair that've fallen at my feet.

"Is everything okay?" she asks. The same stupid question.

"It's fine," I say, an equally stupid answer. Is the fire on my face visible to the eye? Didn't I close the door? Don't I remember turning the lock?

She takes a step closer. Her eyes go squinty as though it's too hard to look. "What are you doing?"

"Just giving myself a trim."

"You used to go to a salon."

I set the scissors down. "Could I go to one now?" I pull at my hair, eager to continue ridding.

"Anything you want." Mom smiles, just "happy" to make me "happy."

I ask if we can go to a place an hour away—as if miles make a difference when one is national news. Mom agrees, also playing along with my idea of making up stage names (since she's getting her hair done too) and paying in cash. And so, while I'm Jane Lane (because, why not), she's Veronica Lake, an old movie actress whose hair she envies.

I like Plum Salon from the moment I open the door. Everything inside is purple—walls, floors, ceilings, furniture—right down to the curling wands. While Mom gets whisked away for hair washing, I get seated with Maven, a stylist with ear spacers the size of quarters. A tall purple Mohawk divides her head in two.

She grabs the ends of the hair I hacked, where it's at least five inches shorter than all the rest. "What happened here? You lookin' to edge out, trying to self-start? Glad you thought twice and came to Ms. Maven. So what's your flavor?"

"My flavor?"

"You in the mood for the traditional chocolate or strawberry? Or something a bit more exotic, like peppermint stick or salted caramel pretzel?"

"Um, what?"

"Well, you've got this major mane." She holds the bulk of my hair in a ponytail. "Might as well pig out on it, right? Except, on second thought"—she gives my hair an extra feel— "we may have to err on the side of vanilla, at least a little . . . unless you're open to some serious deep conditioning, because, holy hemlocks, honey. I mean, no offense or anything, but what happened here? Your hair used to be in dreads or something? Is that what urged you to self-start?"

Maven makes no sense, but it doesn't even matter. What matters is that she doesn't know me—doesn't recognize me from the news or give a shit about how much time I spend in my room. To Maven, I'm nothing more than hair on a cone.

"So what's the verdict?" she asks.

I picture my old self, BIWM, with smooth, dark tresses and caramel-colored highlights. "I think we need to start fresh."

"As in losing some of this weight? How much are you feeling?"

"Can you cut off all the deadness?"

Maven's barbell-pierced eyebrow shoots straight up. "You sure? Because that's going to leave you short—like pixie short."

I nod, beyond ready to look like someone else—not the old me, but maybe a newer version of me, whoever that is, whatever that means.

"Okay, this could be fun." Maven cracks her knuckles. Her fingers are loaded with rubber rainbow rings that remind me of Life Savers. "We could do something totally 'rageous with color to funk it up. How bold are you feeling? Red, blue, pink, jet black?"

"Platinum," I say, nodding to a poster on the wall—a woman with her fists raised high, as though to fight. She looks as fierce as fuck. I suddenly want to be her.

"Hot," Maven agrees.

Once my hair is washed, I sit back in the chair and avoid looking at my face. Instead, I focus on the twelve inches of dead weight that gets severed from my head. In the end, my hair is about a half-inch all around, plus the palest shade of blond I've ever seen.

"Like it?" Maven asks.

I run my hand over the short, glowy layers. "Love it," I say, relieved to look like someone other than a victim. I get up and move toward the seating area, anxious to show my mom, and to see her hair as well. But I'm intercepted en route.

"Excuse me," a woman says. Ten-inch foil tentacles branch out from her scalp like a sci-fi version of Medusa. "I don't mean to intrude, but I've been watching you for a bit and . . . Are you that girl?"

"That *girl?*" I ask, knowing fully well what she means.

"Sorry." She laughs. "I've been wanting to ask if you were *that girl* from the moment I sat down."

I shake my head. A gut reaction, not the smartest response.

"The one on TV," she persists. "The girl that was taken . . ."

I shake my head some more. The room seems loud. Why is everyone staring? It takes me a beat to realize I've got my hands cupped over my ears.

The woman takes a step back as though to give me space. "I don't mean to . . . I just couldn't *not* come over here and tell you how brave I think you are. I followed your case; it was on all of the news channels . . ." She continues to blather on—something about her sister—but I only catch a few words: "—truly an inspiration."

If only she knew.

Or actually saw.

Or really listened.

Or thought before speaking.

"Jane?" My mother's voice. She's standing at my side now. Her hand slides over mine. I flinch at the sensation—like skin to fire.

Mom releases her grip and encircles my wrist instead. The next thing I know, she's leading me out the door onto the sidewalk; stone pavement rather than purple tile is suddenly beneath my feet.

We walk four full blocks as I count all my steps, imagining plucking tissues for each one.

One hundred ten tissues.

Collected on the ground.

Paving my way to normal breath.

Finally, I stop in front of a store. The exterior is shiny, with a mirror finish. I go right up, able to see my reflection. The birthmark on my neck is more visible now with this shorter cut. It's the size of a bumblebee and a perfect match to my dad's.

I search my face for more familiar features: my tiny earlobes, my pointed chin, and the pale blond freckles across the bridge of my nose. The scar below my eye is new, but so is my hair.

"Are you okay?" Mom asks. Her hair is suddenly the color of nutmeg.

"I will be," I mutter, almost believing it's the truth. A new cut, color, and blowout obviously aren't the cure-alls, but maybe they're a start. Like a symbolic shedding of skin, maybe they'll help me emerge into the person I'm supposed to become.

Or maybe not.

THEN

55

A long-legged spider slid down from the ceiling on its silken thread, stopping just inches above my chest. Lying in bed, I admired the spider's shimmering legs; they glistened in the air, reminding me of Christmas tree tinsel.

I couldn't help but wonder if the spider was Tiger, if he'd somehow followed me here to the hospital—crawled inside the hood of my sweatshirt to watch over me like a guardian angel.

"Tiger?" I asked, noting his shimmering brown stripes. I held out my finger to see if he would crawl onto my hand.

Tiger landed on my thumb, crept into the center of my palm, and wove a heart-shaped web.

"Jane?" Tiger asked, staring at me with his pearly black eyes. "Are you awake?"

"*Tiger?*" I repeated, excited he could talk.

"Jane?" A different voice—a female one.

"I think she's still sleeping," Tiger said.

A banging noise throttled my heart. A slamming trunk? I startled awake. My eyes snapped open.

Hovering over me were Special Agents Thomas and Brody—not Tiger the spider. There was no car trunk.

Special Agent Thomas sat down beside my bed. "Do you always talk in your sleep?"

Brody assumed his usual position at the door with a notebook.

I sat up, struggling to catch my breath. What had made that sound? "Did you find Mason?" I asked.

"That's why we're here."

"*You found him?*"

"Unfortunately, no. There's no sign of him."

"What do you mean *no sign?* Did you search inside the air ducts? Did you knock down walls?"

"We found a body," she said.

"*What?*" I blinked hard, digesting the word. "*Whose body? Where was it?*"

"We have reason to believe it's the body of the man who abducted you. It appears he shot himself. The wound looks self-inflicted."

"*What?* Are you sure?"

"I wouldn't have said anything if I wasn't sure. His fingerprints are all over the house—they're on all of the cups and bowls in your room, on the food trays, the doorknobs; they're all over the rooms upstairs . . . Plus, he matches your description."

"With the tree tattoo on his arms?"

"Except the tattoo," she said. "It isn't so uncommon for a perpetrator to fake a tattoo, a scar, or some other distinguishable marking."

"Like a wig, colored contacts, or glasses . . . ," Brody adds.

"Exactly," Agent Thomas says. "They do it to trick the victim."

"To trick them into what?" I grabbed at the throb in my head. I needed a moment to process.

"Let's replay the scenario," she said. "You escaped, came to us, described your abductor as having those tattoos. What if we held on to that detail? We'd only be looking for suspects with tattoos, regardless of whether or not the tattoo in question was fake. Thankfully, we now have scientific evidence: DNA. We don't have to rely on details that may or may not have been fabricated."

"And Mason's DNA?" Could it reveal some clue as to his whereabouts?

She fished in her pocket for a phone. "There's something I want to show you." She searched for a photo and then flashed me the screen: a picture of a note (a torn spiral notebook page with black block lettering).

PLEASE FORGIVE ME.
I NEVER MEANT TO HURT ANYONE.

"What do you think of this?" she asked.

"Where did you find it?"

"On a table, in the study—the one with the pocket door, almost concealed in the wall . . ."

"Did you find any signs of Mason in that room?"

"As I said, we didn't uncover any signs of Mason anywhere, which brings me to my next question. You mentioned before being in a building . . . a warehouse. What made you think that?"

"Because of how spread apart we all sounded."

"By 'we all,' do you mean those you believed were also being kept captive?"

I nodded. "Our voices sounded far apart—like on different floors. Plus, Mason said he'd gotten to the third floor of the building. He told me about a window with bars. Did you find it?"

"A barred window? No. The house is a traditional split-entry ranch. It consists of a main floor and a basement. A drop-down ladder leads to a small attic space for storage."

"Is there a window up there?"

"Yes, but not with bars."

Had Mason even said there were bars? Or was that something I made up? I'd been so out of it at the time—when he was telling me about the window. "Did you search the heating vents?" I asked yet again.

"There are no vents big enough to accommodate a full-sized person. Did you happen to notice the baseboard heating unit in your room . . . how tiny it was?"

"You must not have looked thoroughly. What about air filtration vents? In the drop-down ceiling . . . ?"

"*Jane . . .*"

"*What?*" My skin itched. Had someone cranked the heat?

"There are no traces of anyone else at that house—no fingerprints, no DNA, no articles of clothing or other personal belongings—other than the homeowner (the man who shot himself) and you."

My head fuzzed. "What does that mean?" What happened to the others? "Maybe they all escaped together—Mason and the others, I mean." But how would that explain the lack of fingerprints or DNA?

"We should take a break." She pocketed her phone. "Can I get you something to eat?"

"I don't need a break."

"I think you probably do." She stood up and nodded to Brody. He got up as well, tucked his notebook inside his pocket.

"Tell me," I insisted, picturing Mason in the house, balled up in the corner of some hidden room, completely unconscious, unable to answer anyone's call.

"We'll be back tomorrow," she said.

Tomorrow? What day was it? How long had I slept? "I want to talk now."

Agent Thomas grabbed the call switch and buzzed the nurse.

Some guy came in not two seconds later, wearing blue scrubs and a hospital name tag. "Is everything okay in here?"

Agent Thomas whispered to him as she left the room—something about the victim.

"Just relax," the guy said, checking my monitor. "How are you feeling? Would you like some hot tea?"

I slunk down on my pillow. My heart wouldn't stop palpitating. Behind my eyes was a steel cage, locking me in, keeping me out.

A few seconds later, my dad came into the room. I could hear his voice—could hear him and the nurse talking as though I weren't even there:

"I'll get her an extra blanket. Would you like something too? Water? Tea?"

"Thank you. Tea would be great."

"She could probably use some rest."

"Couldn't we all. I haven't slept in days."

"Tell me about it. This is a double for me. Oh, and FYI: Her last dose was a couple of hours ago, so she may still be a little groggy."

"I'll just sit and keep her company."

"Lucky girl."

Lucky.

Girl.

She, her, the victim.

Where was I?

No one asked.

THEN

56

When I woke up again, my parents were sitting on opposite corners of the hospital bed. The expressions on their faces made me think that someone had died.

"Did something happen?" I asked them.

"We should call the woman," Mom said.

"Call who?" I asked.

Mom's face wilted into a balled-up tissue.

Dad angled away from me. "We have to tell her."

Tell me what? I squeezed my eyes shut, picturing anchors strapped to my feet, pulling me underwater. Mason was down there too, beneath the surface. He swam to me. I wove my fingers with his.

It's going to be okay, Mason said. *You were always okay. That's what drew me to you.* He cradled my face in his hands and kissed my mouth, giving me his last breath.

I sat up with a jolt.

Special Agent Thomas was standing at the foot of my bed,

a dark red folder tucked beneath her arm. "Good morning, or *afternoon,* I should say." She checked her watch.

"Where's Mason?" I asked, noticing others were there too: Mom, Dad, Agent Brody, a nurse, and some other woman. Who was she?

Agent Thomas nodded to the nurse. Somehow, he knew that was his cue to leave.

"I can stay," said the woman, flashing an awkward smile. She wore a name badge I couldn't read, as well as a navy-blue suit that didn't quite fit; pants and sleeves too short, a blouse that hung too low.

"Would you like it if Ms. Davis stayed in the room?" Agent Thomas asked me.

I shook my head. Who was Ms. Davis? I wanted them all to go. Why were they even there? And why was the light so bright?

Dad: "I'm going to take a walk."

Mom: "I'll stay."

Ms. Davis: "I'll stop by a little later to check in."

Special Agent Thomas took her usual seat by my bed, while Mom sat in the corner, and Agent Brody took notes by the door.

How many more times?

Would we have to repeat.

This same scenario.

Before they would tell me about Mason?

"Did you find him?" I asked.

"We found some other things," she said.

"*What* other things?"

"Audio equipment. The voices we believe you heard while in captivity were from audio clips of people screaming . . . from horror movies and Halloween-centric playlists. We'll have you verify to be sure, but—"

"Wait, *what?*"

"It seems you were the only one in captivity."

"Aside from Mason."

"As I said before, we couldn't find evidence that anyone, except for you and the suspect, were in that house."

"Have you looked for fingerprints inside the air ducts? I didn't think so." Why were they wasting my time?

"We found something else." She pulled a photo from her folder: a picture of the emerald bracelet—the one the monster had pretended to buy. Beside the bracelet was a silver box and a purple ribbon.

"Have you seen this before?" Agent Thomas asked.

"It's from Norma's Closet."

"It was in the suspect's office. We found the bracelet wrapped up on his desk." She showed me a photo of the tag attached. It had my name written across it, as well as the words *Love always, Mason*.

"How did Mason get this bracelet?"

"The suspect's name was Martin Gray."

Agent Thomas pulled out another photo: a picture of the guy who took me, the one from Norma's. The photo only showed him from the shoulders up, but still I recognized his dark brown eyes, his wavy hair, and his squarish chin.

"Do you recognize this man?" she asked.

"That's him," I said.

"The man who abducted you?"

"Yes."

"Martin Gray was twenty-four years old, had one prior felony, and owned the house where you were being kept. Was that day at Norma's the first time you ever saw him? Or might you have seen him sometime before that?"

I shook my head. "I'm not really sure."

"Are you saying that you *may have seen* the suspect *prior* to the day he took you?"

"I'm saying that I've racked my brain—for the past seven months—trying to remember if I knew him from someplace or saw him somewhere . . . But I just don't know."

"We'll have more pictures for you to look at. Maybe one of them will jog your memory."

Did I even trust my memory?

"The house had been passed down to the suspect when his father died years ago," she continued. "According to a neighbor, the mother left some years before that. We're still trying to create a timeline and find the mother's whereabouts. It seems things went downhill shortly after her departure, when the father started drinking."

"How do you know all this?"

"The house had been a working farm at one point," Agent Thomas said. "The owners had supplied eggs and honey to local farm stands and suppliers. They'd also sold produce and baked goods. Does any of this ring a bell?"

"No," I lied. They'd gotten things wrong, twisted all around.

"In the suspect's office, we found more items: pictures of you, some poetry you'd published in the school's literary magazine." She read from a list. "There was also a green scarf, a pair of mittens, a red hair comb . . . We'd like to see if you can ID some of the items."

"A green scarf," I said, thinking aloud, remembering having lost a cashmere one, the color of spearmint. I had a red comb too, but I was pretty sure it was in my running bag, back home.

"There's one last thing before we call this a day." Agent Thomas took another photo from the folder: a picture of Mason's hand.

I recognized the scar on his thumb, his crooked fourth finger, the deep creases of his knuckles, and the honey-colored hair that sprouted from his wrist, where there was also a spray of freckles.

My eyes welled up. "You *did* find him."

Agent Thomas shook her head. "This is a photo of the suspect's hand, the owner of the house, the man who shot himself."

"No," I argued, shaking my head.

She looked back at my mom, which was obviously the cue; Mom came and joined me on the bed.

"This isn't right," I told them. "I'm not giving up. As soon as I'm out of here, I'm going to look for Mason."

"For now, you should rest," Mom said, pressing the nurse's call switch. Time to drug me up some more.

57

I spent the next several weeks in the mental health wing of the hospital, where I met a handful of therapists, all of varying age, at varying points in their careers. But still their messages were mostly the same: *I'd been through a lot. The mind is an amazing coping device; it compartmentalizes the truth until we're ready to accept it. It was okay to be angry, as long as my anger was directed at the right person.* As soon as I'd direct it elsewhere—at the police, at myself, at my parents, at Shelley—the therapist would start to write.

The nurse would soon come in.

I'd be given more meds.

Another day would get added to my stay.

One morning, after group, yet another therapist came into my room. She was younger than the others, so I thought I'd give her a try. She wore red Doc Martens, in lieu of old lady nurse clogs, so I wondered if she marched to her own beat. She brought me a bottle of purple nail polish, because she'd clearly done her homework. And so when she asked me about Mason, I told her the truth:

"I really, really miss him."

"What do you miss the most?"

"The way he made me feel—like everything else could've been wrong in my world, and it obviously was, but he made me feel like it wasn't."

"It sounds like you two really had a connection."

I grabbed my pillow and hugged it to my middle, relieved it seemed she believed that he existed. Not all of the therapists did.

"Would you say that you loved him?" She scooted closer in the chair, making a scraping sound against the floor. "I ask because sometimes we feel protective of the ones we love."

"Okay, but obviously I *didn't* protect him."

"Did you love him?" she asked again.

Love? "I don't know. I'm not really sure." Did I? I think I did.

"Did your relationship ever get physical?"

"We never actually saw one another. We talked through a wall."

"But your file says you touched."

"Hands," I clarified. "We touched and held hands."

"Are you sure that's all it was?" She stared at me—*hard*—studying my every blink, shudder, and twitch. "I only ask because physical contact tends to imprint itself on the brain, intensifying whatever emotions we're experiencing at the time. Experts say these imprints are even more pronounced in the female brain, explaining why some girls get particularly attached to a partner after physical intimacy."

"We held hands," I repeated.

She continued to study me, her eyes narrowing into slits, as though I were bacteria in a petri dish about to morph into something mutant. "Have you *ever* been physically intimate?"

I grabbed another pillow, subconsciously erecting a wall. "Well, I've dated before."

"And so maybe you can relate."

"*Relate?*"

"When you've engaged in past relationships . . . with a former boyfriend, for example . . . did you find that your emotional feelings intensified with physical intimacy?"

What was she doing?

How was this relevant?

"There's nothing to feel ashamed of," she insisted. "Did you and Mason ever touch beyond just hand-holding?"

Didn't I already answer that question?

"Okay, let's put a pin in that question and move on to another," she said. "Did Mason ever engage in conversations that made you second-guess some of your other relationships?"

"What other relationships?"

"Those with your friends, your parents, your teachers, a boyfriend . . . Because it wouldn't have been uncommon for someone like him to ask you pointed or loaded questions regarding those you care about. It would've been his way of trying to manipulate those relationships—to change the way you feel about them."

Someone like him?

"Think about it," she continues. "Did he ask any questions that made you reconsider someone's character?"

Did he?

"It would've been a way for him to make you feel as though he were the only worthy, reliable person in your life," she said.

"Okay."

"Okay, *and . . .*"

I looked toward the door, desperate to leave, wanting some air. Sweat dripped down the back of my neck. "I don't think he did that."

"You don't *think,* but you're not sure? Have you ever heard of something called Stockholm syndrome?"

I had. We read a book in English class about a soldier who was taken hostage. By the end of the book, when the soldier could've escaped, he no longer wanted to because he cared too much about the man who'd held him captive. "That's not *this*."

"What do you think *this* is?"

I turned away, faced the wall, and grabbed a box of tissues.

"Rome wasn't built in a day," she continued, "so we'll just start brick by brick. Sound good?"

I didn't answer.

"I'll be back tomorrow," she said.

Four, pluck. Five, pluck. There was no way—*six, pluck*—I was going—*seven, pluck*—to talk to that woman ever again—*eight, pluck.*

When I told my mother she'd been assigned to me, had made me uncomfortable and probed into my dating history, my mother donned her superwoman cape, just like old times, and saved the day by having me released and threatening to sue, saying the woman had tried to violate my privacy.

Before we left, I changed into the clothes she'd brought for me: purple sweats, plain cotton underwear, and a new pair of Uggs. "Thank you," I told her on the car ride home.

Mom filled up yet again. "I'll do whatever you want. Just tell me whatever you want."

I just wanted for her not to feel my pain.

Before she turned onto our street, she told me to keep myself hidden. "In case reporters are lingering about. I'll pull right into the garage."

I did as she said, curling up on the floor of the car as she cranked the stereo loud.

We entered the house through the interior garage door. Dad was already home. He wrapped his arms around me. A welcome sign hung on the wall behind him. For just a second, I wondered whom it was for.

"I hope you're hungry," Dad said. "I'm making my famous grown-up mac 'n' cheese."

The house smelled like boiled chicken. I suddenly wanted to throw up. Mom walked me up to my room, as if I were just moving in or had forgotten where it was. A basket of fresh toiletries sat at the foot of the bed. Pajamas and slippers were laid out on my changing bench. And there was an unopened bottle of water on my bedside table. But aside from those additions, Mom had kept the room looking just as it always had, with my tulip-embroidered bedcovers with the matching pillowcases, the *Les Mis* posters taped over my desk, and the assortment of hairbrushes lined up on my vanity. I picked up one of them, noticing my hair strands still intact.

The book I'd been reading, *All the Pretty Horses,* remained on my night table with a bookmark holding my place, as had the journal I'd been using. I flipped it open. The pages were full of poetry bits and unfinished stories. I ran a finger over the last lines I'd written.

And when my silver lining tore,
I took your shred of hope and used it as a patch.
I stitched the seams
with a hanging thread
and borrowed faith,
using the needle
from my wounds.

I was no longer the poet who'd written those lines.

No longer the bookworm who'd read the novels on the shelf.

No longer the fashionista who'd owned the array of shoes in the closet.

I looked at the bulletin board full of photos. Images of the old me smiled back: toasting marshmallows on a camping trip two summers before; with friends at a Mardi Gras–themed dinner; and posing with Jack at the junior prom, when I wore a coveted Tory Burch dress that my mom had surprised me with.

I gazed in the mirror at the person staring back—dark hair, dark eyes, and dark lips from chewing at the skin—and felt as if I were wearing a costume.

"I was careful not to move anything," Mom said. "I wanted you to feel right back at home, like you'd never left."

"Thanks." I nodded. Except I *had* left. I'm still "gone." And none of these things could ever bring me back.

"So if you're okay for a bit, I'm going to help Dad set up dinner."

While she went downstairs, I stretched out on my bed—on the pretty spring flowers, only they felt more like dried-out stems poking into my skin. I stared up at the ceiling, just as I had on so many nights too excited to fall asleep. To think I'd spent seventeen years in the spirited bubble that was my life . . . it took only seven months to pop that bubble. And to break that spirit.

Into a million tiny pieces.

Shards of mirrored glass that reflected just what I'd become: a distorted version of the person I used to be.

THEN

58

During those first weeks home, it felt like something inside me had died, like my insides were decomposing as hundreds of hungry mealworms ate away at my rotting heart. I'd sit by the window, waiting for Mason to come. Only others came instead—reporters, photographers, neighbors, friends of my parents, Norma from the shop . . . Each time a car pulled up to the curb, I'd sit up, hoping it'd be Mason. But when the person exited the car, another bite would get taken from my heart.

When Mom called me down from my room for meals, I'd push the food around on the plate, my stomach tangled in knots. How could I possibly eat when Mason hadn't yet been found?

"Can I make you something else?" Mom would ask, noticing my untouched food.

My answer was always the same: "I'm not really hungry."

"But you've lost so much weight."

"I'll take the plate up to my room."

And so began the procession of food trays up and down the

stairs, which wasn't as terrible as it sounds, because at least it gave me an excuse for needing a table in my room.

Sitting behind the window curtain, I'd shrink up into a ball, wishing there were a hole I could stick my hand through. With my forehead pressed against the rug, I counted tissues inside my mind—until the room stopped spinning and I could finally control my breathing.

I'd close my eyes, picturing the *Welcome Home* banner, and hear a montage of voices:

"Are these the screams you heard while in captivity? You're absolutely sure? Okay, well, these screams are from an audio track. The CD is sold commercially at novelty shops around Halloween."

"I made a cake to celebrate your return, Jane!"

"Everyone is super excited to see you, Jane. Will you come back to school?"

"It isn't so uncommon for a perpetrator to fake a tattoo, a scar, or some other distinguishable marking."

"At least you're back in time for prom, right? And as an added bonus: You managed to miss midterms."

"Yikes! What happened to your hand?"

"Welcome home, Jane!"

Welcome.

Home.

My first night back home, I tried to sleep in my bed, but it didn't feel secure enough. Not with the windows. I'd bolted both and drawn down the shades. I also locked my door, even though I knew how easy it was to pick. I'd tried it as a kid—just to see if I could—using a butter knife and a bobby pin. Both worked.

And so, I lay in bed, watching the knob, anticipating a turn, able to see a sliver of night through the window, along the side—the part the shade didn't cover.

I got up and took my pillow and blanket into the closet. I

stretched out on the floor, among the shoes and sweaters, leaving a six-inch gap in the sliding door, so I could still peek out.

Finally, I nodded off. But when I woke up, hours later, Mom was sitting on my bed, watching me sleep, with tears running down her face. At first, I assumed they were tears of joy—that she was so happy to have me home.

I sat up and slid the door open wider, about to tell her about my sleep—that I'd managed to somehow get at least a couple of hours of rest. But before I could, Mom's hand flew to her face.

"What did he do to you!" she cried, shaking her head, unable to look at me: the daughter who could no longer sleep in a bed.

On Easter Sunday, my relatives came: my three grandparents, two aunts, an uncle, and four cousins. The adults played it safe, talking about the chilly weather, Uncle Pete's Tokyo trip, and some new cooking show that Grandma Jean would've loved. None of them mentioned my time away, which somehow made things more awkward.

While my male cousins mostly ignored me, opting to play basketball on the street, I remained inside with Jenny, who'd just turned seven. We played gin rummy on the living room sofa while the adults looked on from the dining room table. Mom did lots of soft-talking, while Dad made sure everyone's wineglass was full with a batch he'd made himself.

I tried my best to focus on my cards and not Aunt Suzy's grimace or my Uncle Pete's constant repetition of the word *bastard*.

Bastard.

BASTARD.

Bas.

Tard.

Flash-forward to one rainy night when I couldn't seem to get warm. Mom came up to my room with a bowl of chicken soup.

I knew she'd meant well, but the sight of the soup as I stirred the broth—the chalky-white bits, the thick layer of chicken fat that bubbled at the surface, and the nubby pieces of carrot—made me heave, right there on the rug, thinking about how sick I'd gotten in captivity.

As I helped her clean up the mess, the smell of the boiled chicken parts churned my stomach. I pictured a pot of bones and gristle, and my mouth refilled. I spat out in a spare bowl Mom had brought, convinced the liquid was the residual chicken soup from my time in captivity—that it'd somehow lingered in my body from weeks before.

"Go lie down," Mom said.

I did as told and curled up on my bed.

Mom brought me a warm compress and pulled up a chair. "Is there anything else I can get for you? Hot tea? A heating blanket?"

"Where's Dad?" I asked.

"Working."

"He's always working." I snuggled an extra pillow.

"I know." She sighed. "But after you went missing, it was his work that kept him going."

"And *before* I went missing?"

"Before, he was always trying to prove himself at work."

"At the bank where he'd already worked for a number of years?"

Mom looked at me like the ghost that I was. "Your father hasn't worked at the bank in more than three years. He's in advertising now."

Advertising?

What'd happened to processing mortgages and car loans?

"He's at Langston Young . . . ," she said, her face crumpled like paper. "Initially, it was the career change that prompted him to put in such long hours. He didn't want his bosses thinking they'd made a mistake by hiring someone with a banking back-ground, rather than in something like marketing or sales."

How did I not know? Had no one ever told me? Or had I been so self-involved, BIWM, that I'd never actually listened?

Mom stood up before I could ask more. She tucked me in and clicked off the light.

When I woke up (either days or weeks later), it was prom night. Shelley asked if I wanted to go, suggesting we get a big group together and all wear fire-engine red. I told her no, opt-ing for the window seat in my room. I sat on my perch, looking out at the street, fantasizing that Mason would pull up to the curb and surprise me with a book of poetry and plans for a pic-nic on the beach.

"*Jane?*" Mom knocked on my open bedroom door.

I turned from the window.

"Shelley just called. She and some friends rented a limo. It's going to be at Big City Hotel, right on the water. They'd be happy to swing by here and pick you up."

"I don't have a ticket."

"Shelley said she has an extra. She's on the prom's planning committee."

Since when? "No, thanks." I swiveled back to the window.

My neighbor and his date were both decked out in tuxes, posing for pictures on the lawn.

"Are you sure?" Mom persisted. "It's your *senior prom*. You don't want to miss out."

"I'm fine here."

"Okay, well, if you change your mind . . ."

After she'd gone downstairs, I got up and opened the closet door. My Tory Burch dress from the junior prom was hang-ing toward the back. I took it out, remembering the day Mom brought it home: a floor-length sheath dress in a deep berry color, made with a silky chiffon fabric.

I closed the door to my room and put it on over my tank and sweatpants. Fistfuls of fabric gathered at my waist and sides. I kept the dress on as I sat by the window, continuing to wait for Mason.

At some point, I fell asleep, only to be woken up by the honking of horns—what sounded like hundreds of them, on the main road, a few streets away. It took me a beat to realize that more time had passed.

Days continued to blur together.

I was no longer in the prom dress. It was now the morning of graduation. A senior tradition was to honk your car horn, announcing your freedom, and then to show up at Cravings in your pajamas for a senior class brunch.

"Are you sure you don't want me to drive you?" Mom asked. "I could honk the car the whole way."

I knew I could text Shelley; she'd pick me up in a heartbeat. I went downstairs, actually considering the idea, checking to see if my track sweatshirt was still hanging on a hook. Mom was talking on her phone in the kitchen. A friend's daughter had just gotten into NYU. Mom was trying to be happy for her, using words like *amazing, deserving,* and *congratulations*. But I could tell the words were forced, that they came out with shards of glass, because NYU had been my dream school ever since I was ten, when I stood in the Washington Square Arch, making a wish with my fallen eyelash that years from then I'd return to the very same spot, but as a student rather than a tourist.

Hearing Mom's angst made me forget all about Cravings, and so I returned to the four gray walls of my room: my spot, for now.

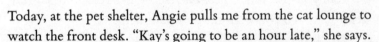

59

Today, at the pet shelter, Angie pulls me from the cat lounge to watch the front desk. "Kay's going to be an hour late," she says.

I look toward the door. There are people lined up outside, waiting for us to open. Adoption hours start in less than three minutes. "Maybe Dan would be a better pick."

"I need Dan to help with shots. Nice 'do, by the way." She nods to my hair. "That color is fierce."

I stand back as Angie lets the customers in. Luckily, they follow her straight to the animals. I grab a rag and begin wiping down counters, spotting a tall white cabinet by Angie's desk.

It's new to the shelter, standing about six feet tall against a stark white wall. I blink hard, figuring I must be seeing things. The doors have a beveled edge, just like the ones in captivity. The knobs are the same too: slightly oblong with engraved spirals. They match the hardware—the tarnished brass hinges. I look down to check the feet: thick wedge slabs, like blocks of wood.

Exactly the same.

I take a step back.

Breathing hard, I feel the floor tilt beneath my feet. Where did this cabinet come from? Who's responsible for bringing it here? Is it chained to the wall? I go to check, but my stomach twists, stopping me in place. Bile squirts into my mouth. And the room starts to spin.

I go to grab a corner of Angie's desk. Something crashes. A potted plant: a present from Angie's husband.

The colors in the room swirl around me—a mix of tans, grays, and greens like inside a washing machine. Only I'm not wet.

"I'm here," says a female voice.

I'm crouched on the floor. A motor clicks on inside my chest, making my insides rev. My nerves start racing.

"Can you hear me?" the woman asks; her voice is beside me, in my ear. "Do you want me to call for help?"

"No. It's just . . ."

"A panic attack," she says, speaking for me.

I try my best to catch my breath, to not pass out, to stop from panting. The woman takes my hand and gives it a squeeze. Her grip reminds me of Mason's—warm, strong, secure. I don't pull away.

"Would you like me to help you?" she asks.

I think I nod. Maybe I let out a sputter.

"My name is Molly. I want you to focus on my voice. We're going to get through this together, okay? It's important for you to know that it's your thoughts creating this panic, not your body. Remember that. You're not going to faint. You're not going to stop breathing. You're going to be just fine." She continues to talk, telling me about her afternoon at the park, watching dogs play. It made her miss her childhood pet, an English bulldog named Presley, who loved stealing slippers and sitting on everyone's feet.

We remain like that, huddled on the floor, until the swirling colors fade and the motor inside my chest slows to a steady hum.

I look down at our hands, surprised to find the woman is no longer squeezing my palm. Instead, I'm squeezing hers.

"Better?" she asks.

I look up into her face. It's speckled with sunspots. The lines in her skin make a web of sorts, outlining her pale blue eyes. I nod, embarrassed. A lump forms in my throat. Something shatters inside my chest.

The woman places her hand on my back; the warmth radiates to my spine.

"I'm glad I could help." She smiles, like it was nothing—like assisting a perfect stranger with her mental and physical breakdown is no more unusual than lending someone a pen.

"Thank you," I say, reluctantly letting her hand go. I start to get up.

The woman helps, gripping around my shoulders, telling me not to rush. "Life isn't a race. You go at your own pace, okay?"

"Do you know me?" I ask. *Why is she being so kind?*

"I don't think so. This is my first time here."

She doesn't ask me my name or what caused my sudden panic. Instead, she grabs a broom to help me sweep up the broken pieces.

Before she leaves, she hands me a business card from her wallet:

Molly Blue, Ph.D.
Licensed Psychologist
123 Newbury Street
Big City, New England State
(617) 555-3109 call or text

"Healing starts the moment we feel heard."

NOW

60

Later—when all of the shelter doors are locked, and only Angie and I are left inside the building (and she's busy with vaccinations)—I go back into the dog wing, armed with a container of treats.

Squatting down in front of Brave's cage, I place my face up to the bars. Brave's barks begin almost instantly, firing like bullets, as if there's anything left in me to hurt. "Good girl," I say, tossing her a heart.

She gobbles it up and looks for more. I set the container in front of the cage—close enough to sniff, but too far to reach with her tongue. Brave growls, wanting more.

I jiggle the treats, releasing the biscuit scent. Brave responds by sticking out her tail, lowering her head to meet my eyes, and making deep, guttural barks. It doesn't matter that outsiders can see her wounds, that it'll likely take her years to recover or trust, or that she's always on guard. She keeps on fighting, following her instinct to survive.

"You're so brave," I tell her, feeding her more treats and encouraging her barks—*jiggle, jiggle, jiggle*. Some of the other dogs begin barking as well. I toss biscuits into their cages too, then bark right along with them—as loud as I can, exhilarated to unleash.

My voice is nearly indistinguishable from the pack. But still, it's there: long-overdue screaming that's palpable inside my chest, that burns like fire in my throat, and that reminds me I'm alive.

61

I wasn't sure how much time had passed (time remained as ominous as my future), but sometime after my escape, I went back to the four white walls. My parents hated the idea, but Agent Thomas said it might actually be healing.

That was the magic word.

Mom walked me to the door, gave me a sweater for the chill. "If this is going to help give you closure . . ."

But it had nothing to do with closure and everything to do with showing Agent Thomas the air vents and finding Mason once and for all.

Mom had wanted to come, but Agent Thomas didn't think that would be a good idea. "Visiting the space where your daughter was forced to dwell for more than seven months might not be the healthiest."

"Okay, so then *I'm* coming," Dad said, not waiting for a rebuttal.

I sat in the back seat as Agent Thomas drove us along the main highway, through several small towns, and down a long, winding road carved out from a sea of trees. Eventually, we pulled up in front of a tiny white house, wrapped in police tape, and with a wooden porch on the front.

Despite the tape, my gut reaction was surprise. In my mind, I still pictured a giant abandoned warehouse. Was this even the right place?

"Ready?" Agent Thomas asked.

I got out of the car and gazed toward the street. The enclave looked somewhat familiar: the dirt-paved clearing with woods all around it. But the trees were budding now. And the snow that'd blanketed the scene weeks or months before had all melted, giving way to a grassy lawn and pops of green.

Dad placed his hand on my shoulder. "Are you sure you're okay to do this?"

I wasn't okay to do much of anything. But we went inside anyway, ducking beneath the tape. A piano faced us in the entryway. It doubled as a storage shelf. A family portrait hung above it: a woman, a man, and a little boy—no one I recognized. Nothing familiar. The smell of honeycomb candles lingered in the air—that musty-earthy scent. It made me want to heave.

I went into the kitchen—a small, square room with cream-colored walls and a linoleum-tiled floor—and moved toward the sink, noticing the sliding glass doors. They froze me in place and flashed me right back to that racing sensation inside my chest as I'd tried to get the door latch to open and pry the butter knife from the floor track.

"Jane?" Dad asked.

I nodded that I was fine and turned away. The fridge faced me—the strawberry magnet and the blank square space where my photo and poem used to be. Someone must've taken them for evidence, leaving a frame of sticky-note reminders—for things like crackers and toothpaste.

Agent Thomas stood in the doorway watching me. "Not exactly a warehouse," she said.

I hated her for it—hated her smug little grin and slouching posture. Why was she just standing there? A better detective would still be searching.

"Shall we go downstairs?" she asked, opening the door to the basement.

I stomped my way down, half hoping that Mason would hear me. The children's drawings remained on the walls in the hallway, along with the *I'm sorry* messages.

"Children were here," I told her.

"We have no evidence of that."

"*This* is evidence." Why wasn't she seeing it? I nodded to a crayon-drawing of a stick-figure boy playing with stick-figure animals.

"Those markings aren't recent," she replied. "Testing of the paint suggests they were drawn more than twelve years ago."

Which proved *what?* My head hurt.

Agent Thomas opened the door to my room. "Ready?" she asked. That question again.

I took a step closer, feeling my knees shake.

"Maybe this isn't right," Dad said.

"We can leave anytime Jane wants."

"No," I blurted, determined to find a clue. I took a step into my room, noticing right away how much smaller it looked than before. The mattress had been taken. The drawers looked empty. The cabinet door squeaked open, as though by a lingering spirit: the ghost of the old me. Gone was the hole Mason had made. Heaps of drywall collected on the floor, in its place.

I stood over the rubble, spotting a star-shaped piece. I picked it up from the heap. Dark, crooked slash marks were lined up in rows, as though marching across the surface—too many slashes to count, but not nearly enough to add up to the total number of days I'd spent in the room.

"Those are your tally marks," Agent Thomas said—a statement, not a question.

Dad didn't comment. Instead, he placed his hands on the vertical planks of wood that separated the two rooms, checking out the wall's construction. "Just drywall?" he said, thinking aloud, stopping my breath.

No concrete layer, or wire mesh, or steel bars to keep me in.

Just.

Drywall.

A chalky, crumbly cardboard mess. A smarter girl would've busted out sooner.

"I'm really sorry," I told him, hugging the broken piece, unsure if my words were actually audible, because Dad didn't respond.

He just continued to inspect the wall, stepping through the planks to get into the other room.

The ceiling tiles had been torn free, exposing water pipes and what looked to be an air duct that traveled across the ceiling, but it was no wider than a two-liter soda bottle.

"Are any of the ducts bigger?" I asked.

Agent Thomas shook her head. "They're all like this one."

"How about passageways behind the walls?"

More head shaking. "Behind these walls, you'll find insulation, electrical wiring, copper pipes . . . but no secret passageways. We called in two contractors and a heating company to be sure."

"There must've been some other way."

"Jane." Her eyes narrowed.

"What?" I snapped.

"Mason told you this was a warehouse."

"Because he truly thought it was."

"And that it had three floors . . ."

"He must've believed that too." I looked at Dad, hoping he'd help me out. But he was staring at the dismantled desk now, wondering maybe why I hadn't used the cement blocks sooner.

"You need to check the floors," I insisted, stomping my foot against the cement.

"This is the basement," she said. "The only thing beneath our feet is dirt."

"Then you'd better get digging." I scanned the room, looking for another possible answer—some unturned corner or crevice.

"How do you explain the lack of bars on windows?" Agent Thomas continued. "Or the audio equipment with the horror-centric sound bites that you identified? Let's also not forget about the lack of DNA."

I wasn't forgetting.

I couldn't explain it.

I really wanted my coil spring.

"You said Mason claimed to have been taken two to three months prior to your disappearance," she persisted. "How come there are no missing-persons cases fitting his profile?"

My father finally met my eyes, but his face showed no expression, as though he'd heard this all before—as if I were the outsider looking in.

"He'd been at a party, right?" she asked. "Thrown by a girl named Haley. We checked out that detail too, but there were no girls named Haley within a three-hundred-mile radius who would admit to hosting a party in which a male was taken."

"Maybe Haley didn't know that anyone was taken."

"You don't think news reports about a missing person would've tipped her off? Especially considering that such reports include a photo of the missing person."

"Maybe you should check beyond three hundred miles. And maybe the party wasn't in May or June."

She gave me a look—eyes bulging, brows raised. "You identified a photo of Martin Gray's hand."

I shook my head.

Why was she still talking?

What was I still doing listening?

I moved back through the wall and stood at the foot of the bed. There were scratch marks on the bedpost—long, narrow gouges.

Had I made them?

Why did I think I had?

I looked down at my thumb, able to feel the sensation of pine beneath the nail as a warm, peppery breath blew behind my ear.

It was all coming back: trying to scratch a web into the wood, convinced that doing so would entice Tiger back. Someone had tugged my hand from the bedpost, stopping me from scratching. And though I'd really wanted Tiger to come visit, another—stronger—part truly wanted to be touched. And so I'd closed my eyes as fingertips glided along the center of my palm, spreading heat all over my skin.

"Jane?" Dad asked, snagging me back to present day.

Both he and Agent Thomas were staring in my direction. Meanwhile, a cold, sticky sensation slithered down my spine, filling my gut with panic.

"Do you remember something?" Agent Thomas asked.

I shook my head as the medley of whites in the room swirled around me. It was way too bright and all too confusing.

"Jane?" Dad insisted; his voice sounded stern.

He said something else, but I wanted them both to go, wanted to close myself up in the room and sit beneath the running shower.

Agent Thomas came closer. Her mouth was moving, but I couldn't process anything. My skin flashed hot. My heart wouldn't stop palpitating. I looked back toward the bedpost with the sudden urge to scratch.

"I want to see the office," I told them.

Agent Thomas gazed at my dad as if seeking his permission.

"*Now,*" I insisted.

"Do you really think that's a good idea?" she asked.

Dad looked back at the crumbled Wall of Separation. "No, I think we've already seen enough."

"It wasn't a question," I told him. "*I want to see it.*"

Dad shook his head, his lips trembling, his nostrils flared, as though no longer able to recognize me. "Whatever she wants," he said quickly, quietly.

I looked toward his neck for the bumblebee birthmark that matched mine. Part of me wanted to point it out—to prove that despite how much I'd changed, I was still his daughter. He was still my father.

"Okay, so let's go," Agent Thomas said, moving toward the door.

Before leaving, I took one last look around the room and felt a wrenching sensation inside my gut, pressing against my spine. I closed my eyes, picturing the hole that was my heart filling with absence—a thick and tarry muck. I didn't want to stay. But I didn't want to leave this place either—as sick and twisted and unexplainable as that was. And so, I held on to my broken piece, determined to take it with me.

Agent Thomas led us back upstairs and down the hallway, toward the office at the end—the one with the pocket door concealed in the wall. She stood outside it and turned to me. "Are you sure you want to go in?"

My eyes locked on the handle, and I flashed back to that

moment—of trying to break in, jamming a knife into the lock. The hardware was barely detectable, concealed by at least several coats of glossy white paint. I gazed at the scars on my forearm, remembering pounding my fists against the door panel, despite my throbbing cut.

Agent Thomas stuck a key into the painted lock and gave it a turn. There was a *click*. She pushed the door open.

I went inside, noticing right away: Police tape outlined the shape of a body where it must've fallen to the floor. But part of the outline—the head part—had been covered by a tarp. I assumed there must be bloodstains beneath it.

"This is the office of Martin Gray," Agent Thomas said. She clicked on his desk lamp and handed me a plastic bag with papers inside it—paystubs with Martin Gray's name.

But what did that prove? I peered around the room, looking for more hidden doors, running my hand along the walls, searching for cracks.

"Here," Agent Thomas said, holding up a plastic bin the size of a laundry basket. Inside were photographs—at least a few hundred of them. She pulled out a handful for show. They were pictures of me, dating all the way back to the summer before high school—candid shots when I'd thought I was alone; personal moments like the time I cried freshman year, in the parking lot at school, after I'd gotten cut from the soccer team tryouts. I was still wearing my tryout number: 23.

"This still doesn't prove anything about Mason," I said.

"Okay, then how about this?" she asked, handing me a photo from the desk, kept in a shiny silver frame.

It was a picture of me with the monster, the guy who took me. We were photoshopped together. "Where did you get this?" I asked as if it weren't already obvious; it'd been kept on the monster's desk. "Are there any others? Photos of Samantha too?"

"Just *your* photos," she reminded me. "*Your* things. A captivity room set up just for *you* . . ."

My hand shook. The frame jittered. The photo looked almost legit, like we'd actually posed together. The picture of me was taken from the sophomore semiformal. I recognized my dress and the flower in my hair. I looked closer, trying to see the guy's arms, but the sleeves of his sweatshirt had been pulled down over his wrists. "It's not Mason," I said, handing it back.

"You're right." Agent Thomas pulled a piece of paper from a manila folder and handed it to me—a photocopy of a driver's license. "It's Martin Gray."

The face in the license picture matched the photoshopped one in the frame. The name read *Martin Gray*.

"Still, what does it prove? That you know the name of the guy that took me? Okay, fine. But that has nothing to do with Mason."

I looked toward Dad, hoping he'd back me up, noticing more plastic bins. They were stacked up around the room, all of them full.

Was that my green scarf?

Were those my yellow mittens?

And my poetry journal from freshman year? I thought I'd lost it.

"Jane?" Agent Thomas asked.

I shook my head and turned to see more. The motion tipped the room onto its side. Dad lunged in my direction, but it was already too late. My knees gave way, and I collapsed to the floor.

NOW

62

I run.

Because I can't sleep.

Because Memory can't catch me if I keep a fast pace.

Because my parents' door is closed, but Night can't shut me out.

Because I'm not supposed to be out at this hour, especially after everything, especially all alone—and so it feels a little like power.

The bells of the town hall chime three times. I run along the pathway that leads to No Name Park. The harbor is the backdrop. It's full of sailboats at this time of year, but the darkness swallows them up. There's only the blinking lamp of the lighthouse, across the way, reminding me where I am.

I walk to the edge of the rock cliff and look out over the harbor, imagining myself as a dab of black paint against the ebony canvas of sea and sky—hidden, invisible, anonymous. The wind tattoos my face, making my eyes water.

Now that I've stopped running, certain questions have caught up; they press into the back of my head. Why did the monster work so hard at stocking my favorite things but didn't do the same for Mason? Why didn't he supply Mason with contact lenses and solution, or at least provide him with a backup pair of glasses? Why did he give Mason mint-flavored antacids despite an allergy? And why were my photos and possessions the only ones found at the house?

The house, not the warehouse.

The glass-paned windows rather than the barred ones.

The unmarked skin, not the tree roots.

Earlier today, I checked my running bag, searching for the red hair comb I'd kept in the side pocket (BIWM), remembering how Agent Thomas said she'd found a similar comb in Martin Gray's office and speculated it was mine. I wanted to show her it wasn't—wanted to prove her theories were somehow wrong.

But the pockets of my bag were empty.

And I couldn't find the comb anywhere—not in my room, not in any drawers or bags either . . .

So, what did that mean? What *does* it mean?

Who is Martin Gray really?

And how did he pick me?

I take another step, picturing myself tumbling forward, in slow motion, wondering if I'd feel my body breaking against the rocks—the sensation of bones snapping and arteries puncturing. Or would I feel nothing at all?

The moon shines down over a patch of sea, giving the illusion of a scrying mirror. In it, I see Grandma Jean wagging her finger back and forth.

She's telling me no.

I blink her away.

My phone vibrates in my pocket. I check the screen, feeling chills rip up my skin. It's an alert to remind me about Grandma

Jean's birthday—as if by fate. It's officially the twenty-seventh. She would've been seventy-five.

There's also a text from Jack. It came in hours ago:

Jack: *Just wanted to make sure you got the CD in your mailbox.*

Me: *I did. Thank you.*

I go to pocket my phone when I notice him texting back— the series of ellipsis points.

Jack: *What are u doing up?*

Me: *I could ask you the same.*

Me: *I went for a run.*

Jack: *At 3AM?*

Jack: *Are you home now?*

Me: *No. I'm at No Name Park.*

Jack: *Do yr parents know?*

Jack: *???*

Me: *What are you doing up?*

Jack: *I wasn't up. Your text woke me.*

Me: *Sorry.*

Jack: *NP. I could've turned down the volume. But I like hearing from u.*

Jack: *U do realize you're just across the harbor from me, right?*

It's true. Jack lives by the lighthouse, down a narrow, winding street that always makes me think of fairy tales. Back in middle school, we used to decorate the street at Halloween, transforming it with fog, cobwebs, and scary music.

Jack: *Hold on a sec. Im going outside.*

Jack: *OK. Im waving at u right now.*

Me: *You don't rly expect me to see u, right?*

Jack: *No. But Im hoping you can cosmically sense my waving.*

Jack: *Can u?*

In some weird way, I can; can also picture him standing on the beach at the end of his street, looking out across the harbor at the very same things I am.

Jack: *Can I join you on the walk home?*

Me: *How do you propose to do that? You're a 20-min swim away.*

Jack: *U can talk to me the whole way back. Unless you'd rather I picked u up.*

Jack: *I won't be able to sleep otherwise.*

Me: *Ok. Let's walk.*

The next thing I know, my phone starts vibrating. Jack's FaceTiming me. I pick it up, able to see him moving through the darkness, with the lighthouse in his background. His hair looks slightly rumpled from having just woken up.

"Hey," he says.

"Hey," I say back, unable to stop the smile on my face.

"Whoa, your hair . . ."

I run my hand over the short spikes. "Oh, right. I got it cut."

"It looks amazing."

"Thanks." I smile wider.

"So shall we walk along the water or take the main road?"

"Are you sure you want to do this?"

"Are you kidding? What else would I want to be doing at 3:00 a.m.?" He sits down on his outside deck, where we've hung out at least a hundred times, doing homework and eating pizza.

"You're really sweet."

"And so are you. So have you left the park yet? I can't quite tell." He squints as though straining to see better.

"I'm leaving now." I turn away from the cliff and begin on my way.

NOW

63

In the kitchen, I nab Dad's chocolate bar from the cabinet. It's 90 percent cocoa, like the kind Mason brought me. I bite off a piece, imagining it was Mason that opened the wrapper—that it's his bite marks in the block rather than my father's.

Mom's cell phone rings from the kitchen island. It's Agent Thomas; her name flashes across the screen. I pick it up, the chocolate wadded in my cheek.

"Mary?" she asks, when I click the phone on.

"No. It's Jane."

"Oh, Jane, hi. It's good to hear your voice. How are you doing?"

"Okay, I guess."

"Are you still going to therapy? Keeping up with your studies? Getting back into the swing of things?"

Which one does she want me to answer? "I guess" applies to at least one of the above.

"Glad to hear. Is your mom around? I'm returning her call."

"She's in the shower, but I'll tell her you called."

"Okay, perfect."

I swallow the bitter syrup taste. "Can I ask you something?" I venture.

"Of course. Anything."

"Did my blood work show signs of being drugged?"

"Excuse me?"

"When I was admitted to the hospital, I mean. Was there a drug in my system?"

"None that was detected, but that doesn't mean much. Some drugs only stay in the system for a matter of hours. Why? What makes you ask?"

"I'll tell my mother you called." I click the phone off. Agent Thomas's words roll like bowling balls inside my brain. *None that was detected, but that doesn't mean much.*

I take another bite. Mom's phone rings again. Agent Thomas. I click the ringer off, but her words continue to play. *None that was detected, but that doesn't mean much.*

Could fever have been to blame for my unconsciousness? Could it have knocked me out? And made me delusional? Are delusions only visual, or do they apply to touch too?

Because when I close my eyes, I can still feel the sticky-wet kisses at the back of my sweat-stained neck, plus the bristle of calves sliding against my bare legs, and the fingertip spirals forming across my back as someone drew invisible roses all over my skin.

"Jane?"

Mom's standing by the fridge. There's a towel wrapped around her head and a carton of eggs in her hand. "Hungry?" she asks. "I was going to make an omelet."

"Why did you call Agent Thomas?"

Mom sets the eggs on the island, along with a plastic mixing bowl; it clamors against the granite and sends shivers over my skin. "Did you talk to her?" She grabs her phone.

"She called while you were in the shower."

Mom sees the missed call. "I was just looking for the name of a trauma expert. She'd mentioned one before, but I never got the number."

"A trauma expert for me?"

"For both of us." She shrugs like it's no big deal, then cracks an egg into a bowl, shells included, and stirs the broken pieces.

NOW

64

Instead of going straight to the shelter, I find myself sitting in the bathroom at the library once again. I'm huddled in the corner with the key clenched in my grip. The door is locked. The air conditioner runs like white noise, but it doesn't blot out the storming inside my head.

Until now, I've kept certain thoughts locked up in a box.

And still now, I remind myself these thoughts may not be true.

But at the same time, now, I wonder if I should face what my mind has labeled sick—what it's quarantined inside my brain.

The door handle jiggles back and forth. I make myself known by shuffling my feet. I also clear my throat and slide my bag toward me, across the tile.

Then I unzip.

And zip.

Unzip.

And zip.

Reaching inside the main compartment, I poke my fingers

through the hole in the lining and pull out the card I got from that woman at the shelter. *Healing starts the moment we feel heard.* I cry for the first time in I don't even know when.

For the loss of a best friend.

(And I don't mean Shelley.)

NOW

65

At the shelter, I avert my gaze as I pass by the cabinet on my way to visit Brave. As usual, she starts barking as soon as I open the door to the dog wing. I sit down outside her cage and toss in a few crumbled hearts from my pocket. I've also brought along my CD player—the handheld kind—with the Gigi Garvey CD already inside.

"How's it going?" Angie asks, coming from around the corner.

"Today's the day. I'm going to let Brave run free in the yard."

"Are you sure she's ready?"

"Definitely sure. I've been walking her every day. She heels, stays, and listens to the word *no*. She also doesn't give me a hard time about coming back inside."

"Sounds like you're doing a great job of taming her."

"Which is all the more reason to let her run wild."

Angie grabs a leash and harness from the hook at the end of the hallway, then unlocks Brave's cage. Brave comes right out, wagging her tail and sniffing Angie all over, while I harness her up.

Angie scoots down to give Brave's mane a pat. "I knew you'd be the one to turn her around."

I take Brave outside. The shelter is lucky to have a decent-sized yard. Dogs run laps around a circular pit—what once used to be a large brick patio. I let Brave go free. Her mouth hangs open as she runs lap after lap; only after at least a hundred or so does she stop to mark her territory, making this her home.

I sit down on a bench and push Play on my CD player. Gigi's voice pours out, singing about an unrecognizable life. I pretend that she means mine.

Moments later, Brave comes over but lingers a few feet away. Her wide eyes blink, and she sniffs the air as though sensing more broken hearts. I extend my hand, and she licks the crumbs from my fingers before running off again. We continue with this back-and-forth game until she finally lays by my feet.

I scrunch down beside her and stroke behind her ears. Brave rests her head in my lap, allowing me to strap on her leash, contented to stay for love, even if it means getting locked up in a cage.

NOW

66

Later, after my shift at the shelter, I find Jack at the front desk signing in for a visit.

"Hey, you," he says when he spots me.

"What are you doing here?"

"What do you think?" He sets the pen down. "I want to adopt a pet."

"Even though your mom is allergic to all four-legged creatures."

"I thought you might know of a two-legged creature I could bring home."

"Right." I smile, feeling my face burn.

"Your mom said you were here," he explains. "I was hoping we could get lunch."

"Sure," I say, even though my gut tells me not to.

We head outside, and Jack leads us to his Jeep. I recognize the eagle wings hanging from his rearview mirror. Jack once told me they symbolize safe travel, that the charm was a gift from his grandfather, who'd spent most of his life in the sky as an air force pilot.

I stop at the front bumper, thinking about all the nights Jack and I spent in this Jeep, driving around, talking until the windows fogged over. I know it's perfectly safe, but I don't want to feel caged.

"Do you mind if we walk?" I ask.

"Not at all," Jack says. "There's no parking on Main Street anyway."

On our way downtown, we pass by Shelley's house. Her car is parked in the driveway. I look up at her bedroom window, remembering Monopoly marathons, campouts in her bedroom tent, and the time she patted my back and listened while I got all emo over not making it into the Honors Club (something that seems so insignificant now).

"You haven't seen much of Shelley, have you?" Jack follows my gaze.

"What makes you say that?"

"Word travels. Care to share?"

"It's kind of hard to explain."

"Try me."

"Even if it defies logic?"

"Logic is way overrated, in my opinion."

"Okay. Well, I know Shelley loves me, that she's only ever wanted what's best for me . . . but a part of me still associates her with that day."

"Maybe you're not as illogical as you think."

"What do you mean?"

"I mean, I get it. At least on some level. After Becky died, it was a while before I could even look at my aunt. She'd been the one driving the car that night. And logically, yeah, I knew it wasn't her fault. The trucker had fallen asleep at the wheel when my aunt's car got hit, but that didn't stop me from blaming my aunt. Why did she get to live? Why did Becky have to die?"

"Were you ever able to forgive your aunt?"

"Yeah, but it didn't happen overnight. And my brain played all kinds of tricks: What if my aunt had swerved to save my sister? Was it my aunt's gut instinct to turn the wheel—to protect herself? But eventually those voices quieted, and I was able to accept that it wasn't really anyone's fault."

"Except the trucker's."

"Yeah, but even *him* . . . I mean, who's to say? Maybe he'd been forced to work a double. Maybe he hadn't slept in days because he'd had his own demons . . . I couldn't really rely on blame; it just made everything harder. Living without my sister was already hard enough."

"Wow," I say, stopping a moment, turning to face him. "You sound really . . . *evolved*."

"Evolved in a good way, I hope . . . rather than in a way that might make you want to gag."

"No gagging here. You might actually be the only one who gets me."

Jack's eyes crinkle up in a half smile. "Well, I'm here whenever you want me to get you. Just give yourself a break. Your whole sense of trust has been knocked on its ass. It's going to take some time."

"How much time?"

Jack turns and plucks a dandelion from the ground. Its cottony white threads wave in the breeze. "Make a wish, but not for something monumental, like finishing school or going back to normal. Wish for something actually attainable within the next sixty minutes."

"Something like spinach enchiladas?"

"Exactly like spinach enchiladas. I just heard that Casa Abuela got a five-star review in *Eat This*. What do you say we be the judges?"

I blow the dandelion threads. They float above our heads like tiny thought bubbles. If only I knew what the words read inside his. "And what happens after sixty minutes?"

"No one knows. We all have to wait."

"How long will *you* wait?"

"Don't worry about me. I just want to be in your life, wherever you have room." He picks another dandelion and blows all the threads.

"Have I told you lately how grateful I am for your friendship? I feel really lucky."

"Luck has nothing to do with it. I'm only friends with amazing individuals."

"How can you possibly say that?"

"Are you forgetting who was there after I broke my arm in the fourth grade while playing Tarzan? Who volunteered to sit out with me in gym class and stay in with me at recess while the arm was healing? How about the person who came to my house and played Battleship with me for hours on end after Becky died? Who helped get me through freshman bio with sadistic Mr. Webber? And stayed up talking to me until 4:00 a.m. after Darla forwarded those love texts I sent her to everyone in our seventh-grade class?"

"Okay, I get it."

"It was *you*. Every time. So don't forget it, okay? Now, shall we get those enchiladas?"

"Definitely." I smile. And for just an instant, as we walk by the street with the cookie bakery I like and the indie bookstore where I used to shop, I feel like a dog off a leash, with a life I'm starting to recognize.

NOW

67

I can't sleep. Memories creep like spiders across my skin: They're there, but I don't always know it. It's not until I see one that I want to swat it away.

Lying in bed, listening to Gigi Garvey's music, I remember. That day.

It was the summer following eighth grade. I was at the beach with some friends—not good friends (like Shelley) but girls I'd wanted to be my friends. The sun was sinking fast, and these girls had other plans. Marlo was meeting a boy. Cece was waiting to get picked up by her boyfriend, who drove. And Lucy was trying to convince some guy at the snack bar to take her for a ride on his new moped.

"What happened to getting food?" I asked them.

When Cece had texted me that afternoon, dinner and a swim had been the plan. But clearly the joke was on me, because I was the only hungry one wearing a swimsuit.

"Maybe another time," Marlo said. "Oh, and if my mom happens to call you—and I seriously think she might—just tell her I'm in the water and then text me, and I'll call her back."

"Ditto for me." Cece laughed. "My mom totally trusts you, so she'll believe whatever you say."

After they'd given me my orders, dubbing me their new best friend—and designated alibi—they left me on my own.

But I wasn't alone—not really. Some guy was there, sitting two benches over, sipping an iced coffee. He was cute—*really* cute. A college boy with wavy brown hair and sun-kissed skin. He'd looked my way a couple of times while Cece and the others were talking. At one point, he even flashed me a knowing grin, silently telling me that he got it—got that these girls were self-absorbed brats, got that I deserved so much better. And, admittedly, his attention made me feel just a little less lonely.

As soon as the girls were gone, however, everything changed. The sky had turned dark. The beach had emptied out. What was I still doing there? And why, more important, was that guy lingering as well?

"Rough night?" he asked as I gathered up my things.

I shot him an awkward grin, suddenly desperate to leave. I stuffed my keys, my beach towel, a Frisbee, and a can of bug spray into my bag, then stepped into my flip-flops.

I began across the parking lot, able to feel him watching me somehow—the sensation of his gaze crawling over my skin. I pulled out my phone and fumbled for Shelley's number.

She picked up right away. "Hey there."

"Can you talk?"

"Is everything okay?"

"I'm just feeling a little freaked. I'm walking home alone."

"Why *alone?*"

"You were right about Marlo and her clan of clones. They totally ditched me."

"Ugh, sorry. Want me to ask my mom to come pick you up?"

"No. It's fine. I'm only down the street from my house."

Shelley proceeded to make me feel better, telling me about how Kenney had gotten a nosebleed in math class and asked Marlo for a tissue from her bra-stuffing (much to Marlo's mortification).

Once I'd finally arrived home, I didn't give the incident at the beach another thought—not until now.

I sit up in bed and grab my phone to text Shelley:

Me: *Hey.*

Me: *There are a couple of things I need to tell u . . .*

Me: *First, thank u for always being there.*

Me: *Second, while I was in captivity, I pretended u were with me.*

Me: *I know that doesn't make sense, but I talked to u and had meals with u. I kept you with me. I'm not sure I would've made it otherwise.*

Me: *Your friendship has always meant the world to me. I know things haven't been great between us. But I hope one day they can be good again.*

Me: *I just need time and space, and I hope whenever I'm ready, you'll still be willing.*

I go to set the phone back on my night table, but it vibrates right away. Shelley writes back:

Shelley: *!!!!*

Shelley: *So good to hear from u!!!*

Shelley: *I'm glad I was able to be with you—so to speak—while you were gone. That rly means a lot to me—knowing the thought of our friendship made you feel a little less alone . . .*

Shelley: *And just so u know, I'll always be here—day or night, now or in 50 years. Just lmk. I love u like a sister—now and always. xoxoxo*

I set the phone down and turn up the volume on Gigi Gar-

vey as she sings about lost innocence. I'm pretty sure she's referring to a former love, but still the lyrics seem fitting. I'll never
be the same friend I was with Shelley, BIWM. But maybe that's
okay. Or maybe it simply just is.

NOW

68

Still unable to sleep—even after what feels like hours later—I go down the hall and peek into my parents' room. Dad's sleeping on the pullout couch. The bed is unmade and vacant.

A book lies splayed open on the table beside him. I move closer and shine my phone's flashlight over the title: *Father Failure.* He's dog-eared a page to a chapter called "Absence."

Mom is absent too. I go downstairs and find her sitting in the living room with my doll in her lap. The full moon streams in through the window glass, blanketing her with light.

I clear my throat to get her attention.

She looks up, startled to see me. Her fingers curl around Pammy's leg.

"Why are you up?" I ask her.

"I couldn't really sleep."

"Was Dad tossing too much? I saw him on the pullout."

She manages a smile, but her eyes can't lie. "Your father and I have been on two entirely different schedules lately. Sometimes it's just easier to sleep in separate beds so we don't disturb one another."

I feel the tears all the way to my gut; a chain reaction that causes my stomach to convulse, my throat to constrict, and my upper lip to tremble—and not because of the obvious problems my parents are having but more because, despite her own angst, she's still trying to protect me.

I turn away so she can't see my face, trying to protect her too. "Do you still talk to Dr. White?"

"I do, and Daddy's going to start coming to sessions too. Would you like to make another appointment?"

"I think I may have someone else in mind."

"Anyone I know?"

"Can we talk about it tomorrow? I should really get back to bed."

"Want me to make you some Sweet Dream Tea? Remember? Like when you were little . . ."

I do remember. On nights when I was convinced that ghouls and goblins lived under my bed, Mom would make the magical tea, and I'd drift off to heavenly sleep. "You used to sit by my bed until I nodded off."

Mom snuggles Pammy closer and kisses the crown of her head.

"Do you think you could do that now?" I ask. "Sit by my bed until I fall asleep?"

Mom looks up as though checking to see if she heard me right. When I don't say anything to correct the words, her eyes fill.

She stands up, setting Pammy down, still hesitating, still not quite believing. She places her hand over the hole that is her heart.

We go upstairs. Mom lies beside me on my bed. It takes me a

moment to notice the box of brownies between us, as well as the broken piece of drywall propped against my headboard—the one with the tally marks. Mom doesn't mention either of them, and neither do I. We simply face one another like bookends with a library of self-help topics between us.

She begins to hum the song about favorite things from *The Sound of Music*. I close my eyes and picture some of those things (gold-trimmed notebooks, blue-frosted cake, gel pens, novels, and Lemon's wide hazel eyes), remembering how, back when I was little and Mom used to sing the song, she'd add in all of my favorite items, the way Maria does in the movie.

Part of me is tempted to share my current list so she could do the same now. But instead I roll onto my side and drift off to sleep.

NOW

69

I get off the train and walk several blocks, watching for cars and faces, listening for thwacks and whimpers. My cell phone clutched like a coil spring in my hand, I use the navigation app to find my way.

I know the general vicinity. Whenever Shelley and I used to come into the city, we'd always stop by Stationery Sweets—not only because it has the coolest notebook supplies but also because it doubles as a cupcake shop.

The building I need is a few doors down.

I count my steps along the way—fifty-six—and enter through a turnstile door. There are sixteen steps until I get to the elevator. I take it up seven flights, holding my breath, eyeing the numbers.

Suite sixteen is at the end of the hall, nine offices down. My mom offered to take me, but I wanted to do this on my own as part of a personal quest to find my lucky number seven: someone who doesn't fall asleep or scratch his groin when I talk, someone who really, truly listens without telling me how to feel or making faces at what I say.

Dr. Molly's name glistens from a golden door plaque. I'm in the right place. I go inside.

"Hey there," she says, crossing the room to water a plant.

There are three windows and rose-colored walls. The room smells like spearmint candy—the kind with the thick wax paper that I used to get out of the coin machine at the supermarket.

Dr. Molly's hair is tied back. She's wearing a summer dress. Her smile is just as warm as it was on the day we met, when she sat by my side, telling me about her bulldog, Presley. "Can I get you something to drink? I have water, tea, seltzer, hot cocoa . . ."

"Hot cocoa," I say, despite the warm weather.

She makes me a cup with some fancy machine, and we sit down across from one another on tan velvet couches.

"I'm glad you called," she says.

I force a smile, realizing that I'm sitting on the edge of the sofa, a sniffle away from slipping onto the floor.

She leans back in her seat as though to give me more space.

"Sorry," I say, scooting back. "I guess I'm really nervous." I eye the box of tissues on the table between us.

"What do you feel most nervous about?"

"Facing the truth, I guess."

"The truth about . . ."

"What happened when I was taken." I study her face, trying to figure out if she knows my story, if she saw it on the news or read it in the papers.

But unlike most of the others, she shows no expression. "Why don't you tell me what you think happened?"

"That's just it; I don't know."

"Not any of it?"

"Well, certain things I know, like how I probably trusted the wrong person."

Dr. Molly pushes the tissue box toward me. "Before we begin, there's something you need to keep in mind. You're human, and humans make mistakes. I'm not saying that you made one in this case, but something you just said . . . about trusting the wrong person; it puts all the blame on you. You need to be kind to yourself—to allow yourself to be human. Does that make sense?"

"I just feel so out of control." I pluck a tissue. "I mean, this isn't like me—like the way I was before everything happened."

"Let's focus on the way you feel at this moment."

"Confused. I just have so many questions."

"Can you tell me at least a few of them? Even if you don't think they'll make any sense to me . . . Don't stop to explain or self-edit. Just say whatever questions come to the forefront of your mind."

"Who was that guy? Why did he choose me? Did he first see me that day at the beach? Or was it before that?" Is there something else I'm not remembering?

"Very good," she says. "What else do you want to know?"

"How I could possibly have been so blind—unable to see what had clearly been all around me."

"Anything else?"

"Yes." I nod. "I want to know what happened while I was unconscious." Was it holding and cuddling, or something more? Does the distinction even matter? "Would the violation be any less?"

"Violation?"

"Sorry." I pluck another tissue. "I'm making no sense."

"Don't apologize. Your thoughts are coming out, probably quicker than you're able to process them. This is a safe space for that to happen."

A safe space? I peer around the room, making sure the windows are still there: one, two, three. Why didn't I think to check the door lock? Would it be weird to get up and check it now—to make sure the knob turns?

"Jane?"

I scratch my palm—raw, cracked skin—weighing the effects of my unspoken words.

"Jane."

"I have half memories."

"Half, not whole?"

"Snippets," I explain. "And I guess I'm scared I may never have enough of them to piece the truth together."

"You may never have all the snippets. Or you may. There are no certainties. Sometimes we simply don't get the answers we want. Other times, we get them, but not until we're ready."

"So maybe I'm just not ready?"

"Maybe not."

"Because of how broken I feel?"

"You won't always feel this way."

"But what if I do?"

"We're all broken in some way; it's part of that being-human thing I was talking about before. The key is to learn how to carry your broken pieces as you move forward day by day."

"And when the pieces get too heavy?"

"I hope to make them lighter, but try not to think of them as solely negative. Our broken pieces are what make us whole."

I take a deep breath, suddenly realizing I'm sitting on the floor. Dr. Molly is squatted in front of me holding the box of tissues. I've plucked most of them out. The floor is littered with cotton-candy pink.

"So what do you say?" she asks. "Shall we get started?"

I nod. "I'm ready."

EPILOGUE

Dear Reader(s),

Last night I dreamed Tiger crawled inside my ear and weaved a web of shimmering pink. And as he worked, he told me things, like that Mason had loved me for years.

"And all he wanted was for you to love him back," Tiger said. "He just didn't know how to make that happen. But that's no surprise, right? I mean, you pretty much had that part figured out already, hadn't you? And as for that other question— the one that's been gnawing away inside your mind . . . The answer is yes."

Yes?

"He intentionally made you sick. Another dumb idea. But he wanted to be the one to nurse you back to health. So you'd feel reliant on him. But you suspected that too, didn't you?"

I suppose I did.

"I knew it." Tiger laughed; it sounded like wind chimes— the copper kind like my neighbors have.

"Lastly," Tiger continued, "the haziest part—the question about what happened after you passed out . . . Rest assured, I was there and saw the whole thing."

And?

"And he came into your room to put you to bed, but he couldn't resist the chance to hold you, and smell you, and lie with you in his arms. He cleaned you up too. Don't you remember? When you woke up? You were wearing fresh clothes. Your face was washed. The room no longer smelled like puke . . . I don't really recall anything else—and neither do you, right? At least, I don't see any other memories inside your brain. I've got a nice view from your ear canal, and I've lit things up pretty well with my glowing spinnerets. I can see all the way to your . . . Oh, wait. There is one more thing. Are you aware that you talk in your sleep?"

Agent Thomas had said the same.

"Okay, well, it's true. You talked in your sleep after you went unconscious."

What did I say?

"Just that you love-love-love me . . . unless you were talking to Mason, in which case I don't want to know. I'd prefer that it's me you love-love-love."

In my dream, Tiger continued to weave a web that stretched across my brain and lit it up like stars. When I finally awoke, I checked inside my ear, not fully conscious, half expecting to find a shimmering web.

Before I went missing, I wouldn't have given the dream a second thought, but it's all I can think about now. The mind, like the heart, is an amazingly powerful thing. One day, I hope that both can be open again. Until then . . .

Thanks for "listening,"
Jane

ACKNOWLEDGMENTS

Many thanks to the talented team at Wednesday Books who embraced *Jane Anonymous* from the very beginning and whose critical questions challenged me to dig deeper and search harder in my quest to find Jane's truth. A special thanks to my acquiring editor, Tiffany Shelton. It's been such a pleasure working with you.

Thanks, as always, to my amazing agent, Kathy Green, for believing in my work, cheering me on when I need it, and offering much-needed literary guidance. I am forever grateful for all you do.

Thanks to friends and family members who've read pieces and/or drafts of *Jane* along the way: Ed, Ryan, Shawn, Kathy, Susan, Julianna, Kate, Deb, and Emily. Your time, questions, suggestions, and offers to get me coffee (black, no sugar) are truly invaluable to me.

A very special thanks goes to my friend Susan O., who sat with me for hours on end discussing such topics as trauma, brokenness, and loss. Our conversations helped me get to the core of Jane's story and enabled me to tell it in the most honest way I could.

Thanks to my amazing copy editor, Sara Ensey, for her careful eye, and to Kerri Resnick for creating the most beautiful cover for my work.

And last, huge thanks go to my readers, who've been asking when my next book is coming out. At last, it's here. Thank you *so much* for reading it!